W9-APN-374

NEW PENGUIN SHAKESPEARE
GENERAL EDITOR: T. J. B. SPENCER
ASSOCIATE EDITOR: STANLEY WELLS

All's Well That Ends Well Barbara Everett
Antony and Cleopatra Emrys Jones
As You Like It H. J. Oliver
The Comedy of Errors Stanley Wells
Coriolanus G. R. Hibbard
Hamlet T. J. B. Spencer
Henry IV, Part 1 P. H. Davison
Henry IV, Part 2 P. H. Davison
Henry V A. R. Humphreys
Henry VI, Part 1 Norman Sanders
Henry VI, Part 2 Norman Sanders
Henry VI, Part 3 Norman Sanders
Henry VIII A. R. Humphreys
Julius Caesar Norman Sanders
King John R. L. Smallwood
King Lear G. K. Hunter
Love's Labour's Lost John Kerrigan
Macbeth G. K. Hunter
Measure for Measure J. M. Nosworthy
The Merchant of Venice W. Moelwyn Merchant
A Midsummer Night's Dream Stanley Wells
Much Ado About Nothing R. A. Foakes
The Narrative Poems Maurice Evans
Othello Kenneth Muir
Pericles Philip Edwards
Richard II Stanley Wells
Richard III E. A. J. Honigmann
Romeo and Juliet T. J. B. Spencer
The Sonnets and *A Lover's Complaint* John Kerrigan
The Taming of the Shrew G. R. Hibbard
The Tempest Anne Righter (Anne Barton)
Timon of Athens G. R. Hibbard
Troilus and Cressida R. A. Foakes
Twelfth Night M. M. Mahood
The Two Gentlemen of Verona Norman Sanders
The Two Noble Kinsmen N. W. Bawcutt
The Winter's Tale Ernest Schanzer

WILLIAM SHAKESPEARE

*

THE MERRY WIVES
OF WINDSOR

EDITED BY
G. R. HIBBARD

PENGUIN BOOKS

PENGUIN BOOKS

Published by the Penguin Group
Penguin Books Ltd, 27 Wrights Lane, London W8 5TZ, England
Penguin Books USA Inc., 375 Hudson Street, New York, New York 10014, USA
Penguin Books Australia Ltd, Ringwood, Victoria, Australia
Penguin Books Canada Ltd, 10 Alcorn Avenue, Toronto, Ontario, Canada M4V 3B2
Penguin Books (NZ) Ltd, 182–190 Wairau Road, Auckland 10, New Zealand

Penguin Books Ltd, Registered Offices: Harmondsworth, Middlesex, England

This edition first published in Penguin Books 1973
11 13 15 17 19 20 18 16 14 12

This edition copyright © Penguin Books, 1973
Introduction and notes copyright © G. R. Hibbard, 1973
All rights reserved

Printed in England by Clays Ltd, St Ives plc
Filmset in Monotype Ehrhardt

CONTENTS

INTRODUCTION

ON the stage *The Merry Wives of Windsor* has been, and continues to be, one of the most popular of Shakespeare's plays. For at least three hundred and seventy years it has been drawing audiences to the theatre. When it was first published, in a version that differs widely from the accepted text, in 1602, the title-page stated that this 'most pleasant and excellent conceited comedy' had 'been divers times acted . . . both before her majesty and elsewhere.' James I saw it at the royal palace of Whitehall in 1604; Charles I and his queen attended a performance of it at the Cockpit Theatre in 1638. It was revived immediately after the Restoration; and, unlike so many of Shakespeare's plays, it suffered hardly at all from that vogue for 'improving' his works which was so strong in the later seventeenth and early eighteenth centuries. One attempt was made to bring it up to date, but it met with no response from the public, which preferred the original version. That was in 1702. Since that time it has been played frequently, not only in England but also in many other countries.

The reasons for its wide appeal are not far to seek. It is essentially a play of intrigue, of plots and counter-plots, turning on the age-old theme of 'the biter bit', which, as Sir Francis Bacon remarks of poetry in general, gives 'some shadow of satisfaction to the mind of man in those points wherein the nature of things doth deny it.' The action is consistently lively and often hilariously funny in a direct knock-about manner. Moreover, the play contains scene after scene that could be cited as text-book examples to demonstrate the meaning of the term 'good theatre'. In Act I, scene 4, for instance, Mistress Quickly, learning that her hot-tempered master Doctor Caius is about to enter the house, hides Simple, whom she does not wish him to see, in a closet. Caius, on coming in, orders her to bring him a box from the closet, and she does so with a sigh of relief. Caius is about to make his exit, but recalls at the last moment that he also needs some drugs from the same closet. He goes to get them himself, and discovers Simple. Then there are the scenes in which Ford, under the assumed name of Brook, is told by Falstaff of the progress he has made in his design to seduce Ford's wife and of his very low opinion of Ford himself. These are the situations that the theatre has thrived on for centuries: the first arousing expectations, to thwart and then satisfy them; the second giving rise to complex ironies, springing from Ford's knowledge and Falstaff's ignorance.

This bustling action is carried out by one of the richest groups of highly individualized characters that Shakespeare had yet invented. In themselves these figures are at bottom long-established stage types – the foolish magistrate, his nonentity of a nephew (or 'cousin', as he is regularly called), the garrulous woman who sees herself as a matchmaker, the jealous husband, the huffing soldier, the choleric Frenchman, and so forth – yet each is given a characteristic idiom that we soon come to recognize as his, and his alone. They are sharply differentiated from each other, yet they all belong to the world of the theatre. And, because this is so, actors know almost immediately how to play these roles. Similarly, a European audience feels itself at home with *The Merry Wives of Windsor*, because this comedy, like *The Taming of the Shrew* and unlike Shakespeare's romantic comedies, has its being within that central comic tradition which runs from the Ancients right down to the time of George Bernard Shaw and beyond. More-over, this Shakespeare comedy suffers less, perhaps, than any other from being submitted to the strains of trans-lation, because it is conducted almost entirely in prose. It has the smallest amount of verse of any play in the canon; and such verse as it does employ lacks any real poetic distinction. Translation cannot spoil this verse, since there is nothing in it to be spoiled.

The play can also stand up well to that other form of translation which so often takes place in the theatre: the itch of producers to set their mark on what they are doing by importing highly idiosyncratic 'interpretations' of their own into Shakespeare's text. The main drift of *The Merry Wives of Windsor* is plain and unmistakable, making it singularly resistant to this kind of interference; and the whole nature of the play is so robust and accommodating that it can absorb almost any amount of 'business' without being seriously affected by it. Comedies such as *As You Like It* and *Twelfth Night* are so exquisite in their poise, in the delicate balance they hold between the expression of sentiment and the mockery of sentiment, that one piece of miscasting, a wrong emphasis in a single scene, or even the bad delivery of a few crucial lines can ruin an entire production. With *The Merry Wives of Windsor* this is not the case. The effects it aims at are broad, not subtle, and they gain rather than lose by being underlined. No one who saw the production at Stratford-upon-Avon in 1968 is likely to forget the marvellous tumbling act with which Ford, Page, Caius, and Evans made their re-entry from upstairs after seeking in vain for Falstaff in the buck-basket scene, Act III, scene 3. There is nothing in the text to call for such a display of acrobatics, but equally there is nothing there to forbid it; and it did bring out admirably the affinities between the play and the art of

9

the old music-halls, reminding one in the process that in Shakespeare's England there was no separation between the activities of tumblers, dancers, and so on and the legitimate theatre, as it later came to be called.

*

But, while the place of *The Merry Wives of Windsor* in the theatre is secure and safe enough, criticism of it has for more than two and a half centuries been bedevilled by a powerful yet dubious tradition. In 1702 John Dennis, now better remembered as a critic than as a playwright, published, under the title of *The Comical Gallant*, an adaptation of Shakespeare's play that he had recently made. To it he prefixed a dedication which opens with an attempt to explain why his version had failed on the stage. He says that from the time he began to work on it, his project met with hostility from two different sources. There were, on the one hand, he states, those who believed *The Merry Wives of Windsor* 'to be so admirable that nothing ought to be added to it', and, on the other, those who 'fancied it to be so despicable that anyone's time would be lost upon it'. He then goes on to make a much quoted assertion:

> *That this comedy was not despicable, I guessed for several reasons: first, I knew very well that it had pleased one of the greatest queens that ever was in the world, great not only for her wisdom in the arts of government, but for her knowledge of polite learning, and her nice taste of the drama, for such a taste we may be sure she had, by the relish which she had of the Ancients. This comedy was written at her command, and by her direction, and she was so eager to see it acted that she commanded it to be finished in fourteen days; and was afterwards, as the tradition tells us, very well pleased at the representation.*

Engaged in a piece of special pleading, designed to justify his own action in refurbishing Shakespeare's comedy, Dennis cites no authority, except 'the tradition', to support his confident assertion about that comedy's origins, though it must have been written at least a hundred years before he put pen to paper. Two years later he repeated the story, but with a significant alteration in detail which does not inspire confidence in his reliability. In a polemical essay called *The Person of Quality's Answer to Mr. Collier's Letter*, which was published in 1704, he wrote that Queen Elizabeth 'encouraged playhouses to that degree that she ... commanded Shakespeare to write the comedy of *The Merry Wives*, and to write it in ten days' time'. The way in which fourteen days have shrunk to ten in the course of a couple of years suggests that Dennis had imbibed something of Falstaff's cavalier attitude to numbers from his contact with him.

Nevertheless, the story that the Queen commanded the play to be written seems to have won immediate acceptance. In 1709 Nicholas Rowe produced, as the introduction to his edition of Shakespeare's plays, the first biography of the poet ever to be written. In it he says of Queen Elizabeth:

> She was so well pleased with that admirable character of Falstaff, in the two parts of Henry IV, that she commanded him [Shakespeare] to continue it for one play more, and to show him in love. This is said to be the occasion of his writing The Merry Wives of Windsor. How well she was obeyed the play itself is an admirable proof.

Like Dennis, Rowe offers no evidence for this specific statement, though he does say, later on in the Life, that he was deeply indebted to the actor Thomas Betterton for many of the details in it about Shakespeare's career. Part at least, however, of his comment is suspect, for, as Dr Johnson shrewdly observed, if the Queen really did ask for a play showing Falstaff in love, Shakespeare disobeyed the royal command, since he shows Falstaff merely pretending to be in love for the sake of the money he hopes to win by counterfeiting attachments he does not feel.

Dennis, it will be noticed, says nothing about Falstaff; Rowe nothing about the fourteen days. But it was an easy matter to bring two such attractive stories into harmony with one another, and little time was lost over doing it. In 1710 Charles Gildon edited a volume containing Shakespeare's poems, which had been omitted from Rowe's edition. In it he included *Remarks on the Plays of Shakespeare*. One of the remarks, on *The Merry Wives of Windsor*, is as follows:

> *The Fairies in the fifth Act makes a handsome compliment to the Queen, in her palace at Windsor, who had obliged him to write a play of Sir John Falstaff in love, and which I am very well assured he performed in a fortnight; a prodigious thing, when all is so well contrived, and carried on without the least confusion.*

Thus, by a process of accretion and reconciliation, does a tradition evolve.

Its survival will depend on its usefulness. The tradition about the origin of *The Merry Wives of Windsor* is as strong today as it ever was. It may, therefore, be assumed that it is very useful indeed. So it is. Editors and critics when they avail themselves of it, which they almost invariably do, usually describe it as 'more reliable than most'. What they really mean is 'more convenient than most'. It is no older and no more reliable than another story related by Rowe, to the effect that Shakespeare in his youth often went deer-stealing in the park of Sir

Thomas Lucy at Charlecote Manor near Stratford. Lucy, so the story goes, prosecuted the young poacher, and drove him away from his native Warwickshire, with the result that he went off to London and became the most successful playwright of the time, and, indeed, of all time. Shakespeare, however, far from being grateful to Lucy for this unintentional stimulus to fame and fortune, harboured feelings of resentment against him, and, still according to Rowe, took his revenge by exhibiting his one-time persecutor as Master Justice Shallow in *The Merry Wives of Windsor*, carefully identifying him by the reference to his coat of arms in the first scene of the play.

But, while this part of Rowe's account has met with a good deal of scepticism, the other tradition to which he contributed has not. It is much too helpful to be discarded, having all the qualities so often desired and so rarely found in a maid-of-all-work. It can be used to buttress, or to apologize for, every estimate of the play's worth, ranging from outright approval and admiration at the one extreme to intense dislike and condemnation at the other. Those who think well of the comedy – a small but distinguished minority – agree with Gildon that only a master of his craft could have produced anything of this quality within the time which, according to Dennis, Shakespeare had at his disposal. The loose ends and the confusions in the conduct of the action, of which there are a number despite Gildon's statement to the contrary, are seen, of course, as an inevitable but venial consequence of hurried composition. Those who disapprove of it – a larger and even more distinguished minority, objecting in the main to the treatment of Falstaff in the play – can interpret what they see as its crudity or even brutality as an expression of the resentment Shakespeare felt at having an unwelcome and uncongenial task imposed upon him. The rest – the great majority – are able to justify their indifference to the drama and their feeling that it is very second-rate Shakespeare by regarding it as something he had to do, as distinct from something he wanted to do. In their view, he did what he was asked to do readily enough, but he never became fully engaged with his play. To support their position they point to the preponderance of prose in the comedy and to its lack of the authentic Shakespearian magic.

*

After reading the critics one is left with the conviction that if the tradition had not existed, it would have been necessary to invent it. Perhaps Dennis did. But, if one puts the tradition out of one's mind, and reads *The Merry Wives of Windsor* with no preconceived ideas about how it came into being, one is left with the exact converse of the former impression: had the tradition not existed, no one would ever have seen any need for it whatsoever. The play says in almost every line that it was written for the public theatre, not for a courtly audience. It is clearly intended, more than any other play in the canon, to reflect the life, to meet the expectations, and to endorse the values of the Elizabethan bourgeoisie, the class from which its author came and to which he belonged.

Drawing, no doubt, on his knowledge of Stratford even more than on his knowledge of Windsor, though he was obviously familiar with it, Shakespeare creates an unforgettable picture of life as it was lived in a small country town round about the year 1600. It is in keeping with the whole development of his art that he should. *The Merry Wives of Windsor* grows naturally out of the two parts of *Henry IV* in a much deeper sense than that represented by its carry-over of a number of characters from those plays.

In *Henry IV* he had dramatized the low life of the metropolis in the scenes that take place at the Boar's Head in Eastcheap, and the ordinary everyday life of the countryside in the scenes that take place on Master Justice Shallow's estate in the Cotswolds, using this new material, the distillation of his acute awareness of the world he was living in, as a kind of counterpoint to the political activities of the early fifteenth century which are his main theme. Indeed, it is hard to escape the conclusion that the introduction of this comic matter into the history play probably stemmed from a growing realization that what would now be called social history was a necessary adjunct to political history. He must have perceived, as the histories followed one another, that he was in fact writing a national epic in dramatic form, and that, to make this epic complete, the normal life of the English people, remote from the court and the battlefield, as he knew it in his own day, had to be given its rightful place within the total pattern.

But when he had finished the writing of the histories with the composition, in 1599, of *Henry V*, clearly designed as the keystone to the great arch of historical events stretching from 1398 to 1485, there was still one important section of English society that had been largely omitted from the edifice: the thriving urban middle class. *The Merry Wives of Windsor*, probably more by accident than by deliberate intent, repairs the omission. It is the most English of all the comedies, in the sense that it is the only one that is set wholly and unequivocally in the country he knew best, perhaps the only country that he knew from direct personal experience. In it there are no kings, no nobles, and no politics. The character highest in rank would seem to be young Master Fenton, though his precise social status is never made clear. Then comes Sir

John Falstaff, a knight, it is true, but a very decadent knight. Two other figures – Master Justice Shallow and his 'wise cousin' Slender – can lay some claim to gentility. The rest are either citizens of Windsor and their wives, or servants and hangers-on. Furthermore, the concerns of the play are business and domestic. Money and marriages, not crowns and kingdoms, are the goals of endeavour and the objectives of intrigue.

Windsor, as Shakespeare portrays it, is a solid, comfortable, self-assured community. Page and Ford are substantial citizens, and Page has that pride in his own class which seems to have been characteristic of many members of the Elizabethan bourgeoisie. His main objection to Fenton as a suitor for his daughter's hand is that the young man has no means, but the fact that Fenton is of a much higher rank than Anne also counts with him. He does not wish her to marry out of her class. Mistress Page and Mistress Ford, far from being the submissive partners in marriage recommended by the social theories of the age, are, as merchants' wives often seem to have been, enterprising, independent women, well able to take care of themselves, and, one gets the impression, of their husbands' affairs too, should the need arise. Indeed, if the report Falstaff has heard of them is true, they actually do, since they control the purse-strings. Then there are the two professional men, without whom no community could survive, the doctor and the parson, to minister to the ills of the flesh and the spirit; the Host of the Garter Inn, to provide entertainment, both in the modern sense of amusement and in the Elizabethan sense of food, drink, and accommodation; and, finally, that other essential ingredient in the life of a small town, the born gossip, in the shape of Mistress Quickly. The whole group has a certain representative quality about it.

Exactly what sort of business Page and Ford are engaged in is not revealed. There is no reason why it should be, since the action of the play takes place, very appropriately in view of the kind of play it is, at what appears to be a holiday time. The Court is at Windsor, or so Doctor Caius assures us in Act I, scene 4, and the townsfolk seem to be making the most of the occasion. The accent is on sport. Page has been coursing on the Cotswolds before the first scene opens. Later on, he invites Ford, Caius, and Evans to go 'a-birding' with him. His son, little William, is given a day off from school. The Host of the Garter regards his gulling of the doctor and the parson as sport; the Wives see their fooling of Falstaff in the same light; and, at the end of it all, Mistress Page, who has herself been tricked by this time over the matter of Anne's marriage, will say:

> Good husband, let us every one go home,
> And laugh this sport o'er by a country fire;
> Sir John and all.   V.5.233-5

*

That 'country fire' is not without its significance for the play as a whole. We have heard of something like it before. Near the beginning of the fourth scene of Act I, Mistress Quickly promises her fellow servant John Rugby a posset in the evening 'at the latter end of a sea-coal fire'. The fires are necessary and welcome because the weather of this comedy is English, not Arcadian. It is a 'raw rheumatic day' when Evans and Caius go out into the fields to fight their abortive duel. In such conditions a tale, read or told by the fireside, was a popular way 'to shorten the lives of long winter's-nights', as Thomas Dekker puts it on the title-page of his pamphlet *The Wonderful Year*, published in 1603. About ten years before *The Merry Wives of Windsor* was written, George Peele had put this familiar situation to good dramatic use in his comedy *The Old Wives' Tale*, which opens with two young men settling down to spend a night by the fire listening to a tale told by an old woman. She has barely begun her narrative, however, when the characters in it make their appearance on the stage and enact the rest of it, a charming inconsequential mixture of fairy-tale, folk-lore, and personal satire.

But, while they enjoyed traditional and romantic matter of the sort that Peele exploits so well, the Elizabethans, and particularly, it would seem, the middle class, also had a pronounced taste for the 'merry tales' which provided the staple for the jest-books that had such a vogue in the sixteenth century. A 'merry tale' is a brief anecdote, relating some form of practical joke, trickery, deception, or clever evading action. A considerable number turn on the relations of men and women: how an adulterous wife avoids detection by her husband, how a smart girl eludes the advances of a lecherous friar, and so on. In such stories 'cunning shifts' and 'quick answers' are held up to admiration. 'Merry tales' of this sort can be seen as the much attenuated descendants of the *fabliaux* of the Middle Ages, such as *The Miller's Tale* and *The Reeve's Tale* in Chaucer's *Canterbury Tales*, and many of the stories in Boccaccio's *Decameron*. There are also a number of them which depend for their point on the foreigner's difficulties with the English language. Welshmen in particular are held up to ridicule on this score; and their proverbial fondness for cheese, especially toasted cheese, is regarded as a sure source of mirth. Falstaff alludes to it in the final scene of Shakespeare's play, when, disgusted with himself for the way in which he has been taken in and has laid himself wide open to the moralizings of Parson Evans, he says: 'Am I ridden with a Welsh goat too? . . . 'Tis time I were choked with a piece of toasted cheese' (V.5.136–8).

It is to the kind of literature represented by the *fabliau* and the 'merry tale' that the main plot of *The Merry Wives of Windsor* belongs. Indeed, it seems likely that to an Elizabethan audience the very title of the comedy would have sounded less innocent than it does to modern ears. They would have expected the Wives to have a taste not only for practical jokes but also for more questionable forms of fun. Mistress Page is careful to rule out the latter possibility by saying of Falstaff, when she and Mistress Ford are about to disguise him as the Wise Woman of Brainford:

> *We'll leave a proof, by that which we will do,*
> *Wives may be merry, and yet honest too.*
>
> IV.2.98–9

In the 'merry tale' mirth and honesty, meaning 'chastity', are rarely found in company. They certainly are not in the nearest analogue that has yet been discovered to the story of Falstaff and the Wives: a *novella* in the same collection of tales that Shakespeare had already drawn on for the main plot of *The Merchant of Venice*, Ser Giovanni Fiorentino's *Il Pecorone*, dating from the later fourteenth century, though it was not published until 1558. In the Italian story a student called Bucciuolo, having finished his course in Canon Law at Bologna, asks his professor to give him some instruction in the Art of Love. The professor complies with this request; and his advice is so sound that very soon the student is able to report to him that he is making good progress in his assault on the chastity of a married woman. However, when the student tells his master that he has been given an assignation by the

INTRODUCTION

lady at her house, the professor begins to suspect that she
could well be his own wife. He therefore follows Bucciuolo,
sees his own wife open the door to the apt student, and
promptly returns to the university, in order to get his
sword and dagger. Properly equipped now for the task of
vengeance, he comes home once more, and bangs on the
door, which is bolted. Realizing that it must be her husband outside, the resourceful lady hides Bucciuolo under
a great heap of clothes which are still damp from the
wash-tub – *nascoselo sotto un monte di panni di bucato, i
quali non erano ancora rasciutti.* Then, putting on an air of
injured innocence, she lets in her husband, pretending that
his wild appearance makes her fear for his sanity. The
professor searches the house from top to bottom, but
finds no one. When it is all over, his wife bids him beware
of what must be, she says, a temptation from the devil,
causing him to see things that are not there. Half con-
vinced that she may be right, the husband goes back to
his work. The lady closes the door, and helps Bucciuolo
out from under the washing. Then, after an excellent
meal, the two of them go to bed together.

In the morning Bucciuolo leaves, promising to return
the same evening. He then goes to see the professor, and
tells him of his escape from the husband, of the happy
night he has spent, and of his assignation for the evening.
When he goes again to the house, the professor, fully
armed this time, is close behind him. No sooner has he
been admitted than the professor is hammering on the
door. The wily wife immediately puts out the light, opens
the door, embraces her husband closely, and so enables
Bucciuolo to slip out behind her, unseen by the husband.
She then cries out in a loud voice, saying that the professor
has gone mad, thus bringing the neighbours on to the
scene. They assure him that his wife's conduct is ir-

reproachable. At this point her two brothers arrive. They too are amazed by the professor's accusation that his wife has a lover concealed in the house; but, as he persists in it, they agree to join in the search. The professor goes straight to the heap of clothes, and begins stabbing at it with his sword. This strange action persuades them that he is indeed mad, and, when he becomes furious with them for their incredulity, they cudgel him soundly, chain him up, and, on the following morning, call in a doctor.

Knowing nothing of these events, Bucciuolo goes off to the university as usual, intending to recount the latest development in his love affair to the professor. Only then does he learn that the professor has gone mad. Several of the other students are going to visit the unfortunate man, and he decides to go with them. Not until they reach the house does the truth dawn on him. He tells the professor that he is very sorry to see him in such a sad state, and that he will do anything he can to help. To this the professor replies: 'Bucciuolo, Bucciuolo, go away in God's name, for you have learned all too well at my expense.' The young man takes his advice, and returns to his family in Rome.

That Shakespeare knew this story, or one very like it, seems beyond doubt. Bucciuolo telling the professor about his affair with the professor's wife corresponds to Falstaff telling Ford, whom he knows as Brook, about his intention to seduce Mistress Ford. Both the professor and Ford learn, moreover, from the would-be seducer how he has managed to elude their vigilance. Falstaff's first escape, in the buck-basket, could have been suggested by Bucciuolo's hiding under the washing, and the cudgelling he undergoes at his second attempt may well owe something to the beating the professor receives at the hands of his wife's brothers. There are also several rather unexpected references to Falstaff's learning in the play, which would be more appropriate to Bucciuolo than they are to Falstaff. Ford's behaviour in searching the buck-basket when he makes his second effort to entrap the knight is very like the professor's stabbing of the linen in a similar situation; and, just as the wife in *Il Pecorone* seeks to convince her husband that he has been led by the devil to see things that are not there, so Page asks Ford: 'What spirit, what devil suggests this imagination?' (III.3.202–3), and Evans remarks later: 'Master Ford, you must pray, and not follow the imaginations of your own heart' (IV.2.146–7).

The similarities between the *novella* and the main plot of *The Merry Wives of Windsor* are plain enough; but the differences are even more striking. In the first place, there is nothing in the Italian story to correspond to Falstaff's third adventure, when he appears in Windsor Forest at midnight, disguised as Herne the Hunter. Secondly, while the professor has for a long time no notion that the object of Bucciuolo's pursuit is his own wife, it is Ford's suspicion, aroused by Pistol's betrayal of Falstaff's plan, that the knight is seeking to cuckold him which causes him to disguise himself as Brook, in order to test his wife and to keep abreast of what is going on. The dramatic effect of this change is great. Not only does it lead to scenes between Ford and Falstaff that are rich in complex irony, but it also ensures that the Wives' plot to discomfit and show up Falstaff works even better than they could have hoped. They do not have to pretend that Ford is at the door when Falstaff visits Mistress Ford; he really is. Thirdly, Falstaff, the would-be seducer, is a very different figure from the student Bucciuolo, and he is inspired by very different motives. For Bucciuolo the art of love is something he has to learn in order to complete his education; and he really does fall for the professor's wife. Falstaff, on the other hand, is a middle-aged man, if not an old man, who is in no way interested in the art of love. Dr Johnson makes the point with his characteristic common sense, when, after referring to the tradition that the play was written on the orders of Queen Elizabeth, he continues thus:

> *No task is harder than that of writing to the ideas of another. Shakespeare knew what the Queen, if the story be true, seems not to have known, that by any real passion of tenderness, the selfish trust, the careless jollity, and the lazy luxury of Falstaff must have suffered so much abatement that little of his former cast would have remained. Falstaff could not love but by ceasing to be Falstaff. He could only counterfeit love, and his professions could be prompted, not by the hope of pleasure, but of money.*

> (*Dr Johnson on Shakespeare*,
> edited by W. K. Wimsatt (Harmondsworth, 1969),
> page 110)

The consequences of this alteration are considerable. Falstaff sets out to practise not the art of love but the art of cony-catching. He says so himself when, announcing his plans to Pistol and Nym, he remarks on his penniless state: 'There is no remedy – I must cony-catch, I must shift' (I.3.30–31). This declaration of intent relates the play to yet another field of popular literature. A feature of respectable urban life is the interest taken by the honest, the frugal, and the industrious in the activities of those to whom none of these adjectives applies. Prior to 1591 there had been several pamphlets published, of a more or less sociological kind, dealing with the tricks of card-sharpers, thieves, confidence men, and the like, but in that year Robert Greene produced the first of the numerous pamphlets that he was to write before his death, in September 1592, on the London underworld and its denizens. These cony-catching pamphlets, as they were called, deliberately exploited the sensational possibilities of crime, and, of course, its comic potentialities as well. They are well larded with 'merry tales' about the fleecing of the foolish. According to Greene, pretending to be in love with a girl, usually a serving-maid, was one of the favourite devices used by cony-catchers to gain access to the houses of citizens they intended to rob. Falstaff's plan, as he himself acknowledges, is of much the same order. From the outset he has placed himself in a position for which there can be no sympathy. But it is also a ridiculous position, for he is not content to practise on one woman but actually takes on two. Any Elizabethan would have foreseen the outcome, since one of the commonest proverbs of the time – and it was a time much addicted to proverbs, as the play so amply demonstrates – was 'Hercules himself cannot deal with two'. From the moment that the two women compare the letters he has sent them and decide on a concerted plan of action, his fate is certain. He does, however, enjoy one minor consolation: to the end of the play they are in the dark about his real motives. They have the truth within their grasp, but they miss it. When they realize that the letters Falstaff has sent them are identical, except for the names, Mistress Page comments:

I warrant he hath a thousand of these letters, writ with blank space for different names – sure, more – and these are of the second edition. He will print them, out of doubt. . . .
                                                                    II.1.69–72

She is referring to the practice, fairly common among hack-writers of the time, who were largely dependent for their livelihood on the gifts they received from those to whom they dedicated their works, of leaving a blank space for the name of the dedicatee, to be filled in as the occasion arose, thus securing money from several patrons, each thinking himself the sole object of the author's flattery. Yet, despite this allusion to a form of cheating, it never seems to occur to either of the Wives that it is their money which excites Falstaff's interest in them, not their personal charms. They are not, therefore, without their vanity, even though Mistress Page does recognize that the 'holiday time' of her beauty has passed.

It is almost the only criticism of the Wives that the play offers, and it is by no means a very obvious criticism. The reason for this is that *The Merry Wives of Windsor*, as well as being about citizens and their way of life, is written from the citizens' point of view. In the *novella* ordinary morality is at a discount. No sympathy is wasted on the professor, who should have known better than to instruct a young student in the science of seduction; and there is no condemnation of the wife. She shows the readiness of wit expected of a woman in her position. But in Shakespeare's play the Wives exercise their powers of invention, not to deceive their husbands, but to administer a lesson – several lessons, in fact – to the man who threatens their whole way of life. It was the middle class in Elizabethan England that seems to have set the highest value on the marriage tie; and in this respect, as in so many others, Mistress Page and Mistress Ford are typical of that class. They are broad-spoken and quite ready to indulge in bawdy jests, but their reputations as honest married women really do matter to them. There is no mistaking the sense of affront and outrage which informs their speeches in Act II, scene 1. What they say about Falstaff is comic in its picturesque exaggeration. 'What a Herod of Jewry is this!' exclaims Mistress Page. 'What tempest,

I trow, threw this whale, with so many tuns of oil in his belly, ashore at Windsor?' demands Mistress Ford. But when they move off together to consult 'against this greasy knight', they are bent on revenge. Falstaff is to be taught that citizens' wives are not the simple-minded creatures of easy virtue that he takes them for.

*

The Merry Wives of Windsor is, in fact, a revenge play, but of a very unusual kind. Placed in a bourgeois setting, inspired by trivial motives, and seen from a middle-class point of view, revenge becomes a subject for comedy not tragedy. The revenge motive is present from the outset, and serves to bind together the various elements of which the play is composed, giving them a certain thematic unity. Looked at in terms of plot development, the opening appears to be a false start. Shallow expresses his determination to have redress for the injury Falstaff has done him in stealing his deer; but nothing comes of it. Falstaff meets the accusation with a brazen admission of guilt: 'I will answer it straight. I have done all this. That is now answered' (I.1.109–10). Shallow is nonplussed; and that is the end of the matter. Nevertheless, the idea of revenge has been announced, and it is taken further when Slender brings his charges against Falstaff and his three henchmen, with much the same results. When the motives for revenge are stolen deer, a broken head, and a picked pocket, the whole notion of revenge looks ridiculous. It looks even more so when the would-be avengers are as spineless and ineffectual as Shallow and Slender show themselves to be.

The next pair of avengers to appear prove slightly more formidable and considerably more effective. Ordered by Falstaff to act as his messengers to the Wives, Nym and Pistol rather unexpectedly resent the idea of being used as

panders, and refuse to do his bidding. Falstaff promptly
turns them out of his service. Thereupon they make the
proper gestures and take the appropriate oaths. 'Wilt thou
revenge?' asks Pistol, to which Nym answers 'By welkin
and her star!' (I.3.85). It is, of course, sheer parody of the
usual revenger's gestures and utterance, as are the plans
they proceed to announce; but in this citizen world even
such cardboard figures as Nym and Pistol can enjoy a
limited success. Their design to embroil Page with Falstaff
gets nowhere. Page's common sense and his trust in his
wife make him immune to Nym's suggestions. But Ford is
another matter. Jealous by temperament, he listens to
Pistol's insinuations, and becomes a comic Othello.

The next revenger to appear on the scene is Doctor
Caius. Discovering Simple hidden in his closet, he quickly
extracts the truth from him, that he has come as an
emissary from Parson Evans to ask Mistress Quickly to use
her influence with Anne Page in the interest of the new
suitor Slender. In love with Anne himself, Caius cannot
brook the idea of a rival or of interference. He therefore
pens a challenge to Evans, who accepts it. The absurdity
of this is patent to all Windsor; and the Host's plan that it
be turned into a jest meets with a ready acceptance. In the
end, this revenge action, like those of Shallow and
Slender, fizzles out, but not before it has begotten another
revenge action. The Doctor and the Parson are reconciled,
but both are smarting at the way in which they have been
gulled by the Host. Consequently, Caius falls in quickly
and eagerly with Evans's suggestion: 'let us knog our
prains together to be revenge on this same scald, scurvy,
cogging companion, the host of the Garter' (III.1.109–11).
The precise manner in which they bring their revenge
about is not shown; but the evident delight with which they
announce to the Host that three cozening Germans are

active in the district, and that the preparations he has made to entertain a German duke and his followers are all in vain, since no German duke is coming to Windsor, are a clear enough indication that they have played their part in cheating him.

Ford is yet another revenger. Disguised as Brook, he goes to see Falstaff in Act II, scene 2, skilfully worms Falstaff's plans out of him, at the price of hearing some very uncomplimentary things about himself, and decides to be revenged. He is, most thoroughly; but on the first two occasions he is completely unaware at the time of the satisfaction he is getting. He does not know that Falstaff is sweating with fear in the buck-basket, or that the old woman he cudgels so soundly is Falstaff in disguise. It is only at the very end that he is able, with the help of the Wives, to savour the pleasures of triumph to the full, as he gloats over his one-time tormentor and administers the final stab with his sharp reminder that Falstaff still faces the pain of paying back the money he has obtained on the false pretence of being able to seduce Mistress Ford. Not the least of the play's ironies is that the fat knight's plan to fill his pockets leaves him more deeply in debt than ever.

Even Falstaff, the main target of revenge, comes for a short time to see himself in the role of the avenger. Having been twice deluded by the machinations of the two women, he ignorantly attributes his failures and tribulations to the intervention of Ford. Embarking on his third assault on Mistress Ford's virtue, he tells her disguised husband: 'Follow me. I'll tell you strange things of this knave Ford, on whom tonight I will be revenged' (V.1.25–6). His 'revenge' recoils, of course, on his own head.

The Wives, the avengers in chief, plan and execute the

most thorough and fitting piece of revenge that even
Elizabethan drama has to offer. They are not satisfied with
one act of retribution for Falstaff's slight on their honour.
Nothing less than three will do for them. Each involves the
use of the complicated intrigues normal in revenge tragedy,
including a good deal of play-acting; each works without a
hitch; and the final one actually takes the form of a masque,
the commonest of all devices for bringing about the
denouement in serious revenge plays. Moreover, it is
wonderfully appropriate, because it exhibits the would-be
cuckold-maker as the great archetype of cuckolds. Un-
inhibited by scruples, because their aim is sport not blood,
the Wives give a highly efficient practical demonstration
of 'how to do it' that makes many a melancholy stage
avenger look like a bungling amateur. *The Merry Wives of
Windsor* is surely a most consummate piece of burlesque.
Shakespeare, soon to write *Hamlet*, has transformed the
revenge convention by shifting it into a middle-class
setting and submitting it to a middle-class point of view.
To rephrase the Prince of Denmark slightly, it may be said
of the Wives: 'they do but jest, revenge in jest; no offence
i'th'world'.

*

It is not only the revenge play that undergoes a meta-
morphosis in *The Merry Wives of Windsor*. At the opening
of the final scene, Falstaff makes his entry disguised as
Herne the Hunter, with a huge set of buck's horns upon
his head. Fully aware of his transformation, he soliloquizes
about it in one of the richest speeches in the play:

> *The Windsor bell hath struck twelve; the minute draws on.
> Now, the hot-blooded gods assist me! Remember, Jove,
> thou wast a bull for thy Europa. Love set on thy horns. O
> powerful love, that in some respects makes a beast a man,*

29

in some other a man a beast. You were also, Jupiter, a swan
for the love of Leda. O omnipotent love, how near the god
drew to the complexion of a goose! A fault done first in
the form of a beast – O Jove, a beastly fault – and then
another fault in the semblance of a fowl – think on't,
Jove, a foul fault! When gods have hot backs, what shall
poor men do? For me, I am here a Windsor stag, and the
fattest, I think, i'th'forest. Send me a cool rut-time, Jove,
or who can blame me to piss my tallow?   V.5.1–14

This is Ovid, not moralized, as he was in the Middle
Ages, but vulgarized to suit citizen taste. It is no accident
that he should be referred to here, as the play reaches its
climax, for he has already made a large contribution to it.
Characteristically, Falstaff, who never suffers from undue
modesty, sees himself as Jove, but it is not in this form that
Shakespeare presents him. The egregious Pistol provides
the clue to the figure from the *Metamorphoses* who really
matters in this play. Taking his revenge on Falstaff by
warning Ford that the knight has designs on Mistress Ford,
Pistol responds to Ford's question, 'Love my wife?',
with these words:

> *With liver burning hot. Prevent. Or go thou*
> *Like Sir Actaeon he, with Ringwood at thy heels.*
>   II.1.110–11

Actaeon was the hunter in classical mythology who accidentally came upon Diana, the goddess of chastity, as she
was bathing in a woodland fountain. Enraged at this intrusion upon her privacy, the goddess promptly turned
him into a stag. Actaeon fled, but his hounds pursued him
and tore him to pieces.
    It is a myth which admits of more than one interpre-
tation. Shakespeare, who knew and loved the *Metamor-*

phoses, offers a singularly beautiful one in the opening lines of *Twelfth Night*. Asked by Curio whether he intends to hunt the hart, Orsino replies:

> *Why, so I do, the noblest that I have.*
> *O, when mine eyes did see Olivia first,*
> *Methought she purged the air of pestilence.*
> *That instant was I turned into a hart,*
> *And my desires, like fell and cruel hounds,*
> *E'er since pursue me.*

I.i.19–24

Actaeon here is the unrequited lover, a prey to insistent longings that give him no rest. But in the popular mind Actaeon, because he was given the horns of a stag, became the type of the cuckold. This is the fate with which Pistol threatens Ford. It is not a fate that Ford is ever in danger of suffering; but his interviews, as Brook, with Falstaff convince him that he is, and he becomes the quarry of his own tormenting suspicions that almost drive him mad. There is, thus, something of Actaeon about him. But the real Actaeon of the comedy is Falstaff. Making his entry into the play as a hunter and stealer of deer, he soon casts himself for the part of a hunter and stealer of women, driven to it by the emptiness of his purse and drawn to it by his vanity, which leads him to interpret the Wives' courteous reception of him as an invitation to immorality. Oblivious at their first meeting with him of the effect they are having on him, the Wives, like Diana, are outraged when they discover what he really thinks of them. Taking the course that she did, they pursue him with vengeance. The hunter has become the hunted. Ford is both huntsman and hound, frequently resorting to hunting language as he takes up the chase. 'I'll warrant we'll unkennel the fox'

(III.3.153-4), he says in his huntsman's role, and 'If I cry out thus upon no trail, never trust me when I open again' (IV.2.185-6) in his role as hound.

The action of the play moves forward, like a hunt, at an ever-increasing pace, to reach its climax in the final scene, where Falstaff dons the buck's head of his own accord, and greets Mistress Ford as 'My doe'. A self-confessed Actaeon, wearing the horns he sought to graft on another man's head, he is brought to bay by the characters in the masque, subjected to pinching and burning, and exposed, unresisting, to the taunts and gibes of Ford, Evans, and the rest. The travesty of the Ovidian myth is complete.

*

Most critics regard *The Merry Wives of Windsor* as a pure farce. That it is the most farcical play Shakespeare ever wrote, more so even than *The Comedy of Errors* and *The Taming of the Shrew*, may be admitted at once. The tricks that are played on Falstaff – his concealment in the buck-basket, his precipitation into the cold waters of the Thames, his cudgelling at the hands of Ford, and the pinching and burning he suffers – all these incidents are not only uproariously funny but they also have that violent aggressive quality which is so characteristic of farce. So have the actions and the ravings of Ford when he searches his own house for Falstaff, throwing unoffending linen this way and that in his frenzy. Yet to list these incidents is to be reminded of something else. We do not see Falstaff being thrown into the river; we hear about it from his own lips in a superb piece of comic narrative, which gains enormously from the fact that it is being related to Ford, the man from whom he escaped in the buck-basket. Here is what he says:

Nay, you shall hear, Master Brook, what I have suffered to bring this woman to evil for your good. Being thus crammed in the basket, a couple of Ford's knaves, his hinds, were called forth by their mistress to carry me in the name of foul clothes to Datchet Lane. They took me on their shoulders, met the jealous knave their master in the door, who asked them once or twice what they had in their basket. I quaked for fear lest the lunatic knave would have searched it; but Fate, ordaining he should be a cuckold, held his hand. Well, on went he for a search, and away went I for foul clothes. But mark the sequel, Master Brook. I suffered the pangs of three several deaths: first, an intolerable fright to be detected with a jealous rotten bell-wether; next, to be compassed like a good bilbo in the circumference of a peck, hilt to point, heel to head; and then, to be stopped in, like a strong distillation, with stinking clothes that fretted in their own grease. Think of that, a man of my kidney – think of that – that am as subject to heat as butter; a man of continual dissolution and thaw. It was a miracle to 'scape suffocation. And in the height of this bath, when I was more than half stewed in grease, like a Dutch dish, to be thrown into the Thames, and cooled, glowing hot, in that surge, like a horse-shoe. Think of that – hissing hot – think of that, Master Brook!

III.5.87–112

It is Falstaff's use of poetic images that makes the speech. Simile follows simile in an inexhaustible stream, transforming both what we have seen – the carrying out of Falstaff in the buck-basket – and what we have not seen – his being thrown into the Thames – from incident into art. In *The Merry Wives of Windsor* farcical happenings occur as much for the sake of what can be made out of them as for their own intrinsic appeal. They become the occasions

33

for comic prose arias. It is this, more than anything else, that makes the role of Ford the richest and the most rewarding, as many actors have realized, in the whole play. To begin with, Ford is that perennial butt of laughter, the jealous husband. But circumstance and his own capacity for a twisted yet logical train of thought combine to transform him into something much more interesting. The initial impetus is given by Pistol, whose accusations of Falstaff tie in so beautifully with Ford's suspicions that he actually describes Pistol of all people as 'a good sensible fellow' (II.1.137). Page's expressions of confidence in his wife, smacking as they do of *hubris*, help to confirm Ford's doubts about his, leading to his decision to adopt a disguise, in order to find out what Falstaff is really up to. It has all the appearance of a wager that must pay off. As he puts it, in the first of those soliloquies which are such a feature of the part: 'If I find her honest, I lose not my labour. If she be otherwise, 'tis labour well bestowed' (II.1.219–21).

Ford's aim is to find out the truth. From the time of his first interview with Falstaff, he is, therefore, in a position from which there can be no escape, for what he learns is the truth – not all of it, since he knows nothing of Mistress Ford's motives, but as much as is available – that his wife has given the knight an assignation. In due course, he learns further how Falstaff escaped his vigilance, with the help and connivance of Mistress Ford. Everything conspires to convince him of his rightness and to give him a sense of power, yet all the time he is caught in a trap of his own making. Triumph and frustration are inextricably mingled, finding their expression in speeches and soliloquies in which one rhetorical question follows another and in which the imagery of cuckoldry wells up in an irrepressible stream. Knowing that his suspicions are completely unjustified, and that his wife has it in her power to disabuse him of them whenever she chooses, an audience can enjoy the absurdity of his perverted logic and conflicting feelings; but there are moments when the reader, if not the spectator, is forced to recognize that this portrayal of the obsessed mind anticipates what Shakespeare was to do later in his depiction of Othello and Leontes.

As well as fun of this aggressive and, in the case of Ford, disturbing kind, there is also in *The Merry Wives of Windsor* fun of another sort, such as is not usually to be found in farce. Slender's wooing of Anne Page, if wooing it can be called, is comedy in its purest and most blessed state, utterly without a trace of malice, rejoicing delightedly in the absurdities of which human beings are capable. Hazlitt, in an inspired phrase, calls Slender 'a very potent piece of imbecility'. It is his utter incapacity to play the role of lover, for which Evans and Shallow cast him – indeed his inability to play any role whatever – that makes Slender so delightful. Inarticulate, except when the subject is bears, bashful, unused to the society of women, Slender is at once comic and pathetic. His is the vanity of innocence; and innocence is a rare and even a precious quality in this play, where everyone else is busy plotting and scheming against someone or other. Urged on by Shallow, who tries to encourage him by saying 'O boy, thou hadst a father!', Slender begins his wooing of Anne with a splendidly fatuous effort to get Shallow to do the job for him, telling her:

> *I had a father, Mistress Anne. My uncle can tell you good jests of him. Pray you, uncle, tell Mistress Anne the jest how my father stole two geese out of a pen, good uncle.*
>
> III.4.38–41

It is a wonderfully goose-like start. Moreover, it is Slender's
constant reiteration of the phrase 'Sweet Anne Page', the
best that he can manage to express his admiration of her,
which does more than anything else to create a sense of
that young woman's personality and presence.

*

The characterization of Ford and Slender, the realism of
the manners, and the artistry so evident in the use of the
revenge motive and of classical myth suggest that *The
Merry Wives of Windsor* may be a true comedy after all,
rather than a pure farce. A consideration of the play's
structure gives further support to this idea. Ignoring the
various underplots, one can discern two main strands in
the fabric of the play: the Wives' revenge on Falstaff,
carrying the business of Ford in disguise with it, and the
matter of Anne Page and her three wooers, Slender, Caius,
and Fenton. In terms of the action, these two plots are
kept carefully separate from one another right up to the
very last scene, where they come together with a complex
reciprocal effect on each other. The exposure of Falstaff
in the masque provides the occasion for Master Fenton
and Anne Page to steal away and get married. The returns,
first of Slender, then of Caius, and finally of Anne and
Fenton, release Falstaff from the baitings he is being
subjected to, and even give him a slight modicum of
revenge, for, after listening to Fenton's account of the
elopement, he is able to say to his tormentors: 'I am glad,
though you have ta'en a special stand to strike at me, that
your arrow hath glanced' (V.5.226–7).

But, though interaction between the two plots is skilfully postponed until the final scene, a thematic link
between them has been established much earlier. Towards
the end of Act III, scene 2, Page tells Slender that he is in

favour of Slender's suit for the hand of his daughter.
Anne herself gives us the reason, two scenes later, when,
as she goes to speak to Slender, she says:

> *This is my father's choice.*
> *O, what a world of vile ill-favoured faults*
> *Looks handsome in three hundred pounds a year!*
>
> III.4.31–3

Having told Slender of his attitude, Page goes on to say
that his wife favours Caius as a husband for Anne.
Thereupon, the Host speaks up on behalf of Fenton.
Page, however, rejects the idea out of hand. Speaking with
considerable animus, he retorts:

> *Not by my consent, I promise you. The gentleman is of
> no having. He kept company with the wild Prince and
> Poins. He is of too high a region, he knows too much. No,
> he shall not knit a knot in his fortunes with the finger of
> my substance. If he take her, let him take her simply. The
> wealth I have waits on my consent, and my consent goes
> not that way.* III.2.65–71

It has often been suggested that the remark about
Fenton's having associated with Prince Hal and Poins is
meant to set the play in the early fifteenth century. If so,
it is singularly ineffective, since the rest of the comedy
says emphatically that it takes place in Shakespeare's
own day. It seems far more likely that it is intended to
serve two other functions. In the first place, it connects Fenton with that other companion of the Prince and Poins, Sir
John Falstaff. Like Falstaff, Fenton is short of money. His
riotous association with the Prince has been a heavy drain
on his estate. At the opening of Act III, scene 4, the only
scene in the play where he appears alone with Anne for a
few moments, Fenton admits that her father's suspicion

about his mercenary motives was, to begin with, a well grounded one. It was Page's money that led him to her. Since that time, however, he has, he pleads, come to see Anne herself as the true gold. He now wants her for herself alone. Fenton, the reformed rake who marries for love and preaches a sermon on the subject that would do credit to a Puritan divine (V.5.212–22), is clearly meant to contrast with Falstaff, the unreformed and irreformable old Adam.

The second reason for the reference to 'the wild Prince and Poins' is that it was probably inserted deliberately, at the time when the play was written, as a kind of insurance policy. Had he been taxed with referring to living people, Shakespeare could have pointed to it as evidence that he was doing no such thing. He almost certainly was. It seems inconceivable that a London audience, seeing *The Merry Wives of Windsor* in 1599 or even a couple of years later, would have failed to connect the story of Anne and Fenton with a wooing, a wedding, and its aftermath, which had all the gossips of the time agog with interest – the affair of Lord Compton, Elizabeth Spencer, and her father.

William, Lord Compton, inherited his father's estate, a very substantial one indeed, in 1589, when he was twenty-one. Apparently a man of winning ways and great charm, Lord Compton became something of a favourite with Queen Elizabeth. But, like many other young aristocrats of the time, he was a great spendthrift, and soon ran deep into debt. By the late 1590s he was selling large portions of the lands he had inherited, yet was still in debt to the tune of £10,000 or more in 1599. By the beginning of that year, however, he could see rescue at hand. He had made up his mind to marry Elizabeth Spencer, a girl much inferior in rank to himself, but with far better financial prospects than he had, for she was the daughter and heiress of Sir John Spencer. Commonly known as 'rich Spencer', and with something of a reputation for parsimony, the lady's father was one of the wealthiest men in the land. A Master of the Clothworkers' Company and an Alderman of the City of London, Spencer, who had been Lord Mayor in 1594, operated as a usurer in addition to his activities as a merchant, lending money on a large scale to improvident members of the aristocracy and reaping corresponding gains.

His daughter, who would, it was thought, bring with her a dowry of £40,000, was, not surprisingly, much sought after. The first suitor in the field was another London alderman, somewhat stricken in years, Anthony Ratcliffe, whom Spencer soon turned down. He appears to have been more impressed by the suit of Sir Arthur Heningham's son, for, if a statement that he made to the Privy Council in March 1599 is to be believed, Elizabeth was actually contracted to this young man. By 1599, however, Lord Compton had become a wooer; and, once the girl had set eyes on the handsome courtier, young Heningham stood no chance. Elizabeth was determined to have Lord Compton. Her father was equally determined that she should do no such thing. The noble lord's terms were far too high. According to John Chamberlain, the great letter-writer and gossip of the time, Lord Compton was asking his prospective father-in-law for a marriage settlement that would include £10,000 in cash down, to help him clear up his debts, and a further £18,000 to redeem his mortgages. The prospect of seeing his 'well-won thrift' dissipated by a man of exactly the same station and habits as the aristocratic prodigals from whom he had acquired so much of it was more than Spencer could bear. He set his face firmly against the match, and tried to hide his daughter away from her lover. Lord Compton retaliated by using his influence with the Privy Council to have Spencer imprisoned in the Fleet. In a letter to Sir Dudley Carleton, dated 15 March 1599, Chamberlain writes:

> *Our Sir John Spenser of London was the last week commit-*
> *ted to the Fleet for a contempt, and hiding away his daughter,*
> *who they say is contracted to the Lord Compton, but he is*
> *now out again and by all means seeks to hinder the match,*
> *alleging a precontract to Sir Arthur Henningham's son;*
> *but upon his beating and misusing her, she was sequestered*
> *to one Barker's, a proctor, and from thence to Sir Henry*
> *Billingsley's, where she yet remains till the matter be*
> *tried. If the obstinate and self-willed fellow should persist*
> *in his doggedness (as he protests he will) and give her*
> *nothing, the poor Lord should have a warm catch.*

(*The Letters of John Chamberlain*, edited by N. E. McClure (Philadelphia, 1939), Volume I, page 73)

Spencer did persist in his doggedness, but in spite of his opposition the young couple were married on 18 April 1599. There was even a rumour that Lord Compton stole the girl away, prior to the marriage, by disguising himself as a baker's boy, and carrying her off in a bread-basket. (For further details of the whole affair, see Lawrence Stone, 'The Peer and the Alderman's Daughter', *History Today*, Volume XI, pages 48–55; and Thomas Dekker, *The Shoemaker's Holiday*, edited by Vittoria Sanna (Bari, 1968), pages 11–13.)

Even if one discounts the final item – though the correspondence between the bread-basket and the buck-basket is a tempting one – the parallels between the story of Anne and Fenton and the historical events leading up to the marriage of Elizabeth Spencer and Lord Compton are too many and too close to be accidental. As well as the basic similarity of a father opposed to his daughter's matching herself with a man of higher rank who is in debt and something of a prodigal, and threatening to give her nothing at her marriage if she disobeys his will, there are a number of other similarities. Just as Sir John Spencer refused Ratcliffe as a suitor to his daughter, so Page disapproves of Caius. The Doctor's age is not given, but Mistress Page tells us that he is 'well moneyed' (IV.4.86), and Anne's reaction to the thought of marriage with him leaves no doubt that she finds him most unattractive. She says of the prospect:

> *Alas, I had rather be set quick i'th'earth,*
> *And bowled to death with turnips.*   III.4.84–5

Page's approval of Slender corresponds to Spencer's approval of Sir Arthur Heningham's son; and there is a touch of parsimony in Page's character, as there was more than a touch of it in Spencer's. Moreover, most people at the time seem to have sympathized with the young lovers, Lord Compton and Elizabeth Spencer – they usually did when the romantic couple were not their own children. Similarly, it is Ford who, at the end of the play, argues that Page should accept what has happened, because

> *In love the heavens themselves do guide the state.*
> *Money buys lands, and wives are sold by fate.*
>   V.5.224–5

The story of Fenton and Anne Page is a version of the Lord Compton–Elizabeth Spencer affair, but, like everything else in the play, that affair has been transferred to a middle-class setting. Fenton is something less than a young

41

peer, and Anne is the daughter of a citizen of Windsor, not of an ex-Lord Mayor of London.

*

It is this same use of a bourgeois setting and a middle-class point of view that accounts for the transformation which the Falstaff of the two parts of *Henry IV* undergoes in this comedy. It has given rise to much critical indignation and protest, as though Shakespeare had not the right to handle a product of his own imagination in whatever way he thought fit. Hazlitt, one of the first to complain, is fairly temperate about the matter. Admitting that the play is 'very amusing', he continues thus:

> *but we should have liked it much better, if any one else had been the hero of it, instead of Falstaff.* . . . *Falstaff in* The Merry Wives of Windsor *is not the man he was in the two parts of* Henry IV. *His wit and eloquence have left him. Instead of making a butt of others, he is made a butt of by them. Neither is there a single particle of love in him to excuse his follies: he is merely a designing, bare-faced knave, and an unsuccessful one.*
>
> (*Characters of Shakespear's Plays* (1817),
> Everyman edition, page 250)

As the nineteenth century went on, however, expressions of dislike for the handling of Falstaff in *The Merry Wives of Windsor* grew stronger, to culminate, early in this century, in A. C. Bradley's outright condemnation of it. Bradley agrees with Hazlitt that the play is amusing, but he then goes on to say that in it Shakespeare 'degraded' Falstaff by representing him

> *assailing for financial purposes, the virtue of two matrons, and in the event baffled, duped, treated like dirty linen,*

42

beaten, burnt, pricked, mocked, insulted, and, worst of
all, repentant and didactic. It is horrible.
('The Rejection of Falstaff', *Oxford Lectures on Poetry*
(London, 1909), page 248)

The assumption underlying these views, and others like
them, is that the Falstaff of the *Henry IV* plays is something not only unique but also immutable, enjoying an
independent existence of his own that extends beyond their
confines. But this is not the case. In the *Henry IV* plays
Falstaff is part of a pattern. What he is depends in no
small measure on what Hal is, to whom he acts, at least in
his own imagination, as a kind of father; on what the
King is, for there is a deliberate contrast between the
monarch of England and the monarch of wit; and, most of
all perhaps, on what Hotspur, his obvious antithesis, is.
Moreover, the Falstaff of these plays is, above everything
else, an actor, assuming one role after another as cir-
cumstances demand. His main one, as Hal cruelly and
forcibly reminds him in the rejection scene at the end of
2 Henry IV, is that of the 'fool and jester'. As such, it is
his function to create amusement and to present truths
and views of an unexpected sort. He carries out these
tasks supremely well, and in doing so he earns the grati-
tude and approval of an audience, for in these plays the
point of view from which things are seen is, to a large
extent, that of those who kept fools and jesters.

In *The Merry Wives of Windsor* this is no longer the
case. It is not Falstaff who has changed, but the world in
which he finds himself. His distinctive idiom, rich in its
vocabulary and shot through and through with poetic
figures of speech, still remains with him. And, to the mind
of at least one of Shakespeare's contemporaries, it was
precisely a man's manner of speaking that established his

character. In his *Discoveries* Ben Jonson writes, adopting
a passage from Erasmus:

> *Language most shows a man: speak, that I may see thee.*
> *It springs out of the most retired and inmost parts of us,*
> *and is the image of the parent of it, the mind. No glass*
> *renders a man's form, or likeness, so true as his speech.*
>
> > (*Ben Jonson*, edited by C. H. Herford and
> > Percy and Evelyn Simpson, Volume VIII
> > (Oxford, 1947), page 625)

Moreover, the Falstaff of *The Merry Wives of Windsor* is
still the trickster that he was in *Henry IV*. The difference
is that his tricks no longer work. His reputation as a
soldier, which led that 'most furious knight and valorous
enemy' Sir John Colville of the Dale to surrender to him
without a blow, cuts no ice with Mistress Page and
Mistress Ford. The role that would have worked with
them, that of Tartuffe, is clearly indicated by Mistress
Ford, when, speaking of her first meeting with him, she
says:

> *And yet he would not swear; praised women's modesty;*
> *and gave such orderly and well-behaved reproof to all*
> *uncomeliness that I would have sworn his disposition would*
> *have gone to the truth of his words.*   II.1.53–7

But, instead of exploiting the possibilities of this approach
further, Falstaff does exactly what shrewd middle-class
wives would expect a penniless captain to do: he becomes
a fortune hunter. But he does it with a difference. The
normal goal of such men was marriage, either to a wealthy
widow or to an heiress – the way that Fenton takes. Falstaff, however, in the older tradition of the *fabliau* hero,

prefers to make his assault on married women who have access to their husbands' purses. Casting himself for the part of the irresistible soldier-lover, he plays it with eloquence and conviction, calling in Sir Philip Sidney and Ovid to assist him. And, once he has adopted it, he finds himself caught in it, especially after he has accepted Brook's money and given his word that Brook shall enjoy the favours of Ford's wife. Both vanity – the vanity of the actor who refuses to be defeated by a role – and prudence demand that he continue with it. Even after he has been cudgelled by Ford he can still boast to Mistress Quickly of his histrionic skill, telling her: 'But that my admirable dexterity of wit, my counterfeiting the action of an old woman, delivered me, the knave constable had set me i'th'stocks, i'th'common stocks, for a witch' (IV.5.108–11). His greatest mistake is that he grossly under-rates the intelligence of the Wives. The women he is in contact with in *Henry IV*, Mistress Quickly and Doll Tearsheet, merit the contempt that he shows for their intellects; he can twist them round his little finger. Mistress Page and Mistress Ford are another matter entirely. Confident in themselves, they resent his low opinion of their minds – a resentment shared today by many women students when confronted with the Falstaff of *Henry IV* – no less than his low opinion of their morals. There could hardly be a stronger confirmation of the idea that the Falstaff of *The Merry Wives of Windsor* is the Falstaff of *Henry IV*, but seen from a middle-class point of view in which the attitude of women counted for much.

Perhaps the play offers a comment on social change. Fenton, who is never in doubt that marriage is the price a gentleman must pay in order to share in the new wealth being created by the bourgeoisie, is successful. Falstaff, another penniless gentleman, who never so much as

45

thinks of paying that price, though he too would like to share in the new wealth, is not.

*

The Falstaff of *The Merry Wives of Windsor* is, then, the Falstaff of *Henry IV*. It is not the character that has changed, but the setting, and with it the angle of vision. But there is one point in the play where his credibility is under a heavy strain. The third adventure, in Windsor Great Park, begins well, with Falstaff's Ovidian speech calling on Jove for his assistance. It reaches its height when Falstaff, finding that Mistress Ford has brought Mistress Page with her, nonchalantly offers himself to both women, saying complacently: 'Divide me like a bribed buck, each a haunch' (V.5.24). Both the wit and the effrontery are in character; so is the joke at his own expense. This cannot be said, however, of what follows. Hearing Quickly and Pistol give their charges to the mock-fairies, Falstaff says:

> *They are fairies; he that speaks to them shall die.*
> *I'll wink and couch; no man their works must eye.*
>
> V.5.47–8

He then falls flat on his face. This will not do. There is no character in Shakespeare's works less likely to believe in fairies than the logical positivist who makes such short work of the idea of honour in *1 Henry IV*. One might as well expect Professor A. J. Ayer to proclaim his faith in witchcraft. Moreover, how is it that Falstaff fails to recognize the disguised Evans when, noticing the Welsh accent, he actually remarks: 'Heavens defend me from that Welsh fairy, lest he transform me to a piece of cheese'?

But there are some odd features about the entire fairy section of the last scene. In the first place, there is nothing like it in any of the stories, such as that of Bucciuolo, which

46

are similar to the rest of the Falstaff story. Secondly, as many editors and critics have observed, there is no attempt here to indicate Evans's Welsh pronunciation, though it has been heavily emphasized in the brief scene (V.4) in which he gives his fairies their instructions, and though Falstaff notices it in this very scene. Strangest of all is the introduction here into this play of action of matter which has no bearing whatever on that action. Pistol, in his role of Hobgoblin, begins it when he says to one of the fairies:

> Cricket, to Windsor chimneys shalt thou leap.
> Where fires thou findest unraked and hearths unswept,
> There pinch the maids as blue as bilberry.
> Our radiant Queen hates sluts and sluttery.   V.5.43–6

It seems evident that these words refer at least as much to Queen Elizabeth in Windsor Castle as they do to the Fairy Queen. Even more explicit are the references in the speech from Mistress Quickly, disguised as the Fairy Queen, which starts at line 55 with the words: 'About, about! | Search Windsor Castle, elves, within and out.' Beginning with praise of Queen Elizabeth, it goes on to pay a handsome and extended compliment to the Order of the Garter, that has no relevance at all to the rest of the scene.

It is here, of course, that most scholars today, who believe that the play was written for a royal occasion, find their main evidence. The lead was given by Leslie Hotson in his book *Shakespeare versus Shallow*, where he argues that *The Merry Wives of Windsor* was written for performance at a Garter Feast, and that it was given its first performance on St George's Day, 23 April 1597, when the feast was held at Whitehall Palace in Westminster, a month before the formal installation of the new knights at St George's Chapel in Windsor, a ceremony which the Queen did not attend. Hotson further points out that a performance by Shakespeare's company on this occasion would have been peculiarly appropriate, since it was at the Garter celebrations of 1597 that George Carey, Lord Hunsdon, the patron of the company, was made a member of the Order.

There are, however, grave difficulties in the way of accepting 1597 as the date of composition for Shakespeare's comedy. The first scene of the play introduces Shallow, Bardolph, Nym, and Pistol, none of whom has any really significant part in the later action. It looks very much as though they have been brought on at the beginning to attract spectators who were already familiar with them and wanted to see more of them. But, if this is indeed the case, 1597 is much too early a date for *The Merry Wives of Windsor*. Bardolph is the only one of the four to appear in *1 Henry IV*, which is usually assigned to the year 1597. Shallow and Pistol are added in *2 Henry IV*, probably written in 1598; and Nym in *Henry V*, which can be dated, with quite unusual accuracy, as having been composed in the summer of 1599. The theory that the play cannot have been written before 1599 is further supported by the way in which the Fenton–Anne Page story reflects the affair between Lord Compton and Elizabeth Spencer. Since the comedy ends with the marriage of Fenton and Anne, it must have been completed after 18 April 1599, when the marriage of the couple from real life took place. A final piece of evidence for 1599 or later is the sequence of Welsh characters – Glendower, Fluellen, and Parson Evans. It suggests that there was a Welsh actor in Shakespeare's company, or at least an actor who could give a convincing imitation of English as spoken by a Welshman; and that Shakespeare gradually perceived the comic possibilities of this manner of speech, and exploited it more and more. The least comic of the three is Glendower, who appears in *1 Henry IV*. There are no indications of a Welsh accent in his speeches, but it seems likely that his lines would be spoken with the characteristic Welsh lilt, since this would give ironical point to his boast when he tells Hotspur: 'I can speak English, lord, as well as you' (*1 Henry IV*, III.i.116). The Welsh peculiarities of Fluellen, who appears in *Henry V*, are carefully spelled out – the muddles over 'p' and 'b', the constant use of 'look you', the fondness for a string of near-synonyms loosely connected together by one 'and' after another, and the confusions of singular and plural forms. They are all there in one brief speech. Demanding that Pistol eat the leek he has scorned, Fluellen says:

> *I peseech you heartily, scurvy, lousy knave, at my desires, and my requests, and my petitions, to eat, look you, this leek. Because, look you, you do not love it, nor your affections, and your appetites, and your digestions, doo's not agree with it, I would desire you to eat it.*
>
> *Henry V*, V.i.21–6

Many of the characteristics of Evans's utterance are present here, but Fluellen has not the Parson's capacity for malapropisms, and he is not wholly comic. Evans must be the last term in the series; and *The Merry Wives of Windsor* must have followed *Henry V*.

How then are the indications that point to the Garter Feast of 1597 as the occasion for the play to be reconciled with all the other evidence that points to a much later date; and what are the references to the Queen and the Order of the Garter doing in a play that seems to have been written for the public theatre? The references occur in one part of one scene. Some exceptional features of this section have already been noticed; but there is another: it is singularly masque-like. The Fairy Queen, the fairies, the Satyr, Hobgoblin – all these are exactly the kind of figures that are to be found in several of the royal 'Entertainments' that have survived. These entertainments are masque-like shows which were put on for the Queen's amusement when she visited the homes of her more important subjects during the course of her annual progresses. Even Herne the Hunter would not be out of place in such a show. When she was staying at Cowdray in Sussex in 1591, part of the entertainment she was regaled with took the form of a speech made by a wild man of the woods underneath a great oak. In the same year, at Elvetham in Hampshire, the fourth day's proceedings began with a speech from the Fairy Queen, after which she and her fairy maids danced about Elizabeth, and then sang a song in praise of her. We are told that 'This spectacle and music so delighted her majesty that she desired to see and hear it twice over' (*The Complete Works of John Lyly*, edited by R. W. Bond (Oxford, 1902), Volume I, page 450).

It therefore seems a reasonable hypothesis that either Hunsdon or the Queen may well have asked Shakespeare and his company to put together such an entertainment for the Garter celebrations of 1597. It would certainly be something that they could do within a fortnight, and it would fit the occasion. Then later, when it was all long over, Shakespeare, with the economy so characteristic of him, salvaged the entertainment, made the necessary changes to fit Falstaff into it, did not bother to insert indications of Welshness into the Satyr's speeches when they were handed over to Evans, and used it for the denouement of his new comedy. It is not a theory that is capable of outright proof, but it is more consistent with the play – and with the way in which traditions grow – than is Dennis's story.

FURTHER READING

Editions and Editorial Problems

THE central problem that every editor of *The Merry Wives of Windsor* has to face is that of establishing the nature of the relationship between the Quarto of 1602 and the text, nearly twice as long, that was first published in the Folio of 1623. For those who wish to try their hands at the fascinating game of literary detection that is involved, both texts are readily available in facsimile form: the first as *The Merry Wives of Windsor 1602*, edited by W. W. Greg (Oxford, 1957, 1963); and the second in *The Norton Facsimile: The First Folio of Shakespeare*, edited by Charlton Hinman (New York and London, 1968). The theory most widely accepted by scholars today, that the Quarto is a reported version of the play, was first advanced by W. W. Greg, some sixty years ago, in his earlier edition of the Quarto (Oxford, 1910). William Bracy, on the other hand, takes the view, in his *The Merry Wives of Windsor: The History and Transmission of Shakespeare's Text* (Columbia, Missouri, 1952), that the Quarto represents a carefully abridged version of the original play.

The most recent scholarly edition is the new Arden (London, 1971), by H. J. Oliver, to which the present editor is much indebted. Based uncompromisingly on the Folio, it admits very few readings from the Quarto. The New Cambridge edition, by Sir A. T. Quiller-Couch and J. Dover Wilson (Cambridge, 1921), the Pelican edition, by Fredson Bowers (Baltimore, 1963), reprinted in *The Complete Pelican Shakespeare* (Baltimore and London, 1969), and the Signet edition, by William Green (New York, Toronto, and London, 1965), are all considerably less austere in this respect.

The Occasion of the Play and Possible Topical References

Early references to *The Merry Wives of Windsor*, including those cited on pages 10, 11, and 12 of the Introduction, are collected in E. K. Chambers's *William Shakespeare: A Study of Facts and Problems* (2 volumes, Oxford, 1930), Volume 2, pages 262-9. The tradition that the play was written in a fortnight, on the orders of Queen Elizabeth herself, has, not surprisingly, given rise to much speculation on the part of scholars as to the specific occasion on which it was first produced before her. The possibility of a reference to Sir Thomas Lucy in the first scene has also excited a great deal of interest; so have the mysterious words, 'there is three sorts of cosen garmombles, | *Is* cosen all the Host of Maidenhead & Readings', which Sir Hugh Evans speaks to the Host in the Quarto equivalent of IV.5.69-72. In his book *Shakespeare versus Shallow* (London, 1931) Leslie Hotson sought to show that Shallow was not intended, as had been thought ever since the time of Rowe (1709), for Sir Thomas Lucy, but for a certain William Gardiner, a Justice of the Peace in the county of Surrey, with whom Shakespeare appears to have become embroiled in 1596. In the same work Hotson also puts forward the theory that the comedy was first performed at the Garter Feast, in Whitehall Palace, on 23 April 1597, and relates this idea to the supposed allusion, first noticed in 1839, to Frederick, Count of Mömpelgart, contained in the words 'cosen garmombles'. The two latter notions are developed further, with much circumstantial detail about the Order of the Garter, by William Green in his *Shakespeare's 'Merry Wives of Windsor'* (Princeton, 1962). The main difficulty in the way of accepting this hypothesis is that 1597 seems too early a date for *The Merry Wives of Windsor*. The objections to it are well put by J. M. Nosworthy in his *Shakespeare's Occasional Plays* (London, 1965), where he goes on to argue that Shakespeare, writing in great haste to meet the royal demand, refashioned a lost play by Henry Porter, entitled *The Two Merry Women of Abingdon*, which must have been more or less complete at the time of Porter's death in June 1599. Nosworthy, however, can only guess what Porter's play was like, and he fails to explain why the Admiral's Men, for whom Porter wrote his play, should have handed it over to their great rivals the Lord Chamberlain's Men, the company to which Shakespeare belonged.

Criticism

The occasion that led, perhaps, to the writing of *The Merry Wives of Windsor*, together with the elucidation of the many topical references that it seems to contain, have absorbed so much scholarly effort and ingenuity that little has been left over for any serious consideration of it as a play in its own right. Furthermore, much of that little has been expended in fierce diatribes against Shakespeare for his treatment of Falstaff, or against Queen Elizabeth for demanding the impossible of him by asking him to show Falstaff in love. Critics in the late seventeenth and early eighteenth centuries approved of the comedy because it obeyed the 'rules', coming much closer than most of Shakespeare's comedies do to observing the celebrated unities of Action, Time, and Place. Dryden liked it because it was 'regular'; and Rowe described it as 'pure Comedy'. Dr Johnson drew attention to some of the weaknesses in the plotting, but then added that its general power 'is such that perhaps it never yet had reader or spectator who did not think it too soon at an end' (*Dr Johnson on Shakespeare*, edited by W. K. Wimsatt (Penguin Shakespeare Library, 1969), page 111). Johnson wrote these words in 1773. Four years later Maurice Morgann brought out an extended essay 'On the Dramatic Character of Sir John Falstaff' (1777), in which he seeks to defend Falstaff against the charge of cowardice, much as though Falstaff were a personal friend of his who had been unjustly attacked. There is no mention whatever in it of the Falstaff of *The Merry Wives of Windsor*. Either Morgann regarded him as an entirely different character from the Falstaff of *Henry IV*, or else he realized that his defence was bound to collapse if it had to cover the fat knight of the comedy.

Morgann's essay is symptomatic of the change that was beginning to take place in the whole climate of critical opinion. The depiction of character, rather than the conduct of an action, was coming to be looked on as the main purpose of the drama; and to the Romantics, interested as they were in Shakespeare's poetry, *The Merry Wives of Windsor*, written almost entirely in prose, had little to offer. Coleridge, the most perceptive and profound of the romantic critics, comes close to ignoring it altogether. The main trends of nineteenth-century criticism of the play are already apparent in William Hazlitt's comment on it in his *Characters of Shakespear's Plays* (1817). Half of what he has to say is devoted to an expression of his regret that the Falstaff of this play is not the Falstaff of *Henry IV*. The rest of it deals with some of the other characters, and is especially good on Slender. But there is no escaping the fact that Hazlitt regards the play as decidedly second-rate. The lead given by Hazlitt was followed up by Coleridge's son Hartley, who transfers the responsibility for the conversion of Falstaff into 'a big-bellied impostor' from Shakespeare to 'Queen Bess . . . a gross-minded old baggage' (quoted from Edward Dowden, *Shakspere: A Critical Study of his Mind and Art* (London, 1875), page 371). Dowden himself in the very influential book referred to – it had gone through ten editions by 1892 – is even more condemnatory of the Queen and her court. He accuses the Queen of a 'lust for gross mirth'; describes the play as designed to meet the taste of 'the barbarian aristocrats with their hatred of ideas, their insensibility to beauty, their hard efficient manners, and their demand for impropriety'; and then adds:

Shakspere did not make a grievance of his task. He threw himself into it with spirit, and despatched his work quickly, – in fourteen days, if we accept the tradition. But Falstaff he was not prepared to recall from heaven or from hell. He dressed up a fat rogue, brought forward for the occasion from the back premises of the poet's imagination, in Falstaff's clothes. . . . But the Queen and her Court laughed as the buck-basket was emptied into the ditch, no more suspecting that its gross lading was not the

incomparable jester of Eastcheap, than Ford suspected the woman
with a great beard to be other than the veritable Dame Pratt.

(pages 369–71)

In the best known piece of criticism that has ever been
written about the play, the opening of his celebrated essay 'The
Rejection of Falstaff' (*Oxford Lectures on Poetry* (London, 1909),
pages 247–75), A. C. Bradley refrains from blaming the Queen
and her Court, but he is in complete agreement with Dowden
that the Falstaff of *The Merry Wives of Windsor* is not the
Falstaff of *Henry IV*, and calls the treatment Falstaff is subjected to 'horrible'. Bradley's disciple, H. B. Charlton, attempts
to outgo his master in his display of indignation, accusing
Shakespeare of slaughtering his 'own offspring' and of making
a 'contemptible caricature' of the true original Falstaff
(*Shakespearian Comedy* (London, 1938; paperback edition,
1966), pages 192–8).

A strong counterblast to complaints of the kind just listed
was made by E. K. Chambers, an unfailing fountain of good
common sense, in the chapter he devotes to the play in his
Shakespeare: A Survey (London, 1925). His argument is that it
is not Falstaff who has changed, but the characters against whom
he is now pitted. Looking at the play in terms of the theatre,
Chambers finds it 'admirably constructed' and credits it with
'astonishing vitality and go'. Much more recently Bertrand
Evans has reached a rather similar conclusion. His main concern in *Shakespeare's Comedies* (Oxford, 1960) is with Shakespeare's exploitation of different levels of awareness among the
characters in a play. Seen from this point of view, *The Merry
Wives of Windsor* proves to be one of the most complex and
most skilfully constructed of all the comedies. Moreover, the
structure is rich in irony, for it is Mistress Quickly, of all
people, who is best informed as to what is really going on, while
Falstaff knows less about what is happening than anyone else in
the play. Anne Righter, in her *Shakespeare and the Idea of the
Play* (London, 1962; Penguin Shakespeare Library, 1967), has a
brief but illuminating section (reprinted in *Shakespeare's*

FURTHER READING

Comedies: An Anthology of Modern Criticism, edited by
Laurence Lerner, Penguin Shakespeare Library, 1967) on the
use of disguise and of plays-within-the-play in the comedy;
while Brian Vickers writes with insight and enthusiasm about
the rich variety of prose styles that Shakespeare employs in
order to differentiate the characters from each other. He is
particularly good on the subject of Ford, whom he sees as 'the
centre of the imaginative exploration in this play'; but the
whole section on *The Merry Wives of Windsor* in his book *The
Artistry of Shakespeare's Prose* (London, 1968) must rank as one
of the best things on the play that have yet been written.

It will be noticed that the defenders of the play, those who
write about it with zest and appreciation, are all interested in
techniques of various kinds, rather than in 'character' or in
Shakespeare as a source of perennial wisdom. Perhaps the
critical era which began with Maurice Morgann's 'Essay on the
Dramatic Character of Sir John Falstaff' is coming to an end.
Confirmation that this may indeed be the case is provided by the
very lively and suggestive chapter on *The Merry Wives of
Windsor* that forms the centre-piece of Muriel C. Bradbrook's
book *Shakespeare the Craftsman* (London, 1969). Untroubled
by what has happened to Falstaff, and not much impressed by
the supposed topicalities, Miss Bradbrook looks at the play as a
play, and brings in a verdict that one can fully concur with when
she describes it as 'the very best second-best Shakespeare'.

Since the above was written, a complete book on the play has
appeared: Jeanne Addison Roberts's *Shakespeare's English
Comedy* (Lincoln, Nebraska, and London, 1979). It has its uses,
since it dutifully surveys most of what has been written about
the play; but its lack-lustre prose is sadly out of keeping with
the vitality of Shakespeare's comedy. Leo Salingar's treatment
of it in his *Shakespeare and the Traditions of Comedy* (Cambridge,
1974) breaks much fresh ground in a brief space; and Alexander
Leggatt puts it into the right context, as well as doing justice
to its positive achievements, in his *Citizen Comedy in the Age of
Shakespeare* (Toronto, 1973).

G. R. H.
April 1980

THE MERRY WIVES OF WINDSOR

THE CHARACTERS IN THE PLAY

GEORGE PAGE, a citizen of Windsor
MISTRESS PAGE, his wife
ANNE PAGE, their daughter
WILLIAM PAGE, their son, a schoolboy
FRANK FORD, another citizen of Windsor
MISTRESS FORD, his wife
JOHN ⎫
ROBERT ⎭ Ford's servants
SIR HUGH EVANS, a Welsh parson
DOCTOR CAIUS, a French physician and suitor for the
    hand of Anne Page
MISTRESS QUICKLY, Doctor Caius's housekeeper
JOHN RUGBY, Doctor Caius's servant
THE HOST OF THE GARTER INN
Several children of Windsor

FENTON, a young gentleman and suitor for the hand of
    Anne Page

SIR JOHN FALSTAFF
ROBIN, Falstaff's page
BARDOLPH ⎤
PISTOL ⎬ Falstaff's followers
NYM ⎦

ROBERT SHALLOW, a country justice of the peace
ABRAHAM SLENDER, Shallow's nephew and suitor for
    the hand of Anne Page
PETER SIMPLE, Slender's servant

Enter Justice Shallow, Slender, and Sir Hugh Evans

SHALLOW Sir Hugh, persuade me not. I will make a Star-Chamber matter of it. If he were twenty Sir John Falstaffs, he shall not abuse Robert Shallow, Esquire.

SLENDER In the county of Gloucester, justice of peace and Coram.

SHALLOW Ay, cousin Slender, and Custalorum.

SLENDER Ay, and Ratolorum too. And a gentleman born, master parson, who writes himself Armigero – in any bill, warrant, quittance, or obligation, Armigero. 10

SHALLOW Ay, that I do, and have done any time these three hundred years.

SLENDER All his successors gone before him hath done't; and all his ancestors that come after him may. They may give the dozen white luces in their coat.

SHALLOW It is an old coat.

EVANS The dozen white louses do become an old coat well. It agrees well, passant. It is a familiar beast to man, and signifies love.

SHALLOW The luce is the fresh fish. The salt fish is an 20 old coat.

SLENDER I may quarter, coz?

SHALLOW You may, by marrying.

EVANS It is marring indeed, if he quarter it.

SHALLOW Not a whit.

EVANS Yes, py'r lady. If he has a quarter of your coat, there is but three skirts for yourself, in my simple

conjectures. But that is all one. If Sir John Falstaff
have committed disparagements unto you, I am of the
Church, and will be glad to do my benevolence, to make
atonements and compromises between you.

SHALLOW The Council shall hear it. It is a riot.

EVANS It is not meet the Council hear a riot. There is no
fear of Got in a riot. The Council, look you, shall desire
to hear the fear of Got, and not to hear a riot. Take your
vizaments in that.

SHALLOW Ha! O'my life, if I were young again, the
sword should end it.

EVANS It is petter that friends is the swort, and end it.
And there is also another device in my prain, which
peradventure prings goot discretions with it. There is
Anne Page, which is daughter to Master George Page,
which is pretty virginity.

SLENDER Mistress Anne Page? She has brown hair, and
speaks small like a woman?

EVANS It is that fery person for all the 'orld, as just as you
will desire. And seven hundred pounds of moneys, and
gold, and silver, is her grandsire upon his death's-bed –
Got deliver to a joyful resurrections! – give, when she is
able to overtake seventeen years old. It were a goot
motion if we leave our pribbles and prabbles, and desire
a marriage between Master Abraham and Mistress Anne
Page.

SHALLOW Did her grandsire leave her seven hundred
pound?

EVANS Ay, and her father is make her a petter penny.

SHALLOW I know the young gentlewoman. She has good
gifts.

EVANS Seven hundred pounds, and possibilities, is goot
gifts.

SHALLOW Well, let us see honest Master Page. Is
Falstaff there?

EVANS Shall I tell you a lie? I do despise a liar as I do
despise one that is false, or as I despise one that is not
true. The knight Sir John is there. And I beseech you be
ruled by your well-willers. I will peat the door for
Master Page. (*He knocks*) What, ho! Got pless your
house here!

PAGE (*within*) Who's there?

EVANS Here is Got's plessing, and your friend, and 70
Justice Shallow; and here young Master Slender, that
peradventures shall tell you another tale, if matters grow
to your likings.

    Enter Page

PAGE I am glad to see your worships well. I thank you
for my venison, Master Shallow.

SHALLOW Master Page, I am glad to see you. Much good
do it your good heart! I wished your venison better – it
was ill killed. How doth good Mistress Page? – And I
thank you always with my heart, la! With my heart.

PAGE Sir, I thank you. 80

SHALLOW Sir, I thank you. By yea and no, I do.

PAGE I am glad to see you, good Master Slender.

SLENDER How does your fallow greyhound, sir? I heard
say he was outrun on Cotsall.

PAGE It could not be judged, sir.

SLENDER You'll not confess. You'll not confess.

SHALLOW That he will not. 'Tis your fault, 'tis your
fault. 'Tis a good dog.

PAGE A cur, sir.

SHALLOW Sir, he's a good dog and a fair dog. Can there 90
be more said? He is good and fair. Is Sir John Falstaff
here?

PAGE Sir, he is within; and I would I could do a good
office between you.

EVANS It is spoke as a Christians ought to speak.

SHALLOW He hath wronged me, Master Page.

PAGE Sir, he doth in some sort confess it.

SHALLOW If it be confessed, it is not redressed. Is not that
so, Master Page? He hath wronged me, indeed he hath,
100   at a word, he hath. Believe me – Robert Shallow,
Esquire, saith he is wronged.

PAGE Here comes Sir John.

Enter Sir John Falstaff, Bardolph, Nym, and Pistol

FALSTAFF Now, Master Shallow, you'll complain of me
to the King?

SHALLOW Knight, you have beaten my men, killed my
deer, and broke open my lodge.

FALSTAFF But not kissed your keeper's daughter?

SHALLOW Tut, a pin! This shall be answered.

FALSTAFF I will answer it straight. I have done all this.
110   That is now answered.

SHALLOW The Council shall know this.

FALSTAFF 'Twere better for you if it were known in
counsel. You'll be laughed at.

EVANS *Pauca verba*, Sir John, good worts.

FALSTAFF Good worts? Good cabbage! – Slender, I
broke your head. What matter have you against me?

SLENDER Marry, sir, I have matter in my head against
you, and against your cony-catching rascals, Bardolph,
Nym, and Pistol. They carried me to the tavern, and
120   made me drunk, and afterward picked my pocket.

BARDOLPH You Banbury cheese!

SLENDER Ay, it is no matter.

PISTOL How now, Mephostophilus?

SLENDER Ay, it is no matter.

NYM Slice, I say. *Pauca, pauca*. Slice! That's my humour.

SLENDER Where's Simple, my man? Can you tell, cousin?

EVANS Peace, I pray you. Now let us understand. There is three umpires in this matter, as I understand – that is, Master Page, *fidelicet* Master Page; and there is myself, *fidelicet* myself; and the three party is, lastly and finally, mine host of the Garter. 130

PAGE We three to hear it, and end it between them.

EVANS Fery goot. I will make a prief of it in my notebook, and we will afterwards 'ork upon the cause with as great discreetly as we can.

FALSTAFF Pistol!

PISTOL He hears with ears.

EVANS The tevil and his tam! What phrase is this, 'He hears with ear'? Why, it is affectations. 140

FALSTAFF Pistol, did you pick Master Slender's purse?

SLENDER Ay, by these gloves, did he – or I would I might never come in mine own great chamber again else – of seven groats in mill-sixpences, and two Edward shovel-boards, that cost me two shillings and twopence apiece of Yed Miller, by these gloves.

FALSTAFF Is this true, Pistol?

EVANS No, it is false, if it is a pickpurse.

PISTOL
Ha, thou mountain-foreigner! – Sir John and master mine,
I combat challenge of this latten bilbo. 150
Word of denial in thy *labras* here!
Word of denial! Froth and scum, thou liest!

SLENDER (*pointing to Nym*) By these gloves, then 'twas he.

NYM Be advised, sir, and pass good humours. I will say 'Marry trap with you', if you run the nuthook's humour on me. That is the very note of it.

SLENDER By this hat, then he in the red face had it. For

though I cannot remember what I did when you made
me drunk, yet I am not altogether an ass.

160 FALSTAFF What say you, Scarlet and John?

BARDOLPH Why, sir, for my part, I say the gentleman
had drunk himself out of his five sentences.

EVANS It is his 'five senses'. Fie, what the ignorance is!

BARDOLPH And being fap, sir, was, as they say, cashiered.
And so conclusions passed the careers.

SLENDER Ay, you spake in Latin then too. But 'tis no
matter. I'll ne'er be drunk whilst I live again, but in
honest, civil, godly company, for this trick. If I be
drunk, I'll be drunk with those that have the fear of
170 God, and not with drunken knaves.

EVANS So Got 'udge me, that is a virtuous mind.

FALSTAFF You hear all these matters denied, gentlemen.
You hear it.

*Enter Anne Page, with wine, Mistress Ford, and
Mistress Page*

PAGE Nay, daughter, carry the wine in – we'll drink
within.

Exit Anne Page

SLENDER O heaven! This is Mistress Anne Page.

PAGE How now, Mistress Ford?

FALSTAFF Mistress Ford, by my troth, you are very well
met. By your leave, good mistress.

He kisses her

180 PAGE Wife, bid these gentlemen welcome. Come, we
have a hot venison pasty to dinner. Come, gentlemen, I
hope we shall drink down all unkindness.

Exeunt all except Slender

SLENDER I had rather than forty shillings I had my Book
of Songs and Sonnets here.

Enter Simple

How now, Simple, where have you been? I must wait

on myself, must I? You have not the Book of Riddles
about you, have you?

SIMPLE Book of Riddles? Why, did you not lend it to
Alice Shortcake upon Allhallowmas last, a fortnight
afore Michaelmas? 190

Enter Shallow and Evans

SHALLOW Come, coz; come, coz; we stay for you. A word
with you, coz. Marry, this, coz – there is as 'twere a
tender, a kind of tender, made afar off by Sir Hugh
here. Do you understand me?

SLENDER Ay, sir, you shall find me reasonable. If it be
so, I shall do that that is reason.

SHALLOW Nay, but understand me.

SLENDER So I do, sir.

EVANS Give ear to his motions. Master Slender, I will
description the matter to you, if you be capacity of it. 200

SLENDER Nay, I will do as my cousin Shallow says. I
pray you pardon me. He's a justice of peace in his
country, simple though I stand here.

EVANS But that is not the question. The question is
concerning your marriage.

SHALLOW Ay, there's the point, sir.

EVANS Marry, is it, the very point of it – to Mistress Anne
Page.

SLENDER Why, if it be so, I will marry her upon any
reasonable demands. 210

EVANS But can you affection the 'oman? Let us command
to know that of your mouth, or of your lips – for divers
philosophers hold that the lips is parcel of the mouth.
Therefore, precisely, can you carry your good will to
the maid?

SHALLOW Cousin Abraham Slender, can you love her?

SLENDER I hope, sir, I will do as it shall become one that
would do reason.

67

EVANS Nay, Got's lords and his ladies! You must speak
220 possitable, if you can carry her your desires towards
her.

SHALLOW That you must. Will you, upon good dowry,
marry her?

SLENDER I will do a greater thing than that, upon your
request, cousin, in any reason.

SHALLOW Nay, conceive me, conceive me, sweet coz –
what I do is to pleasure you, coz. Can you love the maid?

SLENDER I will marry her, sir, at your request. But if
there be no great love in the beginning, yet heaven may
230 decrease it upon better acquaintance when we are
married and have more occasion to know one another.
I hope upon familiarity will grow more content. But if
you say 'Marry her', I will marry her – that I am freely
dissolved, and dissolutely.

EVANS It is a fery discretion answer, save the fall is in the
'ord 'dissolutely'. The 'ort is, according to our meaning,
'resolutely'. His meaning is good.

SHALLOW Ay, I think my cousin meant well.

SLENDER Ay, or else I would I might be hanged, la!
Enter Anne Page
240 SHALLOW Here comes fair Mistress Anne. Would I
were young for your sake, Mistress Anne!

ANNE The dinner is on the table. My father desires your
worships' company.

SHALLOW I will wait on him, fair Mistress Anne.

EVANS 'Od's plessed will! I will not be absence at the
grace.   *Exeunt Shallow and Evans*

ANNE Will't please your worship to come in, sir?

SLENDER No, I thank you, forsooth, heartily. I am very
well.

250 ANNE The dinner attends you, sir.

SLENDER I am not a-hungry, I thank you, forsooth.

(To Simple) Go, sirrah, for all you are my man, go wait
upon my cousin Shallow.   *Exit Simple*
A justice of peace sometime may be beholding to his
friend for a man. I keep but three men and a boy yet,
till my mother be dead. But what though? Yet I live
like a poor gentleman born.

ANNE I may not go in without your worship – they will
not sit till you come.

SLENDER I'faith, I'll eat nothing. I thank you as much as   260
though I did.

ANNE I pray you, sir, walk in.

SLENDER I had rather walk here, I thank you. I bruised my
shin th'other day with playing at sword and dagger with
a master of fence – three veneys for a dish of stewed
prunes – and, by my troth, I cannot abide the smell of
hot meat since. Why do your dogs bark so? Be there
bears i'th'town?

ANNE I think there are, sir. I heard them talked of.

SLENDER I love the sport well, but I shall as soon quarrel   270
at it as any man in England. You are afraid if you see the
bear loose, are you not?

ANNE Ay, indeed, sir.

SLENDER That's meat and drink to me, now. I have seen
Sackerson loose twenty times, and have taken him by
the chain. But, I warrant you, the women have so cried
and shrieked at it, that it passed. But women, indeed,
cannot abide 'em – they are very ill-favoured rough
things.

    Enter Page

PAGE Come, gentle Master Slender, come. We stay for   280
you.

SLENDER I'll eat nothing, I thank you, sir.

PAGE By cock and pie, you shall not choose, sir! Come,
come.

SLENDER Nay, pray you lead the way.

PAGE Come on, sir.

SLENDER Mistress Anne, yourself shall go first.

ANNE Not I, sir. Pray you keep on.

SLENDER Truly, I will not go first, truly, la! I will not do
290 you that wrong.

ANNE I pray you, sir.

SLENDER I'll rather be unmannerly than troublesome.
You do yourself wrong, indeed, la!   *Exeunt*

I.2   *Enter Evans and Simple*

EVANS Go your ways, and ask of Doctor Caius's house
which is the way. And there dwells one Mistress Quickly,
which is in the manner of his nurse, or his dry nurse,
or his cook, or his laundry, his washer, and his wringer.

SIMPLE Well, sir.

EVANS Nay, it is petter yet. Give her this letter, for it is a
'oman that altogether's acquaintance with Mistress Anne
Page. And the letter is to desire and require her to
solicit your master's desires to Mistress Anne Page.
10 I pray you be gone. I will make an end of my dinner –
there's pippins and cheese to come.   *Exeunt*

I.3   *Enter Falstaff, Host, Bardolph, Nym, Pistol, and*
Robin

FALSTAFF Mine host of the Garter –

HOST What says my bully rook? Speak scholarly and
wisely.

FALSTAFF Truly, mine host, I must turn away some of
my followers.

HOST Discard, bully Hercules, cashier. Let them wag;
trot, trot.

FALSTAFF I sit at ten pounds a week.

HOST Thou'rt an emperor – Caesar, Keisar, and Pheazar.
I will entertain Bardolph; he shall draw, he shall tap.   10
Said I well, bully Hector?

FALSTAFF Do so, good mine host.

HOST I have spoke. Let him follow. (*To Bardolph*) Let me
see thee froth and lime. I am at a word. Follow.   *Exit*

FALSTAFF Bardolph, follow him. A tapster is a good trade.
An old cloak makes a new jerkin; a withered servingman
a fresh tapster. Go, adieu.

BARDOLPH It is a life that I have desired. I will thrive.

PISTOL
O base Hungarian wight! Wilt thou the spigot wield?
Exit Bardolph

NYM He was gotten in drink. Is not the humour con-   20
ceited?

FALSTAFF I am glad I am so acquit of this tinderbox.
His thefts were too open. His filching was like an
unskilful singer – he kept not time.

NYM The good humour is to steal at a minute's rest.

PISTOL
'Convey', the wise it call. 'Steal'? Foh,
A fico for the phrase!

FALSTAFF Well, sirs, I am almost out at heels. (money)

PISTOL
Why then, let kibes ensue.

FALSTAFF There is no remedy – I must cony-catch, I must   30
shift.

PISTOL
Young ravens must have food.

FALSTAFF Which of you know Ford of this town?

PISTOL
I ken the wight. He is of substance good.

FALSTAFF My honest lads, I will tell you what I am about.

PISTOL Two yards, and more.

FALSTAFF No quips now, Pistol. Indeed, I am in the
waist two yards about. But I am now about no waste –
I am about thrift. Briefly, I do mean to make love to
40 Ford's wife. I spy entertainment in her. She discourses,
she carves, she gives the leer of invitation. I can construe
the action of her familiar style; and the hardest voice
of her behaviour – to be Englished rightly – is 'I am
Sir John Falstaff's'.

PISTOL He hath studied her will, and translated her will –
out of honesty into English.

NYM The anchor is deep. Will that humour pass?

FALSTAFF Now, the report goes she has all the rule of
her husband's purse. He hath a legion of angels.

PISTOL
50 As many devils entertain! And 'To her, boy', say I.

NYM The humour rises – it is good. Humour me the
angels.

FALSTAFF I have writ me here a letter to her; and here
another to Page's wife, who even now gave me good eyes
too, examined my parts with most judicious œillades.
Sometimes the beam of her view gilded my foot, sometimes my portly belly.

PISTOL (aside)
Then did the sun on dunghill shine.

NYM (aside) I thank thee for that humour.

60 FALSTAFF O, she did so course o'er my exteriors with
such a greedy intention that the appetite of her eye did
seem to scorch me up like a burning-glass. Here's
another letter to her. She bears the purse too. She is a
region in Guiana, all gold and bounty. I will be cheaters
to them both, and they shall be exchequers to me. They
shall be my East and West Indies, and I will trade to
them both. (To Pistol) Go, bear thou this letter to

Mistress Page; (*to Nym*) and thou this to Mistress Ford.
We will thrive, lads, we will thrive.

PISTOL

    Shall I Sir Pandarus of Troy become –   70
    And by my side wear steel? Then Lucifer take all!

NYM I will run no base humour. Here, take the humour-
    letter. I will keep the haviour of reputation.

FALSTAFF (*to Robin*)

    Hold, sirrah, bear you these letters tightly;
    Sail like my pinnace to these golden shores.
    Rogues, hence, avaunt! Vanish like hailstones, go!
    Trudge, plod away o'th'hoof, seek shelter, pack!
    Falstaff will learn the humour of the age,
    French thrift, you rogues – myself and skirted page.

                                Exeunt Falstaff and Robin

PISTOL

    Let vultures gripe thy guts! For gourd and fullam holds, 80
    And high and low beguiles the rich and poor.
    Tester I'll have in pouch when thou shalt lack,
    Base Phrygian Turk!

NYM I have operations which be humours of revenge.

PISTOL

    Wilt thou revenge?

NYM   By welkin and her star!

PISTOL

    With wit or steel?

NYM   With both the humours, I.

    I will discuss the humour of this love to Page.

PISTOL

        And I to Ford shall eke unfold
           How Falstaff, varlet vile,
        His dove will prove, his gold will hold,   90
           And his soft couch defile.

NYM My humour shall not cool. I will incense Page to

deal with poison. I will possess him with yellowness, for the revolt of mine is dangerous. That is my true humour.

PISTOL
Thou art the Mars of malcontents. I second thee. Troop on.   *Exeunt*

I.4   *Enter Mistress Quickly and Simple*
MISTRESS QUICKLY (*calling*) What, John Rugby!
          Enter Rugby
I pray thee, go to the casement and see if you can see my master, Master Doctor Caius, coming. If he do, i'faith, and find anybody in the house, here will be an old abusing of God's patience and the King's English.

RUGBY I'll go watch.

MISTRESS QUICKLY Go; and we'll have a posset for't soon at night, in faith, at the latter end of a sea-coal fire.   *Exit Rugby*

10   An honest, willing, kind fellow, as ever servant shall come in house withal; and, I warrant you, no tell-tale, nor no breed-bate. His worst fault is that he is given to prayer. He is something peevish that way, but nobody but has his fault. But let that pass. – Peter Simple you say your name is?

SIMPLE Ay, for fault of a better.

MISTRESS QUICKLY And Master Slender's your master?

SIMPLE Ay, forsooth.

MISTRESS QUICKLY Does he not wear a great round
20   beard like a glover's paring-knife?

SIMPLE No, forsooth. He hath but a little wee face, with a little yellow beard – a Cain-coloured beard.

MISTRESS QUICKLY A softly-sprighted man, is he not?

SIMPLE Ay, forsooth. But he is as tall a man of his hands

as any is between this and his head. He hath fought with
a warrener.

MISTRESS QUICKLY How say you? – O, I should remember him. Does he not hold up his head, as it were,
and strut in his gait?

SIMPLE Yes, indeed, does he.   30

MISTRESS QUICKLY Well, heaven send Anne Page no
worse fortune. Tell Master Parson Evans I will do
what I can for your master. Anne is a good girl, and I
wioh –

    Enter Rugby

RUGBY Out, alas! Here comes my master.

MISTRESS QUICKLY We shall all be shent. Run in here,
good young man; go into this closet. He will not stay
long.

    She shuts Simple in the closet

What, John Rugby! John, what, John, I say! Go, John,
go inquire for my master. I doubt he be not well, that   40
he comes not home.   *Exit Rugby*

    She sings

       And down, down, adown-a, etc.

    Enter Doctor Caius

CAIUS Vat is you sing? I do not like dese toys. Pray you go
and vetch me in my closet *un boîtier vert* – a box, a
green-a box. Do intend vat I speak? A green-a box.

MISTRESS QUICKLY Ay, forsooth, I'll fetch it you.
(*Aside*) I am glad he went not in himself. If he had
found the young man, he would have been horn-mad.

                       Exit to the closet

CAIUS Fe, fe, fe, fe! *Ma foi, il fait fort chaud. Je m'en
vais à la cour – la grande affaire.*   50

    Enter Mistress Quickly with the box

MISTRESS QUICKLY Is it this, sir?

CAIUS *Oui, mette-le au mon* pocket. *Dépêche*, quickly. Vere is dat knave Rugby?

MISTRESS QUICKLY What, John Rugby! John!

Enter Rugby

RUGBY Here, sir.

CAIUS You are John Rugby, and you are Jack Rugby. Come, take-a your rapier, and come after my heel to the court.

RUGBY 'Tis ready, sir, here in the porch.

60 CAIUS By my trot, I tarry too long. 'Od's me! *Qu'ai-je oublié?* Dere is some simples in my closet, dat I vill not for the varld I shall leave behind.   *Exit to the closet*

MISTRESS QUICKLY Ay me, he'll find the young man there, and be mad.

CAIUS *(within)* O, *diable, diable!* Vat is in my closet? Villainy! *Larron!*

Enter Caius, pulling Simple out of the closet

Rugby, my rapier!

MISTRESS QUICKLY Good master, be content.

CAIUS Wherefore shall I be content-a?

70 MISTRESS QUICKLY The young man is an honest man.

CAIUS What shall de honest man do in my closet? Dere is no honest man dat shall come in my closet.

MISTRESS QUICKLY I beseech you, be not so phlegmatic. Hear the truth of it. He came of an errand to me from Parson Hugh.

CAIUS Vell?

SIMPLE Ay, forsooth, to desire her to –

MISTRESS QUICKLY Peace, I pray you.

CAIUS Peace-a your tongue. *(To Simple)* Speak-a your
80 tale.

SIMPLE To desire this honest gentlewoman, your maid, to speak a good word to Mistress Anne Page for my master in the way of marriage.

MISTRESS QUICKLY This is all, indeed, la! But I'll ne'er put my finger in the fire, and need not.

CAIUS Sir Hugh send-a you? – Rugby, *baille* me some paper. (*To Simple*) Tarry you a little-a while.

He writes

MISTRESS QUICKLY (*aside to Simple*) I am glad he is so quiet. If he had been throughly moved, you should have heard him so loud and so melancholy. But notwith- 90 standing, man, I'll do you your master what good I can. And the very yea and the no is, the French doctor, my master – I may call him my master, look you, for I keep his house; and I wash, wring, brew, bake, scour, dress meat and drink, make the beds, and do all myself –

SIMPLE (*aside to Mistress Quickly*) 'Tis a great charge to come under one body's hand.

MISTRESS QUICKLY (*aside to Simple*) Are you avised o'that? You shall find it a great charge – and to be up early and down late. But notwithstanding – to tell you 100 in your ear, I would have no words of it – my master himself is in love with Mistress Anne Page. But not-withstanding that, I know Anne's mind. That's neither here nor there.

CAIUS You, jack'nape, give-a this letter to Sir Hugh. By gar, it is a shallenge. I will cut his troat in de park, and I will teach a scurvy jackanape priest to meddle or make. You may be gone. It is not good you tarry here. *Exit Simple* By gar, I will cut all his two stones. By gar, he shall not have a stone to throw at his dog. 110

MISTRESS QUICKLY Alas, he speaks but for his friend.

CAIUS It is no matter-a ver dat. Do not you tell-a me dat I shall have Anne Page for myself? By gar, I vill kill de Jack priest. And I have appointed mine host of de Jarteer to measure our weapon. By gar, I will myself have Anne Page.

MISTRESS QUICKLY Sir, the maid loves you, and all shall be well. We must give folks leave to prate. What the good-year!

120 CAIUS Rugby, come to the court with me. (*To Mistress Quickly*) By gar, if I have not Anne Page, I shall turn your head out of my door. Follow my heels, Rugby.

Exeunt Caius and Rugby

MISTRESS QUICKLY You shall have An – fool's-head of your own. No, I know Anne's mind for that. Never a woman in Windsor knows more of Anne's mind than I do, nor can do more than I do with her, I thank heaven.

FENTON (*off stage*) Who's within there, ho?

MISTRESS QUICKLY Who's there, I trow? Come near the house, I pray you.

Enter Fenton

130 FENTON How now, good woman, how dost thou?

MISTRESS QUICKLY The better that it pleases your good worship to ask.

FENTON What news? How does pretty Mistress Anne?

MISTRESS QUICKLY In truth, sir, and she is pretty, and honest, and gentle – and one that is your friend. I can tell you that by the way, I praise heaven for it.

FENTON Shall I do any good, thinkest thou? Shall I not lose my suit?

MISTRESS QUICKLY Troth, sir, all is in His hands above.
140 But notwithstanding, Master Fenton, I'll be sworn on a book she loves you. Have not your worship a wart above your eye?

FENTON Yes, marry, have I. What of that?

MISTRESS QUICKLY Well, thereby hangs a tale. Good faith, it is such another Nan – but, I detest, an honest maid as ever broke bread. We had an hour's talk of that wart. I shall never laugh but in that maid's company. But, indeed, she is given too much to allicholy and musing. But for you – well – go to –

FENTON Well, I shall see her today. Hold, there's money 150
for thee; let me have thy voice in my behalf. If thou
seest her before me, commend me –

MISTRESS QUICKLY Will I? I'faith, that we will. And I
will tell your worship more of the wart the next time
we have confidence, and of other wooers.

FENTON Well, farewell. I am in great haste now.

MISTRESS QUICKLY Farewell to your worship.

Exit Fenton

Truly, an honest gentleman. But Anne loves him not,
for I know Anne's mind as well as another does. Out
upon't! What have I forgot?   *Exit* 160

*

Enter Mistress Page, with a letter   II.1

MISTRESS PAGE What, have I 'scaped love-letters in the
holiday time of my beauty, and am I now a subject for
them? Let me see.

(*She reads*)

*Ask me no reason why I love you, for though Love use
Reason for his precisian, he admits him not for his coun-
sellor. You are not young, no more am I. Go to, then,
there's sympathy. You are merry, so am I. Ha, ha, then
there's more sympathy. You love sack, and so do I. Would
you desire better sympathy? Let it suffice thee, Mistress
Page – at the least if the love of soldier can suffice – that I* 10
*love thee. I will not say, pity me – 'tis not a soldier-like
phrase – but I say, love me. By me,*

Thine own true knight,
By day or night,
Or any kind of light,

> *With all his might*
> *For thee to fight,*
>
>   *John Falstaff.*

20 What a Herod of Jewry is this! O, wicked, wicked world! One that is well-nigh worn to pieces with age to show himself a young gallant! What an unweighed behaviour hath this Flemish drunkard picked – with the devil's name! – out of my conversation, that he dares in this manner assay me? Why, he hath not been thrice in my company. What should I say to him? I was then frugal of my mirth – heaven forgive me! Why, I'll exhibit a bill in the parliament for the putting down of men. How shall I be revenged on him? For revenged I will be, as sure as his guts are made of puddings.

Enter Mistress Ford

30 MISTRESS FORD Mistress Page! Trust me, I was going to your house.

MISTRESS PAGE And, trust me, I was coming to you. You look very ill.

MISTRESS FORD Nay, I'll ne'er believe that. I have to show to the contrary.

MISTRESS PAGE Faith, but you do, in my mind.

MISTRESS FORD Well, I do, then. Yet I say I could show you to the contrary. O Mistress Page, give me some counsel.

40 MISTRESS PAGE What's the matter, woman?

MISTRESS FORD O woman, if it were not for one trifling respect, I could come to such honour.

MISTRESS PAGE Hang the trifle, woman, take the honour. What is it? Dispense with trifles. What is it?

MISTRESS FORD If I would but go to hell for an eternal moment or so, I could be knighted.

MISTRESS PAGE What? Thou liest. Sir Alice Ford? These

knights will hack, and so thou shouldst not alter the article of thy gentry.

MISTRESS FORD We burn daylight. Here, read, read. 50 Perceive how I might be knighted. I shall think the worse of fat men as long as I have an eye to make difference of men's liking. And yet he would not swear; praised women's modesty; and gave such orderly and well-behaved reproof to all uncomeliness that I would have sworn his disposition would have gone to the truth of his words. But they do no more adhere and keep place together than the Hundredth Psalm to the tune of 'Greensleeves'. What tempest, I trow, threw this whale, with so many tuns of oil in his belly, ashore at Windsor? 60 How shall I be revenged on him? I think the best way were to entertain him with hope till the wicked fire of lust have melted him in his own grease. Did you ever hear the like?

MISTRESS PAGE (*comparing the two letters*) Letter for letter, but that the name of Page and Ford differs. To thy great comfort in this mystery of ill opinions, here's the twin-brother of thy letter. But let thine inherit first, for I protest mine never shall. I warrant he hath a thousand of these letters, writ with blank space for different names 70 – sure, more – and these are of the second edition. He will print them, out of doubt; for he cares not what he puts into the press, when he would put us two. I had rather be a giantess and lie under Mount Pelion. Well, I will find you twenty lascivious turtles ere one chaste man.

She gives her letter to Mistress Ford

MISTRESS FORD Why, this is the very same: the very hand, the very words. What doth he think of us?

MISTRESS PAGE Nay, I know not. It makes me almost ready to wrangle with mine own honesty. I'll entertain 80

81

myself like one that I am not acquainted withal; for, sure, unless he know some strain in me that I know not myself, he would never have boarded me in this fury.

MISTRESS FORD 'Boarding' call you it? I'll be sure to keep him above deck.

MISTRESS PAGE So will I. If he come under my hatches, I'll never to sea again. Let's be revenged on him. Let's appoint him a meeting, give him a show of comfort in his suit, and lead him on with a fine-baited delay till he
90 hath pawned his horses to mine host of the Garter.

MISTRESS FORD Nay, I will consent to act any villainy against him that may not sully the chariness of our honesty. O that my husband saw this letter! It would give eternal food to his jealousy.

MISTRESS PAGE Why, look where he comes, and my good man too. He's as far from jealousy as I am from giving him cause – and that, I hope, is an unmeasurable distance.

MISTRESS FORD You are the happier woman.

100 MISTRESS PAGE Let's consult together against this greasy knight. Come hither.

They retire
Enter Ford with Pistol, and Page with Nym

FORD Well, I hope it be not so.

PISTOL
Hope is a curtal dog in some affairs.
Sir John affects thy wife.

FORD Why, sir, my wife is not young.

PISTOL
He woos both high and low, both rich and poor,
Both young and old, one with another, Ford.
He loves the gallimaufry. Ford, perpend.

FORD Love my wife?

PISTOL

    With liver burning hot. Prevent. Or go thou   110
    Like Sir Actaeon he, with Ringwood at thy heels.
    O, odious is the name!

FORD What name, sir?

PISTOL

    The horn, I say. Farewell.
    Take heed, have open eye, for thieves do foot by night.
    Take heed, ere summer comes or cuckoo-birds do sing.
    Away, Sir Corporal Nym!
    Believe it, Page; he speaks sense.   *Exit*

FORD (*aside*)

    I will be patient. I will find out this.

NYM (*to Page*) And this is true. I like not the humour of 120
    lying. He hath wronged me in some humours. I should
    have borne the humoured letter to her, but I have a
    sword and it shall bite upon my necessity. He loves your
    wife. There's the short and the long. My name is
    Corporal Nym. I speak, and I avouch 'tis true. My name
    is Nym, and Falstaff loves your wife. Adieu. I love not
    the humour of bread and cheese – and there's the
    humour of it. Adieu.   *Exit*

PAGE 'The humour of it', quoth 'a! Here's a fellow frights
    English out of his wits.   130

FORD (*aside*) I will seek out Falstaff.

PAGE (*aside*) I never heard such a drawling, affecting
    rogue.

FORD (*aside*) If I do find it – well.

PAGE (*aside*) I will not believe such a Cataian, though the
    priest o'th'town commended him for a true man.

FORD (*aside*) 'Twas a good sensible fellow – well.

    Mistress Page and Mistress Ford come forward

PAGE How now, Meg?

MISTRESS PAGE Whither go you, George? Hark you.

They speak aside

140 MISTRESS FORD How now, sweet Frank, why art thou melancholy?

FORD I melancholy? I am not melancholy. Get you home, go.

MISTRESS FORD Faith, thou hast some crotchets in thy head now. Will you go, Mistress Page?

MISTRESS PAGE Have with you. – You'll come to dinner, George?

Enter Mistress Quickly

(*Aside to Mistress Ford*) Look who comes yonder. She shall be our messenger to this paltry knight.

150 MISTRESS FORD (*aside to Mistress Page*) Trust me, I thought on her. She'll fit it.

MISTRESS PAGE You are come to see my daughter Anne?

MISTRESS QUICKLY Ay, forsooth; and, I pray, how does good Mistress Anne?

MISTRESS PAGE Go in with us and see. We have an hour's talk with you.

Exeunt Mistress Page, Mistress Ford,
and Mistress Quickly

PAGE How now, Master Ford?

FORD You heard what this knave told me, did you not?

PAGE Yes, and you heard what the other told me?

100 FORD Do you think there is truth in them?

PAGE Hang 'em, slaves! I do not think the knight would offer it. But these that accuse him in his intent towards our wives are a yoke of his discarded men – very rogues, now they be out of service.

FORD Were they his men?

PAGE Marry, were they.

FORD I like it never the better for that. Does he lie at the Garter?

PAGE Ay, marry, does he. If he should intend this voyage

toward my wife, I would turn her loose to him; and 170
what he gets more of her than sharp words, let it lie on
my head.

FORD I do not misdoubt my wife, but I would be loath
to turn them together. A man may be too confident. I
would have nothing lie on my head. I cannot be thus
satisfied.

Enter Host

PAGE Look where my ranting host of the Garter comes.
There is either liquor in his pate or money in his purse
when he looks so merrily. – How now, mine host?

HOST How now, bully rook? Thou'rt a gentleman. 180

He turns and calls

Cavaliero justice, I say!

Enter Shallow

SHALLOW I follow, mine host, I follow. Good even and
twenty, good Master Page. Master Page, will you go with
us? We have sport in hand.

HOST Tell him, cavaliero justice; tell him, bully rook.

SHALLOW Sir, there is a fray to be fought between Sir
Hugh the Welsh priest and Caius the French doctor.

FORD Good mine host o'th'Garter, a word with you.

HOST What sayest thou, my bully rook?

They go aside

SHALLOW (*to Page*) Will you go with us to behold it? 190
My merry host hath had the measuring of their weapons,
and, I think, hath appointed them contrary places; for,
believe me, I hear the parson is no jester. Hark, I will
tell you what our sport shall be.

They go aside

HOST Hast thou no suit against my knight, my guest
cavaliero?

FORD None, I protest. But I'll give you a pottle of burnt
sack to give me recourse to him and tell him my name is

Brook – only for a jest.

200 HOST My hand, bully. Thou shalt have egress and
regress. – Said I well? – And thy name shall be Brook.
It is a merry knight. Will you go, Ameers?

SHALLOW Have with you, mine host.

PAGE I have heard the Frenchman hath good skill in his
rapier.

SHALLOW Tut, sir, I could have told you more. In these
times you stand on distance, your passes, stoccadoes,
and I know not what. 'Tis the heart, Master Page;
'tis here, 'tis here. I have seen the time, with my long
210 sword, I would have made you four tall fellows skip like
rats.

HOST Here, boys, here, here! Shall we wag?

PAGE Have with you. I had rather hear them scold than
fight.   *Exeunt Host, Shallow, and Page*

FORD Though Page be a secure fool and stands so firmly
on his wife's frailty, yet I cannot put off my opinion so
easily. She was in his company at Page's house, and what
they made there I know not. Well, I will look further
into't, and I have a disguise to sound Falstaff. If I find
220 her honest, I lose not my labour. If she be otherwise,
'tis labour well bestowed.   *Exit*

II.2   *Enter Falstaff and Pistol*

FALSTAFF I will not lend thee a penny.

PISTOL
⦁ Why then, the world's mine oyster,
Which I with sword will open. –
I will retort the sum in equipage.

FALSTAFF Not a penny. I have been content, sir, you
should lay my countenance to pawn. I have grated upon
my good friends for three reprieves for you and your

coach-fellow Nym, or else you had looked through the grate, like a geminy of baboons. I am damned in hell for swearing to gentlemen my friends you were good soldiers and tall fellows. And when Mistress Bridget lost the handle of her fan, I took't upon mine honour thou hadst it not.

PISTOL
Didst thou not share? Hadst thou not fifteen pence?

FALSTAFF Reason, you rogue, reason. Thinkest thou I'll endanger my soul gratis? At a word, hang no more about me – I am no gibbet for you. Go – a short knife and a throng – to your manor of Pickt-hatch, go. You'll not bear a letter for me, you rogue? You stand upon your honour! Why, thou unconfinable baseness, it is as much as I can do to keep the terms of my honour precise. I, I, I myself sometimes, leaving the fear of God on the left hand and hiding mine honour in my necessity, am fain to shuffle, to hedge, and to lurch; and yet you, you rogue, will ensconce your rags, your cat-a-mountain looks, your red-lattice phrases, and your bold beating oaths, under the shelter of your honour! You will not do it? You!

PISTOL
I do relent. What wouldst thou more of man?
    Enter Robin

ROBIN Sir, here's a woman would speak with you.

FALSTAFF Let her approach.
    Enter Mistress Quickly

MISTRESS QUICKLY Give your worship good morrow.

FALSTAFF Good morrow, good wife.

MISTRESS QUICKLY Not so, an't please your worship.

FALSTAFF Good maid, then.

MISTRESS QUICKLY
I'll be sworn,

87

As my mother was the first hour I was born.

FALSTAFF

I do believe the swearer. What with me?

MISTRESS QUICKLY Shall I vouchsafe your worship a
40 word or two?

FALSTAFF Two thousand, fair woman, and I'll vouchsafe thee the hearing.

MISTRESS QUICKLY There is one Mistress Ford – Sir,
I pray, come a little nearer this ways – I myself dwell
with Master Doctor Caius.

FALSTAFF Well, on. Mistress Ford, you say –

MISTRESS QUICKLY Your worship says very true – I
pray your worship, come a little nearer this ways.

FALSTAFF I warrant thee nobody hears – (indicating
50 Pistol and Robin) mine own people, mine own people.

MISTRESS QUICKLY Are they so? God bless them and
make them his servants!

FALSTAFF Well, Mistress Ford – what of her?

MISTRESS QUICKLY Why, sir, she's a good creature.
Lord, Lord, your worship's a wanton! Well, God forgive
you, and all of us, I pray –

FALSTAFF Mistress Ford – come, Mistress Ford.

MISTRESS QUICKLY Marry, this is the short and the long
of it: you have brought her into such a canaries as 'tis
60 wonderful. The best courtier of them all, when the
court lay at Windsor, could never have brought her to
such a canary; yet there has been knights, and lords,
and gentlemen, with their coaches, I warrant you, coach
after coach, letter after letter, gift after gift, smelling so
sweetly – all musk – and so rushling, I warrant you, in
silk and gold, and in such alligant terms, and in such
wine and sugar of the best and the fairest, that would
have won any woman's heart, and, I warrant you, they
could never get an eye-wink of her – I had myself twenty

angels given me this morning, but I defy all angels in 70
any such sort, as they say, but in the way of honesty –
and, I warrant you, they could never get her so much
as sip on a cup with the proudest of them all, and yet
there has been earls – nay, which is more, pensioners –
but, I warrant you, all is one with her.

FALSTAFF But what says she to me? Be brief, my good
she-Mercury.

MISTRESS QUICKLY Marry, she hath received your
letter, for the which she thanks you a thousand times,
and she gives you to notify that her husband will be 80
absence from his house between ten and eleven.

FALSTAFF Ten and eleven.

MISTRESS QUICKLY Ay, forsooth; and then you may
come and see the picture, she says, that you wot of.
Master Ford, her husband, will be from home. Alas,
the sweet woman leads an ill life with him – he's a very
jealousy man – she leads a very frampold life with him,
good heart.

FALSTAFF Ten and eleven. Woman, commend me to her.
I will not fail her. 90

MISTRESS QUICKLY Why, you say well. But I have
another messenger to your worship. Mistress Page
hath her hearty commendations to you too; and, let me
tell you in your ear, she's as fartuous a civil modest
wife, and one, I tell you, that will not miss you morning
nor evening prayer, as any is in Windsor, whoe'er be
the other. And she bade me tell your worship that her
husband is seldom from home, but she hopes there will
come a time. I never knew a woman so dote upon a
man. Surely, I think you have charms, la! Yes, in 100
truth.

FALSTAFF Not I, I assure thee. Setting the attraction of
my good parts aside, I have no other charms.

MISTRESS QUICKLY Blessing on your heart for't!

FALSTAFF But I pray thee tell me this: has Ford's wife and Page's wife acquainted each other how they love me?

MISTRESS QUICKLY That were a jest indeed! They have not so little grace, I hope – that were a trick indeed! But Mistress Page would desire you to send her your little page, of all loves. Her husband has a marvellous infection to the little page; and, truly, Master Page is an honest man. Never a wife in Windsor leads a better life than she does. Do what she will, say what she will, take all, pay all, go to bed when she list, rise when she list, all is as she will. And, truly, she deserves it; for if there be a kind woman in Windsor, she is one. You must send her your page – no remedy.

FALSTAFF Why, I will.

MISTRESS QUICKLY Nay, but do so, then – and, look you, he may come and go between you both. And in any case have a nay-word, that you may know one another's mind, and the boy never need to understand anything; for 'tis not good that children should know any wickedness. Old folks, you know, have discretion, as they say, and know the world.

FALSTAFF Fare thee well; commend me to them both. There's my purse – I am yet thy debtor. Boy, go along with this woman.

Exeunt Mistress Quickly and Robin

This news distracts me.

PISTOL *(aside)*

This punk is one of Cupid's carriers.

Clap on more sails; pursue; up with your fights;

Give fire! She is my prize, or ocean whelm them all!

Exit

FALSTAFF Sayest thou so, old Jack? Go thy ways. I'll

make more of thy old body than I have done. Will they yet look after thee? Wilt thou, after the expense of so much money, be now a gainer? Good body, I thank thee. Let them say 'tis grossly done – so it be fairly done, no matter.

Enter Bardolph

BARDOLPH Sir John, there's one Master Brook below 140 would fain speak with you, and be acquainted with you; and hath sent your worship a morning's draught of sack.

FALSTAFF Brook is his name?

BARDOLPH Ay, sir.

FALSTAFF Call him in. *Exit Bardolph*
Such Brooks are welcome to me, that o'erflows such liquor. Aha! Mistress Ford and Mistress Page, have I encompassed you? Go to; *via!*

Enter Bardolph, with Ford disguised as Brook

FORD Bless you, sir. 150

FALSTAFF And you, sir. Would you speak with me?

FORD I make bold to press with so little preparation upon you.

FALSTAFF You're welcome. What's your will? (*To Bardolph*) Give us leave, drawer. *Exit Bardolph*

FORD Sir, I am a gentleman that have spent much. My name is Brook.

FALSTAFF Good Master Brook, I desire more acquaintance of you.

FORD Good Sir John, I sue for yours – not to charge 160 you – for I must let you understand I think myself in better plight for a lender than you are, the which hath something emboldened me to this unseasoned intrusion; for they say if money go before, all ways do lie open.

FALSTAFF Money is a good soldier, sir, and will on.

FORD Troth, and I have a bag of money here troubles me.

If you will help to bear it, Sir John, take all, or half, for easing me of the carriage.

FALSTAFF Sir, I know not how I may deserve to be your
170 porter.

FORD I will tell you, sir, if you will give me the hearing.

FALSTAFF Speak, good Master Brook. I shall be glad to be your servant.

FORD Sir, I hear you are a scholar – I will be brief with you – and you have been a man long known to me, though I had never so good means as desire to make myself acquainted with you. I shall discover a thing to you wherein I must very much lay open mine own imperfection. But, good Sir John, as you have one
180 eye upon my follies, as you hear them unfolded, turn another into the register of your own, that I may pass with a reproof the easier, sith you yourself know how easy it is to be such an offender.

FALSTAFF Very well, sir. Proceed.

FORD There is a gentlewoman in this town – her husband's name is Ford.

FALSTAFF Well, sir.

FORD I have long loved her, and, I protest to you, be-stowed much on her, followed her with a doting ob-
190 servance, engrossed opportunities to meet her, fee'd every slight occasion that could but niggardly give me sight of her, not only bought many presents to give her but have given largely to many to know what she would have given. Briefly, I have pursued her as love hath pursued me, which hath been on the wing of all oc-casions. But whatsoever I have merited – either in my mind or in my means – meed, I am sure, I have received none, unless experience be a jewel. That I have pur-chased at an infinite rate, and that hath taught me to
200 say this:

'Love like a shadow flies when substance love pursues,
Pursuing that that flies, and flying what pursues.'

FALSTAFF Have you received no promise of satisfaction
at her hands?

FORD Never.

FALSTAFF Have you importuned her to such a purpose?

FORD Never.

FALSTAFF Of what quality was your love, then?

FORD Like a fair house built on another man's ground, so
that I have lost my edifice by mistaking the place where 210
I erected it.

FALSTAFF To what purpose have you unfolded this to me?

FORD When I have told you that, I have told you all.
Some say that though she appear honest to me, yet
in other places she enlargeth her mirth so far that there
is shrewd construction made of her. Now, Sir John,
here is the heart of my purpose: you are a gentleman of
excellent breeding, admirable discourse, of great admittance, authentic in your place and person, generally
allowed for your many warlike, courtlike, and learned 220
preparations.

FALSTAFF O, sir!

FORD Believe it, for you know it. There is money. Spend
it, spend it; spend more; spend all I have. Only give me
so much of your time in exchange of it as to lay an
amiable siege to the honesty of this Ford's wife. Use
your art of wooing, win her to consent to you. If any
man may, you may as soon as any.

FALSTAFF Would it apply well to the vehemency of your
affection that I should win what you would enjoy? Me- 230
thinks you prescribe to yourself very preposterously.

FORD O, understand my drift. She dwells so securely on
the excellency of her honour that the folly of my soul
dares not present itself. She is too bright to be looked

against. Now, could I come to her with any detection in
my hand, my desires had instance and argument to
commend themselves. I could drive her then from the
ward of her purity, her reputation, her marriage-vow,
and a thousand other her defences, which now are too
240 too strongly embattled against me. What say you to't,
Sir John?

FALSTAFF Master Brook, I will first make bold with your
money; next, give me your hand; and last, as I am a
gentleman, you shall, if you will, enjoy Ford's wife.

FORD O good sir!

FALSTAFF I say you shall.

FORD Want no money, Sir John; you shall want none.

FALSTAFF Want no Mistress Ford, Master Brook; you
shall want none. I shall be with her, I may tell you, by
250 her own appointment. Even as you came in to me, her
assistant, or go-between, parted from me. I say I shall
be with her between ten and eleven, for at that time
the jealous rascally knave her husband will be forth.
Come you to me at night, you shall know how I speed.

FORD I am blest in your acquaintance. Do you know
Ford, sir?

FALSTAFF Hang him, poor cuckoldy knave! I know him
not. Yet I wrong him to call him poor. They say the
jealous wittolly knave hath masses of money, for the
260 which his wife seems to me well-favoured. I will use
her as the key of the cuckoldy rogue's coffer – and
there's my harvest-home.

FORD I would you knew Ford, sir, that you might avoid
him if you saw him.

FALSTAFF Hang him, mechanical salt-butter rogue! I will
stare him out of his wits. I will awe him with my cudgel;
it shall hang like a meteor o'er the cuckold's horns.
Master Brook, thou shalt know I will predominate over

the peasant, and thou shalt lie with his wife. Come to
me soon at night. Ford's a knave, and I will aggravate   270
his style. Thou, Master Brook, shalt know him for
knave and cuckold. Come to me soon at night.   *Exit*
FORD What a damned Epicurean rascal is this! My heart
is ready to crack with impatience. Who says this is
improvident jealousy? My wife hath sent to him, the
hour is fixed, the match is made. Would any man have
thought this? See the hell of having a false woman! My
bed shall be abused, my coffers ransacked, my reputation gnawn at; and I shall not only receive this villainous wrong, but stand under the adoption of abomin-   280
able terms, and by him that does me this wrong.
Terms! Names! Amaimon sounds well; Lucifer, well;
Barbason, well. Yet they are devils' additions, the names
of fiends. But Cuckold! Wittol! – Cuckold! The devil
himself hath not such a name. Page is an ass, a secure
ass. He will trust his wife, he will not be jealous. I will
rather trust a Fleming with my butter, Parson Hugh the
Welshman with my cheese, an Irishman with my
aqua-vitae bottle, or a thief to walk my ambling gelding,
than my wife with herself. Then she plots, then she   290
ruminates, then she devises. And what they think in
their hearts they may effect, they will break their
hearts but they will effect. God be praised for my
jealousy! Eleven o'clock the hour. I will prevent this,
detect my wife, be revenged on Falstaff, and laugh at
Page. I will about it. Better three hours too soon than a
minute too late. Fie, fie, fie! Cuckold, cuckold, cuckold!
                                                    Exit

Enter Doctor Caius and Rugby   II.3
CAIUS Jack Rugby!
RUGBY Sir.

CAIUS Vat is the clock, Jack?

RUGBY 'Tis past the hour, sir, that Sir Hugh promised to meet.

CAIUS By gar, he has save his soul dat he is no come. He has pray his Pible well dat he is no come. By gar, Jack Rugby, he is dead already if he be come.

RUGBY He is wise, sir. He knew your worship would kill
10   him if he came.

CAIUS By gar, de herring is no dead so as I vill kill him. Take your rapier, Jack. I vill tell you how I vill kill him.

RUGBY Alas, sir, I cannot fence.

CAIUS Villainy, take your rapier.

RUGBY Forbear. Here's company.

    Enter Host, Shallow, Slender, and Page

HOST Bless thee, bully doctor!

SHALLOW Save you, Master Doctor Caius!

PAGE Now, good Master Doctor!

SLENDER Give you good morrow, sir.

20 CAIUS Vat be you all, one, two, tree, four, come for?

HOST To see thee fight, to see thee foin, to see thee traverse, to see thee here, to see thee there, to see thee pass thy punto, thy stock, thy reverse, thy distance, thy montant. Is he dead, my Ethiopian? Is he dead, my Francisco? Ha, bully? What says my Aesculapius? My Galen? My heart of elder? Ha? Is he dead, bully stale? Is he dead?

CAIUS By gar, he is de coward Jack priest of de vorld. He is not show his face.

30 HOST Thou art a Castalion-King-Urinal. Hector of Greece, my boy!

CAIUS I pray you bear witness that me have stay six or seven, two, tree hours for him, and he is no come.

SHALLOW He is the wiser man, Master Doctor. He is a curer of souls, and you a curer of bodies. If you should fight, you go against the hair of your professions. Is it not true, Master Page?

PAGE Master Shallow, you have yourself been a great fighter, though now a man of peace.

SHALLOW Bodykins, Master Page, though I now be old 40 and of the peace, if I see a sword out, my finger itches to make one. Though we are justices and doctors and churchmen, Master Page, we have some salt of our youth in us. We are the sons of women, Master Page.

PAGE 'Tis true, Master Shallow.

SHALLOW It will be found so, Master Page. Master Doctor Caius, I am come to fetch you home. I am sworn of the peace. You have showed yourself a wise physician, and Sir Hugh hath shown himself a wise and patient churchman. You must go with me, Master 50 Doctor.

HOST Pardon, guest justice. – A word, Mounseur Mock-water.

CAIUS Mockvater? Vat is dat?

HOST Mockwater, in our English tongue, is valour, bully.

CAIUS By gar, then I have as much mockvater as de Englishman. Scurvy jack-dog priest! By gar, me vill cut his ears.

HOST He will clapper-claw thee tightly, bully.

CAIUS Clapper-de-claw? Vat is dat? 60

HOST That is, he will make thee amends.

CAIUS By gar, me do look he shall clapper-de-claw me, for, by gar, me vill have it.

HOST And I will provoke him to't, or let him wag.

CAIUS Me tank you for dat.

HOST And moreover, bully – (*Aside to the others*) But first, Master guest, and Master Page, and eke Cavaliero Slender, go you through the town to Frogmore.

PAGE Sir Hugh is there, is he?

97

70 HOST He is there. See what humour he is in; and I will
bring the doctor about by the fields. Will it do well?

SHALLOW We will do it.

PAGE, SHALLOW, *and* SLENDER Adieu, good master
Doctor.   *Exeunt*

CAIUS By gar, me vill kill de priest, for he speak for a
jackanape to Anne Page.

HOST Let him die. Sheathe thy impatience; throw cold
water on thy choler. Go about the fields with me
through Frogmore. I will bring thee where Mistress
80 Anne Page is, at a farmhouse a-feasting; and thou shalt
woo her. Cried game? Said I well?

CAIUS By gar, me dank you vor dat. By gar, I love you,
and I shall procure-a you de good guest – de earl, de
knight, de lords, de gentlemen, my patients.

HOST For the which I will be thy adversary toward
Anne Page. Said I well?

CAIUS By gar, 'tis good. Vell said.

HOST Let us wag, then.

CAIUS Come at my heels, Jack Rugby.   *Exeunt*

∗

III.1   *Enter Evans and Simple*

EVANS I pray you now, good Master Slender's servingman, and friend Simple by your name, which way have
you looked for Master Caius, that calls himself Doctor
of Physic?

SIMPLE Marry, sir, the pittie-ward, the park-ward,
every way; Old Windsor way, and every way but the
town way.

EVANS I most fehemently desire you you will also look
that way.

SIMPLE I will, sir. *Exit* 10

EVANS Pless my soul, how full of chollors I am, and
  trempling of mind! I shall be glad if he have deceived
  me. How melancholies I am! I will knog his urinals
  about his knave's costard when I have good opportunities
  for the 'ork. Pless my soul!

> *He sings*
>> To shallow rivers, to whose falls
>> Melodious birds sings madrigals.
>> There will we make our peds of roses,
>> And a thousand fragrant posies.
>> To shallow – 20

Mercy on me! I have a great dispositions to cry.

> *He sings*
>> Melodious birds sing madrigals –
>> Whenas I sat in Pabylon –
>> And a thousand vagram posies.
>> To shallow, etc.

> *Enter Simple*

SIMPLE Yonder he is, coming this way, Sir Hugh.

EVANS He's welcome.

> *He sings*
>> To shallow rivers, to whose falls –

Heaven prosper the right! What weapons is he?

SIMPLE No weapons, sir. There comes my master, Master 30
  Shallow, and another gentleman, from Frogmore, over
  the stile, this way.

EVANS Pray you, give me my gown – or else keep it in
  your arms.

> *He takes a book and reads it*
> *Enter Page, Shallow, and Slender*

SHALLOW How now, Master Parson? Good morrow, good
  Sir Hugh. Keep a gamester from the dice, and a good
  student from his book, and it is wonderful.

SLENDER (*aside*) Ah, sweet Anne Page!

PAGE Save you, good Sir Hugh!

40 EVANS Pless you from his mercy sake, all of you!

SHALLOW What, the sword and the word? Do you study
them both, Master Parson?

PAGE And youthful still – in your doublet and hose this
raw rheumatic day?

EVANS There is reasons and causes for it.

PAGE We are come to you to do a good office, Master
Parson.

EVANS Fery well. What is it?

PAGE Yonder is a most reverend gentleman, who, belike,
50 having received wrong by some person, is at most odds
with his own gravity and patience that ever you saw.

SHALLOW I have lived fourscore years and upward. I
never heard a man of his place, gravity, and learning so
wide of his own respect.

EVANS What is he?

PAGE I think you know him: Master Doctor Caius, the
renowned French physician.

EVANS Got's will and his passion of my heart! I had as
lief you would tell me of a mess of porridge.

60 PAGE Why?

EVANS He has no more knowledge in Hibocrates and
Galen – and he is a knave besides, a cowardly knave as
you would desires to be acquainted withal.

PAGE I warrant you, he's the man should fight with him.

SLENDER (*aside*) O sweet Anne Page!

SHALLOW It appears so by his weapons.

Enter Host, Caius, and Rugby

Keep them asunder; here comes Doctor Caius.

Evans and Caius offer to fight

PAGE Nay, good master Parson, keep in your weapon.

SHALLOW So do you, good Master Doctor.

HOST Disarm them, and let them question. Let them keep 70 their limbs whole and hack our English.

CAIUS I pray you let-a me speak a word with your ear. Verefore vill you not meet-a me?

EVANS (*aside to Caius*) Pray you, use your patience. (*Aloud*) In good time.

CAIUS By gar, you are de coward, de Jack dog, John ape.

EVANS (*aside to Caius*) Pray you, let us not be laughing-stocks to other men's humours. I desire you in friend-ship, and I will one way or other make you amends. (*Aloud*) I will knog your urinals about your knave's cogscombs for missing your meetings and appoint-ments.

CAIUS *Diable!* Jack Rugby, mine host de Jarteer, have I not stay for him to kill him? Have I not, at de place I did appoint?

EVANS As I am a Christians soul, now, look you, this is the place appointed. I'll be judgement by mine host of the Garter.

HOST Peace, I say, Gallia and Gaul, French and Welsh, soul-curer and body-curer. 90

CAIUS Ay, dat is very good, excellent.

HOST Peace, I say. Hear mine host of the Garter. Am I politic? Am I subtle? Am I a Machiavel? Shall I lose my doctor? No; he gives me the potions and the motions. Shall I lose my parson? My priest? My Sir Hugh? No; he gives me the proverbs and the no-verbs. Give me thy hand, terrestrial; so. Give me thy hand, celestial; so. Boys of art, I have deceived you both. I have directed you to wrong places. Your hearts are mighty, your skins are whole, and let burnt sack be the issue. 100 Come, lay their swords to pawn. Follow me, lads of peace; follow, follow, follow.

Exit

SHALLOW Trust me, a mad host. Follow, gentlemen, follow.

SLENDER (*aside*) O sweet Anne Page!

Exeunt Shallow, Slender, and Page

CAIUS Ha, do I perceive dat? Have you make-a de sot of us, ha, ha?

EVANS This is well. He has made us his vlouting-stog. I desire you that we may be friends, and let us knog our prains together to be revenge on this same scald, scurvy, cogging companion, the host of the Garter.

CAIUS By gar, with all my heart. He promise to bring me where is Anne Page. By gar, he deceive me too.

EVANS Well, I will smite his noddles. Pray you follow.

Exeunt

III.2 *Enter Mistress Page and Robin*

MISTRESS PAGE Nay, keep your way, little gallant. You were wont to be a follower, but now you are a leader. Whether had you rather, lead mine eyes, or eye your master's heels?

ROBIN I had rather, forsooth, go before you like a man than follow him like a dwarf.

MISTRESS PAGE O, you are a flattering boy. Now I see you'll be a courtier.

Enter Ford

FORD Well met, Mistress Page. Whither go you?

MISTRESS PAGE Truly, sir, to see your wife. Is she at home?

FORD Ay; and as idle as she may hang together, for want of company. I think, if your husbands were dead, you two would marry.

MISTRESS PAGE Be sure of that – two other husbands.

FORD Where had you this pretty weathercock?

MISTRESS PAGE I cannot tell what the dickens his name

is that my husband had him of. What do you call your
knight's name, sirrah?

ROBIN Sir John Falstaff.   20

FORD Sir John Falstaff?

MISTRESS PAGE He, he. I can never hit on's name. There
is such a league between my good man and he. Is your
wife at home indeed?

FORD Indeed she is.

MISTRESS PAGE By your leave, sir. I am sick till I see her.
                         Exeunt Mistress Page and Robin

FORD Has Page any brains? Hath he any eyes? Hath he
any thinking? Sure, they sleep; he hath no use of them.
Why, this boy will carry a letter twenty mile as easy as a
cannon will shoot point-blank twelve score. He pieces   30
out his wife's inclination. He gives her folly motion and
advantage. And now she's going to my wife, and Falstaff's boy with her. A man may hear this shower sing
in the wind. And Falstaff's boy with her! Good plots!
They are laid; and our revolted wives share damnation
together. Well, I will take him, then torture my wife,
pluck the borrowed veil of modesty from the so-
seeming Mistress Page, divulge Page himself for a
secure and wilful Actaeon; and to these violent proceedings all my neighbours shall cry aim.   40
         The town clock strikes
The clock gives me my cue, and my assurance bids me
search. There I shall find Falstaff. I shall be rather
praised for this than mocked, for it is as positive as the
earth is firm that Falstaff is there. I will go.
         Enter Page, Shallow, Slender, Host, Evans, Caius,
         and Rugby

ALL Well met, Master Ford.

FORD Trust me, a good knot. I have good cheer at home,
and I pray you all go with me.

SHALLOW I must excuse myself, Master Ford.

SLENDER And so must I, sir. We have appointed to dine
50   with Mistress Anne, and I would not break with her for
more money than I'll speak of.

SHALLOW We have lingered about a match between Anne
Page and my cousin Slender, and this day we shall have
our answer.

SLENDER I hope I have your good will, father Page.

PAGE You have, Master Slender – I stand wholly for you.
But my wife, Master Doctor, is for you altogether.

CAIUS Ay, be–gar, and de maid is love–a me – my nursh–a
Quickly tell me so mush.

60 HOST What say you to young Master Fenton? He capers,
he dances, he has eyes of youth, he writes verses, he
speaks holiday, he smells April and May. He will
carry't, he will carry't. 'Tis in his buttons he will
carry't.

PAGE Not by my consent, I promise you. The gentleman
is of no having. He kept company with the wild Prince
and Poins. He is of too high a region, he knows too
much. No, he shall not knit a knot in his fortunes with
the finger of my substance. If he take her, let him take
70   her simply. The wealth I have waits on my consent, and
my consent goes not that way.

FORD I beseech you heartily, some of you go home with
me to dinner. Besides your cheer, you shall have sport –
I will show you a monster. Master Doctor, you shall go.
So shall you, Master Page, and you, Sir Hugh.

SHALLOW Well, fare you well. We shall have the freer
wooing at Master Page's. *Exeunt Shallow and Slender*

CAIUS Go home, John Rugby. I come anon. *Exit Rugby*

HOST Farewell, my hearts. I will to my honest knight
80   Falstaff, and drink canary with him. *Exit*

FORD (*aside*) I think I shall drink in pipe-wine first with him; I'll make him dance. – Will you go, gentles?

ALL Have with you to see this monster.   *Exeunt*

Enter Mistress Ford and Mistress Page

MISTRESS FORD What, John! What, Robert!

MISTRESS PAGE Quickly, quickly! Is the buck-basket –

MISTRESS FORD I warrant. What, Robert, I say!

Enter John and Robert with a great buck-basket

MISTRESS PAGE Come, come, come.

MISTRESS FORD Here, set it down.

MISTRESS PAGE Give your men the charge. We must be brief.

MISTRESS FORD Marry, as I told you before, John and Robert, be ready here hard by in the brew-house. And when I suddenly call you, come forth, and, without any 10 pause or staggering, take this basket on your shoulders. That done, trudge with it in all haste, and carry it among the whitsters in Datchet Mead, and there empty it in the muddy ditch close by the Thames side.

MISTRESS PAGE You will do it?

MISTRESS FORD I ha' told them over and over – they lack no direction. – Be gone, and come when you are called.   *Exeunt John and Robert*

Enter Robin

MISTRESS PAGE Here comes little Robin.

MISTRESS FORD How now, my eyas-musket, what news 20 with you?

ROBIN My master, Sir John, is come in at your back-door, Mistress Ford, and requests your company.

MISTRESS PAGE You little Jack-a-Lent, have you been true to us?

ROBIN Ay, I'll be sworn. My master knows not of your being here, and hath threatened to put me into everlasting liberty if I tell you of it; for he swears he'll turn me away.

30 MISTRESS PAGE Thou'rt a good boy. This secrecy of thine shall be a tailor to thee and shall make thee a new doublet and hose. I'll go hide me.

MISTRESS FORD Do so. (*To Robin*) Go tell thy master I am alone.   *Exit Robin*
Mistress Page, remember you your cue.

MISTRESS PAGE I warrant thee. If I do not act it, hiss me.

MISTRESS FORD Go to, then. We'll use this unwholesome humidity, this gross watery pumpion. We'll teach him to know turtles from jays.   *Exit Mistress Page*
Enter Falstaff

40 FALSTAFF Have I caught thee, my heavenly jewel? Why, now let me die, for I have lived long enough. This is the period of my ambition. O this blessed hour!

MISTRESS FORD O sweet Sir John!

FALSTAFF Mistress Ford, I cannot cog, I cannot prate, Mistress Ford. Now shall I sin in my wish: I would thy husband were dead. I'll speak it before the best lord, I would make thee my lady.

MISTRESS FORD I your lady, Sir John? Alas, I should be a pitiful lady.

50 FALSTAFF Let the court of France show me such another. I see how thine eye would emulate the diamond. Thou hast the right arched beauty of the brow that becomes the ship-tire, the tire-valiant, or any tire of Venetian admittance.

MISTRESS FORD A plain kerchief, Sir John. My brows become nothing else, nor that well neither.

FALSTAFF Thou art a tyrant to say so. Thou wouldst make an absolute courtier, and the firm fixture of thy foot would give an excellent motion to thy gait in a
60 semi-circled farthingale. I see what thou wert if For-

tune, thy foe, were – not Nature – thy friend. Come, thou canst not hide it.

MISTRESS FORD Believe me, there's no such thing in me.

FALSTAFF What made me love thee? Let that persuade thee there's something extraordinary in thee. Come, I cannot cog and say thou art this and that, like a many of these lisping hawthorn-buds that come like women in men's apparel and smell like Bucklersbury in simple-time. I cannot. But I love thee, none but thee; and thou deservest it. 70

MISTRESS FORD Do not betray me, sir. I fear you love Mistress Page.

FALSTAFF Thou mightst as well say I love to walk by the Counter-gate, which is as hateful to me as the reek of a lime-kiln.

MISTRESS FORD Well, heaven knows how I love you, and you shall one day find it.

FALSTAFF Keep in that mind – I'll deserve it.

MISTRESS FORD Nay, I must tell you, so you do, or else I could not be in that mind. 80

Enter Robin

ROBIN Mistress Ford, Mistress Ford! Here's Mistress Page at the door, sweating and blowing and looking wildly, and would needs speak with you presently.

FALSTAFF She shall not see me. I will ensconce me behind the arras.

MISTRESS FORD Pray you, do so. She's a very tattling woman.

Falstaff hides himself
Enter Mistress Page

What's the matter? How now?

MISTRESS PAGE O Mistress Ford, what have you done? You're shamed, you're overthrown, you're undone for 90 ever.

MISTRESS FORD What's the matter, good Mistress Page?

MISTRESS PAGE O well-a-day, Mistress Ford, having an
honest man to your husband, to give him such cause of
suspicion!

MISTRESS FORD What cause of suspicion?

MISTRESS PAGE What cause of suspicion? Out upon
you! How am I mistook in you!

MISTRESS FORD Why, alas, what's the matter?

100 MISTRESS PAGE Your husband's coming hither, woman,
with all the officers in Windsor, to search for a gentleman
that he says is here now in the house, by your consent,
to take an ill advantage of his absence. You are undone.

MISTRESS FORD 'Tis not so, I hope.

MISTRESS PAGE Pray heaven it be not so that you have
such a man here! But 'tis most certain your husband's
coming, with half Windsor at his heels, to search for such
a one. I come before to tell you. If you know yourself
clear, why, I am glad of it. But if you have a friend here,
110 convey, convey him out. Be not amazed, call all your
senses to you, defend your reputation, or bid farewell to
your good life for ever.

MISTRESS FORD What shall I do? There is a gentleman,
my dear friend; and I fear not mine own shame so much
as his peril. I had rather than a thousand pound he were
out of the house.

MISTRESS PAGE For shame, never stand 'you had rather'
and 'you had rather'! Your husband's here at hand.
Bethink you of some conveyance. In the house you
120 cannot hide him. – O, how have you deceived me! – Look,
here is a basket. If he be of any reasonable stature, he
may creep in here; and throw foul linen upon him, as if
it were going to bucking. Or – it is whiting-time – send
him by your two men to Datchet Mead.

MISTRESS FORD He's too big to go in there. What shall I do?

Falstaff rushes out of hiding

FALSTAFF Let me see't, let me see't. O, let me see't! I'll in, I'll in. Follow your friend's counsel. I'll in.

MISTRESS PAGE What, Sir John Falstaff? (*Aside to him*) Are these your letters, knight?   130

FALSTAFF (*aside to Mistress Page*) I love thee, and none but thee. Help me away. Let me creep in here. I'll never –

He gets into the basket; they cover him with foul linen

MISTRESS PAGE (*to Robin*) Help to cover your master, boy. Call your men, Mistress Ford. (*Aside to Falstaff*) You dissembling knight!   *Exit Robin*

MISTRESS FORD What, John! Robert! John!

Enter John and Robert

Go, take up these clothes here. Quickly! Where's the cowl-staff? Look how you drumble! Carry them to the laundress in Datchet Mead. Quickly! Come.   140

Enter Ford, Page, Caius, and Evans

FORD (*to his companions*) Pray you, come near. If I suspect without cause, why then make sport at me; then let me be your jest; I deserve it. (*To John and Robert*) How now? Whither bear you this?

JOHN *and* ROBERT To the laundress, forsooth.

MISTRESS FORD Why, what have you to do whither they bear it? You were best meddle with buck-washing.

FORD Buck? I would I could wash myself of the buck! Buck, buck, buck! Ay, buck! I warrant you, buck – and of the season too, it shall appear.   150

Exeunt John and Robert with the basket

Gentlemen, I have dreamed tonight. I'll tell you my dream. Here, here, here be my keys. Ascend my cham-

bers. Search, seek, find out. I'll warrant we'll unkennel
the fox. Let me stop this way first.

He locks the door

So; now escape.

PAGE Good master Ford, be contented. You wrong yourself too much.

FORD True, Master Page. Up, gentlemen, you shall see
sport anon. Follow me, gentlemen.   *Exit*

160 EVANS This is fery fantastical humours and jealousies.

CAIUS By gar, 'tis no the fashion of France. It is not
jealous in France.

PAGE Nay, follow him, gentlemen. See the issue of his
search.   *Exeunt Page, Caius, and Evans*

MISTRESS PAGE Is there not a double excellency in this?

MISTRESS FORD I know not which pleases me better –
that my husband is deceived, or Sir John.

MISTRESS PAGE What a taking was he in when your
husband asked who was in the basket!

170 MISTRESS FORD I am half afraid he will have need of
washing; so throwing him into the water will do him a
benefit.

MISTRESS PAGE Hang him, dishonest rascal! I would all
of the same strain were in the same distress.

MISTRESS FORD I think my husband hath some special
suspicion of Falstaff's being here, for I never saw him
so gross in his jealousy till now.

MISTRESS PAGE I will lay a plot to try that, and we will
yet have more tricks with Falstaff. His dissolute disease
180 will scarce obey this medicine.

MISTRESS FORD Shall we send that foolish carrion
Mistress Quickly to him, and excuse his throwing into
the water, and give him another hope to betray him to
another punishment?

MISTRESS PAGE We will do it. Let him be sent for

    tomorrow eight o'clock, to have amends.

    Enter Ford, Page, Caius, and Evans

FORD I cannot find him. Maybe the knave bragged of that he could not compass.

MISTRESS PAGE (*aside to Mistress Ford*) Heard you that?

MISTRESS FORD You use me well, Master Ford! Do you? 190

FORD Ay, I do so.

MISTRESS FORD Heaven make you better than your thoughts.

FORD Amen.

MISTRESS PAGE You do yourself mighty wrong, Master Ford.

FORD Ay, ay, I must bear it.

EVANS If there be anypody in the house, and in the chambers, and in the coffers, and in the presses, heaven forgive my sins at the day of judgement. 200

CAIUS By gar, nor I too. There is nobodies.

PAGE Fie, fie, Master Ford, are you not ashamed? What spirit, what devil suggests this imagination? I would not ha' your distemper in this kind for the wealth of Windsor Castle.

FORD 'Tis my fault, Master Page. I suffer for it.

EVANS You suffer for a pad conscience. Your wife is as honest a 'omans as I will desires among five thousand, and five hundred too.

CAIUS By gar, I see 'tis an honest woman. 210

FORD Well, I promised you a dinner. Come, come, walk in the Park. I pray you pardon me. I will hereafter make known to you why I have done this. Come, wife, come, Mistress Page, I pray you pardon me. Pray heartily pardon me.

PAGE Let's go in, gentlemen; but, trust me, we'll mock him. I do invite you tomorrow morning to my house to breakfast. After, we'll a-birding together. I have a fine hawk for the bush. Shall it be so?

220 FORD Anything.

EVANS If there is one, I shall make two in the company.

CAIUS If there be one or two, I shall make-a the turd.

FORD Pray you go, Master Page.

Exeunt all but Evans and Caius

EVANS I pray you now, remembrance tomorrow on the lousy knave, mine host.

CAIUS Dat is good. By gar, with all my heart.

EVANS A lousy knave, to have his gibes and his mockeries.

Exeunt

III.4   *Enter Fenton and Anne Page*

FENTON

I see I cannot get thy father's love;

Therefore no more turn me to him, sweet Nan.

ANNE

Alas, how then?

FENTON   Why, thou must be thyself.

He doth object I am too great of birth,

And that, my state being galled with my expense,

I seek to heal it only by his wealth.

Besides these, other bars he lays before me –

My riots past, my wild societies;

And tells me 'tis a thing impossible

10 I should love thee but as a property.

ANNE

Maybe he tells you true.

FENTON

No, heaven so speed me in my time to come!

Albeit, I will confess, thy father's wealth

Was the first motive that I wooed thee, Anne;

Yet, wooing thee, I found thee of more value

Than stamps in gold or sums in sealèd bags.
And 'tis the very riches of thyself
That now I aim at.

ANNE   Gentle Master Fenton,
    Yet seek my father's love, still seek it, sir.
    If opportunity and humblest suit   20
    Cannot attain it, why then – hark you hither.

       They talk aside
       Enter Shallow, Slender, and Mistress Quickly

SHALLOW Break their talk, Mistress Quickly. My kinsman shall speak for himself.

SLENDER I'll make a shaft or a bolt on't. 'Slid, 'tis but
venturing.

SHALLOW Be not dismayed.

SLENDER No, she shall not dismay me. I care not for
that, but that I am afeard.

MISTRESS QUICKLY (*to Anne*) Hark ye, Master Slender
would speak a word with you.   30

ANNE
    I come to him. (*Aside*) This is my father's choice.
    O, what a world of vile ill-favoured faults
    Looks handsome in three hundred pounds a year!

MISTRESS QUICKLY And how does good Master Fenton?
Pray you, a word with you.

       They talk aside

SHALLOW She's coming. To her, coz. O boy, thou hadst
a father!

SLENDER I had a father, Mistress Anne. My uncle can
tell you good jests of him. Pray you, uncle, tell Mistress
Anne the jest how my father stole two geese out of a pen,   40
good uncle.

SHALLOW Mistress Anne, my cousin loves you.

SLENDER Ay, that I do, as well as I love any woman in
Gloucestershire.

SHALLOW He will maintain you like a gentlewoman.

SLENDER Ay, that I will, come cut and long-tail, under the degree of a squire.

SHALLOW He will make you a hundred and fifty pounds jointure.

50 ANNE Good Master Shallow, let him woo for himself.

SHALLOW Marry, I thank you for it; I thank you for that good comfort. She calls you, coz. I'll leave you.

ANNE Now, Master Slender –

SLENDER Now, good Mistress Anne –

ANNE What is your will?

SLENDER My will? 'Od's heartlings, that's a pretty jest indeed! I ne'er made my will yet, I thank heaven. I am not such a sickly creature, I give heaven praise.

ANNE I mean, Master Slender, what would you with me?

60 SLENDER Truly, for mine own part, I would little or nothing with you. Your father and my uncle hath made motions. If it be my luck, so; if not, happy man be his dole. They can tell you how things go better than I can. You may ask your father; here he comes.

Enter Page and Mistress Page

PAGE

Now, Master Slender. Love him, daughter Anne –
Why, how now? What does Master Fenton here?
You wrong me, sir, thus still to haunt my house.
I told you, sir, my daughter is disposed of.

FENTON

Nay, Master Page, be not impatient.

MISTRESS PAGE

70 Good Master Fenton, come not to my child.

PAGE

She is no match for you.

FENTON

Sir, will you hear me?

PAGE   No, good Master Fenton.
  Come, Master Shallow, come, son Slender, in.
  Knowing my mind, you wrong me, Master Fenton.
                         Exeunt Page, Shallow, and Slender

MISTRESS QUICKLY
  Speak to Mistress Page.

FENTON
  Good Mistress Page, for that I love your daughter
  In such a righteous fashion as I do,
  Perforce, against all checks, rebukes, and manners,
  I must advance the colours of my love
  And not retire. Let me have your good will.   80

ANNE
  Good mother, do not marry me to yond fool.

MISTRESS PAGE
  I mean it not – I seek you a better husband.

MISTRESS QUICKLY That's my master, Master Doctor.

ANNE
  Alas, I had rather be set quick i'th'earth,
  And bowled to death with turnips.

MISTRESS PAGE
  Come, trouble not yourself. Good Master Fenton,
  I will not be your friend, nor enemy.
  My daughter will I question how she loves you,
  And as I find her, so am I affected.
  Till then, farewell, sir. She must needs go in;   90
  Her father will be angry.

FENTON
  Farewell, gentle mistress. Farewell, Nan.
                         Exeunt Mistress Page and Anne

MISTRESS QUICKLY This is my doing now. 'Nay,' said
  I, 'will you cast away your child on a fool, and a
  physician? Look on Master Fenton.' This is my doing.

FENTON

    I thank thee, and I pray thee once tonight

    Give my sweet Nan this ring. There's for thy pains.

MISTRESS QUICKLY Now heaven send thee good fortune!   *Exit Fenton*

100 A kind heart he hath. A woman would run through fire and water for such a kind heart. But yet I would my master had Mistress Anne; or I would Master Slender had her; or, in sooth, I would Master Fenton had her. I will do what I can for them all three, for so I have promised, and I'll be as good as my word – but speciously for Master Fenton. Well, I must of another errand to Sir John Falstaff from my two mistresses. What a beast am I to slack it!   *Exit*

III.5   *Enter Falstaff and Bardolph*

FALSTAFF Bardolph, I say!

BARDOLPH Here, sir.

FALSTAFF Go fetch me a quart of sack – put a toast in't.

                                      Exit Bardolph

    Have I lived to be carried in a basket like a barrow of butcher's offal? And to be thrown in the Thames? Well, if I be served such another trick, I'll have my brains ta'en out and buttered, and give them to a dog for a new-year's gift. The rogues slighted me into the river with as little remorse as they would have drowned a blind

10 bitch's puppies, fifteen i'th'litter. And you may know by my size that I have a kind of alacrity in sinking. If the bottom were as deep as hell, I should down. I had been drowned but that the shore was shelvy and shallow – a death that I abhor, for the water swells a man, and what a thing should I have been when I had been swelled! I should have been a mountain of mummy.

Enter Bardolph with sack

BARDOLPH Here's Mistress Quickly, sir, to speak with you.

FALSTAFF Come, let me pour in some sack to the Thames water, for my belly's as cold as if I had swallowed 20 snowballs for pills to cool the reins. Call her in.

BARDOLPH Come in, woman.

Enter Mistress Quickly

MISTRESS QUICKLY By your leave; I cry you mercy. Give your worship good morrow.

FALSTAFF Take away these chalices. Go, brew me a pottle of sack finely.

BARDOLPH With eggs, sir?

FALSTAFF Simple of itself. I'll no pullet-sperm in my brewage.   *Exit Bardolph*
How now?   30

MISTRESS QUICKLY Marry, sir, I come to your worship from Mistress Ford.

FALSTAFF Mistress Ford? I have had ford enough. I was thrown into the ford. I have my belly full of ford.

MISTRESS QUICKLY Alas the day, good heart, that was not her fault. She does so take on with her men; they mistook their erection.

FALSTAFF So did I mine, to build upon a foolish woman's promise.

MISTRESS QUICKLY Well, she laments, sir, for it, that 40 it would yearn your heart to see it. Her husband goes this morning a-birding. She desires you once more to come to her between eight and nine. I must carry her word quickly. She'll make you amends, I warrant you.

FALSTAFF Well, I will visit her. Tell her so, and bid her think what a man is. Let her consider his frailty, and then judge of my merit.

MISTRESS QUICKLY I will tell her.

FALSTAFF Do so. Between nine and ten, sayest thou?
50 MISTRESS QUICKLY Eight and nine, sir.
FALSTAFF Well, begone. I will not miss her.
MISTRESS QUICKLY Peace be with you, sir. *Exit*
FALSTAFF I marvel I hear not of Master Brook. He sent
me word to stay within. I like his money well. O, here
he comes.

Enter Ford disguised as Brook

FORD Bless you, sir.
FALSTAFF Now, Master Brook, you come to know what
hath passed between me and Ford's wife?
FORD That, indeed, Sir John, is my business.
60 FALSTAFF Master Brook, I will not lie to you. I was at her
house the hour she appointed me.
FORD And sped you, sir?
FALSTAFF Very ill-favouredly, Master Brook.
FORD How so, sir? Did she change her determination?
FALSTAFF No, Master Brook, but the peaking cornuto
her husband, Master Brook, dwelling in a continual
'larum of jealousy, comes me in the instant of our
encounter, after we had embraced, kissed, protested,
and, as it were, spoke the prologue of our comedy; and
70 at his heels a rabble of his companions, thither provoked
and instigated by his distemper, and, forsooth, to
search his house for his wife's love.
FORD What? While you were there?
FALSTAFF While I was there.
FORD And did he search for you, and could not find you?
FALSTAFF You shall hear. As good luck would have it,
comes in one Mistress Page, gives intelligence of Ford's
approach, and, in her invention and Ford's wife's dis-
traction, they conveyed me into a buck-basket.
80 FORD A buck-basket?
FALSTAFF By the Lord, a buck-basket! Rammed me in

with foul shirts and smocks, socks, foul stockings, greasy napkins, that, Master Brook, there was the rankest compound of villainous smell that ever offended nostril.

FORD And how long lay you there?

FALSTAFF Nay, you shall hear, Master Brook, what I have suffered to bring this woman to evil for your good. Being thus crammed in the basket, a couple of Ford's knaves, his hinds, were called forth by their mistress to 90 carry me in the name of foul clothes to Datchet Lane. They took me on their shoulders, met the jealous knave their master in the door, who asked them once or twice what they had in their basket. I quaked for fear lest the lunatic knave would have searched it; but Fate, ordaining he should be a cuckold, held his hand. Well, on went he for a search, and away went I for foul clothes. But mark the sequel, Master Brook. I suffered the pangs of three several deaths: first, an intolerable fright to be detected with a jealous rotten bell-wether; 100 next, to be compassed like a good bilbo in the circumference of a peck, hilt to point, heel to head; and then, to be stopped in, like a strong distillation, with stinking clothes that fretted in their own grease. Think of that, a man of my kidney – think of that – that am as subject to heat as butter; a man of continual dissolution and thaw. It was a miracle to 'scape suffocation. And in the height of this bath, when I was more than half stewed in grease, like a Dutch dish, to be thrown into the Thames, and cooled, glowing hot, in that surge, like a horse- 110 shoe. Think of that – hissing hot – think of that, Master Brook!

FORD In good sadness, sir, I am sorry that for my sake you have suffered all this. My suit, then, is desperate? You'll undertake her no more?

FALSTAFF Master Brook, I will be thrown into Etna, as I have been into Thames, ere I will leave her thus. Her husband is this morning gone a-birding. I have received from her another embassy of meeting. 'Twixt eight
120 and nine is the hour, Master Brook.

FORD 'Tis past eight already, sir.

FALSTAFF Is it? I will then address me to my appointment. Come to me at your convenient leisure, and you shall know how I speed; and the conclusion shall be crowned with your enjoying her. Adieu. You shall have her, Master Brook; Master Brook, you shall cuckold Ford. *Exit*

FORD Hum! Ha! Is this a vision? Is this a dream? Do I sleep? Master Ford, awake; awake, Master Ford!
130 There's a hole made in your best coat, Master Ford. This 'tis to be married; this 'tis to have linen and buck-baskets! Well, I will proclaim myself what I am. I will now take the lecher. He is at my house. He cannot 'scape me. 'Tis impossible he should. He cannot creep into a halfpenny purse, nor into a pepperbox. But, lest the devil that guides him should aid him, I will search impossible places. Though what I am I cannot avoid, yet to be what I would not shall not make me tame. If I have horns to make one mad, let the proverb go with
140 me – I'll be horn-mad. *Exit*

✳

IV.1 *Enter Mistress Page, Mistress Quickly, and William*

MISTRESS PAGE Is he at Master Ford's already, thinkest thou?

MISTRESS QUICKLY Sure he is by this, or will be presently. But truly he is very courageous mad about his throwing into the water. Mistress Ford desires you to come suddenly.

MISTRESS PAGE I'll be with her by and by – I'll but bring my young man here to school. Look where his master comes.

Enter Sir Hugh Evans

'Tis a playing day, I see. How now, Sir Hugh, no school 10 today?

EVANS No. Master Slender is let the boys leave to play.

MISTRESS QUICKLY Blessing of his heart!

MISTRESS PAGE Sir Hugh, my husband says my son profits nothing in the world at his book. I pray you, ask him some questions in his accidence.

EVANS Come hither, William. Hold up your head. Come.

MISTRESS PAGE Come on, sirrah. Hold up your head. Answer your master, be not afraid.

EVANS William, how many numbers is in nouns?   20

WILLIAM Two.

MISTRESS QUICKLY Truly, I thought there had been one number more, because they say ' 'Od's nouns'.

EVANS Peace your tattlings. What is 'fair', William?

WILLIAM *Pulcher*.

MISTRESS QUICKLY Polecats! There are fairer things than polecats, sure.

EVANS You are a very simplicity 'oman. I pray you peace. What is *lapis*, William?

WILLIAM A stone.   30

EVANS And what is 'a stone', William?

WILLIAM A pebble.

EVANS No, it is *lapis*. I pray you remember in your prain.

WILLIAM *Lapis*.

EVANS That is a good William. What is he, William, that does lend articles?

WILLIAM Articles are borrowed of the pronoun, and be

thus declined: *Singulariter, nominativo, hic, haec, hoc.*

EVANS *Nominativo, hig, hag, hog.* Pray you mark:
genitivo, *hujus.* Well, what is your accusative case?

WILLIAM *Accusativo, hinc.*

EVANS I pray you have your remembrance, child.
Accusativo, hung, hang, hog.

MISTRESS QUICKLY 'Hang-hog' is Latin for bacon, I
warrant you.

EVANS Leave your prabbles, 'oman. What is the focative
case, William?

WILLIAM O – *vocativo, O.*

EVANS Remember, William. Focative is *caret.*

MISTRESS QUICKLY And that's a good root.

EVANS 'Oman, forbear.

MISTRESS PAGE Peace!

EVANS What is your genitive case plural, William?

WILLIAM Genitive case?

EVANS Ay.

WILLIAM Genitive – *horum, harum, horum.*

MISTRESS QUICKLY Vengeance of Jenny's case! Fie on
her! Never name her, child, if she be a whore.

EVANS For shame, 'oman.

MISTRESS QUICKLY You do ill to teach the child such
words. He teaches him to hick and to hack, which they'll
do fast enough of themselves, and to call 'horum'. Fie
upon you!

EVANS 'Oman, art thou lunatics? Hast thou no under-
standings for thy cases and the numbers of the genders?
Thou art as foolish Christian creatures as I would
desires.

MISTRESS PAGE Prithee hold thy peace.

EVANS Show me now, William, some declensions of your
pronouns.

WILLIAM Forsooth, I have forgot.

EVANS It is *qui, quae, quod*. If you forget your *quis*, your *quae*s, and your *quod*s, you must be preeches. Go your ways and play. Go.

MISTRESS PAGE He is a better scholar than I thought he was.

EVANS He is a good sprag memory. Farewell, Mistress Page.

MISTRESS PAGE Adieu, good Sir Hugh.   *Exit Evans*
Get you home, boy. Come, we stay too long.   *Exeunt* 80

Enter Falstaff and Mistress Ford   IV.2

FALSTAFF Mistress Ford, your sorrow hath eaten up my sufferance. I see you are obsequious in your love, and I profess requital to a hair's breadth, not only, Mistress Ford, in the simple office of love, but in all the accoutrement, complement, and ceremony of it. But are you sure of your husband now?

MISTRESS FORD He's a-birding, sweet Sir John.

MISTRESS PAGE (*within*) What ho, gossip Ford. What ho!

MISTRESS FORD Step into the chamber, Sir John.

                                        Exit Falstaff

Enter Mistress Page

MISTRESS PAGE How now, sweetheart; who's at home 10 besides yourself?

MISTRESS FORD Why, none but mine own people.

MISTRESS PAGE Indeed?

MISTRESS FORD No, certainly. (*Aside to her*) Speak louder.

MISTRESS PAGE Truly, I am so glad you have nobody here.

MISTRESS FORD Why?

MISTRESS PAGE Why, woman, your husband is in his old lines again. He so takes on yonder with my hus- 20

123

band, so rails against all married mankind, so curses all Eve's daughters, of what complexion soever, and so buffets himself on the forehead, crying 'Peer out, peer out!', that any madness I ever yet beheld seemed but tameness, civility, and patience to this his distemper he is in now. I am glad the fat knight is not here.

MISTRESS FORD Why, does he talk of him?

MISTRESS PAGE Of none but him, and swears he was carried out, the last time he searched for him, in a
30 basket; protests to my husband he is now here, and hath drawn him and the rest of their company from their sport, to make another experiment of his suspicion. But I am glad the knight is not here. Now he shall see his own foolery.

MISTRESS FORD How near is he, Mistress Page?

MISTRESS PAGE Hard by, at street end. He will be here anon.

MISTRESS FORD I am undone. The knight is here.

MISTRESS PAGE Why, then, you are utterly shamed, and
40 he's but a dead man. What a woman are you! Away with him, away with him! Better shame than murder.

MISTRESS FORD Which way should he go? How should I bestow him? Shall I put him into the basket again?
      Enter Falstaff

FALSTAFF No, I'll come no more i'th'basket. May I not go out ere he come?

MISTRESS PAGE Alas, three of Master Ford's brothers watch the door with pistols, that none shall issue out. Otherwise you might slip away ere he came. But what make you here?

50 FALSTAFF What shall I do? I'll creep up into the chimney.

MISTRESS FORD There they always use to discharge their birding pieces.

MISTRESS PAGE Creep into the kiln-hole.

FALSTAFF Where is it?

MISTRESS FORD He will seek there, on my word. Neither press, coffer, chest, trunk, well, vault, but he hath an abstract for the remembrance of such places, and goes to them by his note. There is no hiding you in the house.   60

FALSTAFF I'll go out, then.

MISTRESS PAGE If you go out in your own semblance, you die, Sir John. Unless you go out disguised –

MISTRESS FORD How might we disguise him?

MISTRESS PAGE Alas the day, I know not. There is no woman's gown big enough for him. Otherwise he might put on a hat, a muffler, and a kerchief, and so escape.

FALSTAFF Good hearts, devise something. Any extremity rather than a mischief.

MISTRESS FORD My maid's aunt, the fat woman of 70 Brainford, has a gown above.

MISTRESS PAGE On my word, it will serve him. She's as big as he is; and there's her thrummed hat and her muffler too. Run up, Sir John.

MISTRESS FORD Go, go, sweet Sir John. Mistress Page and I will look some linen for your head.

MISTRESS PAGE Quick, quick! We'll come dress you straight. Put on the gown the while.   *Exit Falstaff*

MISTRESS FORD I would my husband would meet him in this shape. He cannot abide the old woman of 80 Brainford. He swears she's a witch, forbade her my house, and hath threatened to beat her.

MISTRESS PAGE Heaven guide him to thy husband's cudgel, and the devil guide his cudgel afterwards!

MISTRESS FORD But is my husband coming?

MISTRESS PAGE Ay, in good sadness, is he, and talks of the basket too, howsoever he hath had intelligence.

MISTRESS FORD We'll try that; for I'll appoint my men
to carry the basket again, to meet him at the door with
90   it, as they did last time.

MISTRESS PAGE Nay, but he'll be here presently. Let's
go dress him like the witch of Brainford.

MISTRESS FORD I'll first direct my men what they shall
do with the basket. Go up. I'll bring linen for him
straight.

MISTRESS PAGE Hang him, dishonest varlet! We cannot
misuse him enough.
  We'll leave a proof, by that which we will do,
  Wives may be merry, and yet honest too.
100   We do not act that often jest and laugh;
  'Tis old but true: 'Still swine eats all the draff.'

                                  Exit

    Enter John and Robert

MISTRESS FORD Go, sirs, take the basket again on your
shoulders. Your master is hard at door. If he bid you
set it down, obey him. Quickly, dispatch.   *Exit*

JOHN Come, come, take it up.

ROBERT Pray heaven it be not full of knight again.

JOHN I hope not. I had as lief bear so much lead.

    Enter Ford, Page, Shallow, Caius, and Evans

FORD Ay, but if it prove true, Master Page, have you any
way then to unfool me again? Set down the basket,
110   villains. Somebody call my wife. Youth in a basket! O
you panderly rascals! There's a knot, a ging, a pack, a
conspiracy against me. Now shall the devil be shamed.
What, wife, I say! Come, come forth! Behold what
honest clothes you send forth to bleaching!

PAGE Why, this passes, Master Ford. You are not to go
loose any longer. You must be pinioned.

EVANS Why, this is lunatics. This is mad as a mad dog.

SHALLOW Indeed, Master Ford, this is not well, indeed.

FORD So say I too, sir.

Enter Mistress Ford

Come hither, Mistress Ford. Mistress Ford, the honest 120
woman, the modest wife, the virtuous creature, that
hath the jealous fool to her husband! I suspect without
cause, mistress, do I?

MISTRESS FORD Heaven be my witness, you do, if you
suspect me in any dishonesty.

FORD Well said, brazen-face. Hold it out. – Come forth,
sirrah!

He pulls clothes out of the basket

PAGE This passes!

MISTRESS FORD Are you not ashamed? Let the clothes
alone. 130

FORD I shall find you anon.

EVANS 'Tis unreasonable. Will you take up your wife's
clothes? Come away.

FORD Empty the basket, I say.

MISTRESS FORD Why, man, why?

FORD Master Page, as I am a man, there was one conveyed out of my house yesterday in this basket. Why
may not he be there again? In my house I am sure he is.
My intelligence is true. My jealousy is reasonable.
Pluck me out all the linen. 140

MISTRESS FORD If you find a man there, he shall die a
flea's death.

PAGE Here's no man.

SHALLOW By my fidelity, this is not well, Master Ford.
This wrongs you.

EVANS Master Ford, you must pray, and not follow the
imaginations of your own heart. This is jealousies.

FORD Well, he's not here I seek for.

PAGE No, nor nowhere else but in your brain.

FORD Help to search my house this one time. If I find 150

not what I seek, show no colour for my extremity. Let me for ever be your table sport. Let them say of me 'As jealous as Ford, that searched a hollow walnut for his wife's leman'. Satisfy me once more. Once more search with me.   *Exeunt John and Robert with the basket*

MISTRESS FORD What ho, Mistress Page, come you and the old woman down. My husband will come into the chamber.

FORD Old woman? What old woman's that?

160 MISTRESS FORD Why, it is my maid's aunt of Brainford.

FORD A witch, a quean, an old cozening quean! Have I not forbid her my house? She comes of errands, does she? We are simple men; we do not know what's brought to pass under the profession of fortune-telling. She works by charms, by spells, by th'figure; and such daubery as this is beyond our element – we know nothing. Come down, you witch, you hag, you. Come down, I say!

MISTRESS FORD Nay, good sweet husband! – Good gentlemen, let him not strike the old woman.

Enter Falstaff in woman's clothes, and Mistress Page

170 MISTRESS PAGE Come, Mother Prat, come, give me your hand.

FORD I'll prat her.

He beats Falstaff

Out of my door, you witch, you rag, you baggage, you polecat, you ronyon! Out, out! I'll conjure you, I'll fortune-tell you.   *Exit Falstaff*

MISTRESS PAGE Are you not ashamed? I think you have killed the poor woman.

MISTRESS FORD Nay, he will do it. – 'Tis a goodly credit for you.

180 FORD Hang her, witch!

EVANS By yea and no, I think the 'oman is a witch indeed.

I like not when a 'oman has a great peard. I spy a great peard under his muffler.

FORD Will you follow, gentlemen? I beseech you, follow. See but the issue of my jealousy. If I cry out thus upon no trail, never trust me when I open again.

PAGE Let's obey his humour a little further. Come, gentlemen.

Exeunt Ford, Page, Shallow, Caius, and Evans

MISTRESS PAGE Trust me, he beat him most pitifully.

MISTRESS FORD Nay, by th'mass, that he did not. He 190 beat him most unpitifully, methought.

MISTRESS PAGE I'll have the cudgel hallowed and hung o'er the altar. It hath done meritorious service.

MISTRESS FORD What think you? May we, with the warrant of womanhood and the witness of a good conscience, pursue him with any further revenge?

MISTRESS PAGE The spirit of wantonness is sure scared out of him. If the devil have him not in fee simple, with fine and recovery, he will never, I think, in the way of waste, attempt us again. 200

MISTRESS FORD Shall we tell our husbands how we have served him?

MISTRESS PAGE Yes, by all means, if it be but to scrape the figures out of your husband's brains. If they can find in their hearts the poor unvirtuous fat knight shall be any further afflicted, we two will still be the ministers.

MISTRESS FORD I'll warrant they'll have him publicly shamed, and methinks there would be no period to the jest, should he not be publicly shamed.

MISTRESS PAGE Come, to the forge with it, then. Shape 210 it. I would not have things cool. *Exeunt*

IV.3 *Enter Host and Bardolph*

BARDOLPH Sir, the Germans desire to have three of your
horses. The Duke himself will be tomorrow at court,
and they are going to meet him.

HOST What duke should that be comes so secretly? I
hear not of him in the court. Let me speak with the
gentlemen. They speak English?

BARDOLPH Ay, sir. I'll call them to you.

HOST They shall have my horses, but I'll make them pay.
I'll sauce them. They have had my house a week at
10 command. I have turned away my other guests. They
must come off. I'll sauce them. Come.   *Exeunt*

IV.4 *Enter Page, Ford, Mistress Page, Mistress Ford, and*
Evans

EVANS 'Tis one of the best discretions of a 'oman as ever
I did look upon.

PAGE And did he send you both these letters at an instant?

MISTRESS PAGE Within a quarter of an hour.

FORD

Pardon me, wife. Henceforth do what thou wilt.

I rather will suspect the sun with cold

Than thee with wantonness. Now doth thy honour
     stand,

In him that was of late an heretic,

As firm as faith.

PAGE   'Tis well, 'tis well. No more.
10 Be not as extreme in submission

As in offence.

But let our plot go forward. Let our wives

Yet once again, to make us public sport,

Appoint a meeting with this old fat fellow,

Where we may take him and disgrace him for it.

FORD

 There is no better way than that they spoke of.

PAGE How? To send him word they'll meet him in the
 Park at midnight? Fie, fie, he'll never come.

EVANS You say he has been thrown in the rivers, and has
 been grievously peaten as an old 'oman. Methinks there 20
 should be terrors in him, that he should not come.
 Methinks his flesh is punished; he shall have no desires.

PAGE So think I too.

MISTRESS FORD

 Devise but how you'll use him when he comes,

 And let us two devise to bring him thither.

MISTRESS PAGE

 There is an old tale goes that Herne the Hunter,
 Sometime a keeper here in Windsor Forest,
 Doth all the winter-time, at still midnight,
 Walk round about an oak, with great ragg'd horns;
 And there he blasts the tree, and takes the cattle, 30
 And makes milch-kine yield blood, and shakes a chain
 In a most hideous and dreadful manner.
 You have heard of such a spirit, and well you know
 The superstitious idle-headed eld
 Received and did deliver to our age
 This tale of Herne the Hunter for a truth.

PAGE

 Why, yet there want not many that do fear
 In deep of night to walk by this Herne's Oak.
 But what of this?

MISTRESS FORD Marry, this is our device:

 That Falstaff at that oak shall meet with us, 40
 Disguised like Herne, with huge horns on his head.

PAGE

 Well, let it not be doubted but he'll come.
 And in this shape, when you have brought him thither,

What shall be done with him? What is your plot?

MISTRESS PAGE
That likewise have we thought upon, and thus:
Nan Page my daughter, and my little son,
And three or four more of their growth, we'll dress
Like urchins, ouphes, and fairies, green and white,
With rounds of waxen tapers on their heads,
50 And rattles in their hands. Upon a sudden,
As Falstaff, she, and I are newly met,
Let them from forth a sawpit rush at once
With some diffusèd song. Upon their sight,
We two in great amazedness will fly.
Then let them all encircle him about,
And, fairy-like, to pinch the unclean knight,
And ask him why, that hour of fairy revel,
In their so sacred paths he dares to tread
In shape profane.

MISTRESS FORD   And till he tell the truth,
60 Let the supposèd fairies pinch him sound
And burn him with their tapers.

MISTRESS PAGE   The truth being known,
We'll all present ourselves, dis-horn the spirit,
And mock him home to Windsor.

FORD   The children must
Be practised well to this, or they'll ne'er do't.

EVANS I will teach the children their behaviours, and I
will be like a jackanapes also, to burn the knight with
my taber.

FORD
That will be excellent. I'll go buy them vizards.

MISTRESS PAGE
My Nan shall be the Queen of all the Fairies,
70 Finely attirèd in a robe of white.

PAGE

That silk will I go buy. (*Aside*) And in that time
Shall Master Slender steal my Nan away
And marry her at Eton. (*To them*) Go, send to Falstaff
straight.

FORD

Nay, I'll to him again in name of Brook.
He'll tell me all his purpose. Sure, he'll come.

MISTRESS PAGE

Fear not you that. Go get us properties
And tricking for our fairies.

EVANS Let us about it. It is admirable pleasures and fery
honest knaveries. *Exeunt Page, Ford, and Evans*

MISTRESS PAGE

Go, Mistress Ford,   80
Send Quickly to Sir John, to know his mind.
Exit Mistress Ford

I'll to the doctor. He hath my good will,
And none but he, to marry with Nan Page.
That Slender, though well landed, is an idiot;
And he my husband best of all affects.
The doctor is well moneyed, and his friends
Potent at court. He, none but he, shall have her,
Though twenty thousand worthier come to crave her.
Exit

Enter Host and Simple   IV.5

HOST What wouldst thou have, boor? What, thick-skin?
Speak, breathe, discuss; brief, short, quick, snap.

SIMPLE Marry, sir, I come to speak with Sir John Falstaff
from Master Slender.

HOST There's his chamber, his house, his castle, his
standing-bed and truckle-bed. 'Tis painted about with

the story of the Prodigal, fresh and new. Go, knock and call. He'll speak like an Anthropophaginian unto thee. Knock, I say.

10 SIMPLE There's an old woman, a fat woman, gone up into his chamber. I'll be so bold as stay, sir, till she come down. I come to speak with her, indeed.

HOST Ha! A fat woman? The knight may be robbed. I'll call. Bully knight! Bully Sir John! Speak from thy lungs military. Art thou there? It is thine host, thine Ephesian, calls.

FALSTAFF (*above*) How now, mine host?

HOST Here's a Bohemian-Tartar tarries the coming down of thy fat woman. Let her descend, bully, let her des-
20 cend. My chambers are honourable. Fie, privacy, fie!

Enter Falstaff

FALSTAFF There was, mine host, an old fat woman even now with me, but she's gone.

SIMPLE Pray you, sir, was't not the wise woman of Brainford?

FALSTAFF Ay, marry, was it, mussel-shell. What would you with her?

SIMPLE My master, sir, my Master Slender, sent to her, seeing her go thorough the streets, to know, sir, whether one Nym, sir, that beguiled him of a chain, had the
30 chain or no.

FALSTAFF I spake with the old woman about it.

SIMPLE And what says she, I pray, sir?

FALSTAFF Marry, she says that the very same man that beguiled Master Slender of his chain cozened him of it.

SIMPLE I would I could have spoken with the woman herself. I had other things to have spoken with her too, from him.

FALSTAFF What are they? Let us know.

HOST Ay, come. Quick!

SIMPLE I may not conceal them, sir.   40

HOST Conceal them, or thou diest.

SIMPLE Why, sir, they were nothing but about Mistress
    Anne Page: to know if it were my master's fortune to
    have her or no.

FALSTAFF 'Tis, 'tis his fortune.

SIMPLE What, sir?

FALSTAFF To have her or no. Go, say the woman told me
    so.

SIMPLE May I be bold to say so, sir?

FALSTAFF Ay, sir; like who more bold.   50

SIMPLE I thank your worship. I shall make my master
    glad with these tidings.   *Exit*

HOST Thou art clerkly, thou art clerkly, Sir John. Was
    there a wise woman with thee?

FALSTAFF Ay, that there was, mine host, one that hath
    taught me more wit than ever I learned before in my
    life. And I paid nothing for it neither, but was paid for
    my learning.
        Enter Bardolph

BARDOLPH Out, alas, sir, cozenage, mere cozenage!

HOST Where be my horses? Speak well of them, varletto.   60

BARDOLPH Run away with the cozeners. For so soon as
    I came beyond Eton, they threw me off, from behind
    one of them, in a slough of mire; and set spurs and
    away, like three German devils, three Doctor Faustuses.

HOST They are gone but to meet the Duke, villain. Do
    not say they be fled. Germans are honest men.
        Enter Evans

EVANS Where is mine host?

HOST What is the matter, sir?

EVANS Have a care of your entertainments. There is a
    friend of mine come to town tells me there is three   70
    cozen-germans that has cozened all the hosts of Readins,

135

of Maidenhead, of Colebrook, of horses and money. I
tell you for good will, look you. You are wise, and full of
gibes and vlouting-stocks, and 'tis not convenient you
should be cozened. Fare you well.   *Exit*

Enter Caius

CAIUS Vere is mine host de Jarteer?

HOST Here, Master Doctor, in perplexity and doubtful
dilemma.

CAIUS I cannot tell vat is dat. But it is tell-a me dat you
80 make grand preparation for a duke de Jamany. By my
trot, dere is no duke that the court is know to come. I
tell you for good will. Adieu.   *Exit*

HOST Hue and cry, villain, go! Assist me, knight. I am
undone! Fly, run, hue and cry, villain! I am undone!

Exeunt Host and Bardolph

FALSTAFF I would all the world might be cozened, for I
have been cozened and beaten too. If it should come to
the ear of the court how I have been transformed, and
how my transformation hath been washed and cudgelled,
they would melt me out of my fat drop by drop, and
90 liquor fishermen's boots with me. I warrant they would
whip me with their fine wits till I were as crestfallen as a
dried pear. I never prospered since I forswore myself at
primero. Well, if my wind were but long enough to say
my prayers, I would repent.

Enter Mistress Quickly

Now, whence come you?

MISTRESS QUICKLY From the two parties, forsooth.

FALSTAFF The devil take one party, and his dam the
other! And so they shall be both bestowed. I have
suffered more for their sakes, more than the villainous
100 inconstancy of man's disposition is able to bear.

MISTRESS QUICKLY And have not they suffered? Yes, I
warrant; speciously one of them. Mistress Ford, good

heart, is beaten black and blue, that you cannot see a
white spot about her.

FALSTAFF What tellest thou me of black and blue? I
was beaten myself into all the colours of the rainbow;
and I was like to be apprehended for the witch of
Brainford. But that my admirable dexterity of wit, my
counterfeiting the action of an old woman, delivered me,
the knave constable had set me i'th'stocks, i'th'common 110
stocks, for a witch.

MISTRESS QUICKLY Sir, let me speak with you in your
chamber. You shall hear how things go, and, I warrant,
to your content. Here is a letter will say somewhat.
Good hearts, what ado here is to bring you together!
Sure, one of you does not serve heaven well, that you are
so crossed.

FALSTAFF Come up into my chamber.   *Exeunt*

           Enter Fenton and Host   IV.6
HOST Master Fenton, talk not to me. My mind is heavy.
I will give over all.

FENTON
   Yet hear me speak. Assist me in my purpose,
   And, as I am a gentleman, I'll give thee
   A hundred pound in gold more than your loss.

HOST I will hear you, Master Fenton, and I will, at the
least, keep your counsel.

FENTON
   From time to time I have acquainted you
   With the dear love I bear to fair Anne Page,
   Who mutually hath answered my affection,   10
   So far forth as herself might be her chooser,
   Even to my wish. I have a letter from her
   Of such contents as you will wonder at,

137

The mirth whereof so larded with my matter
That neither singly can be manifested
Without the show of both. Fat Falstaff
Hath a great scene. The image of the jest
I'll show you here at large. Hark, good mine host:
Tonight at Herne's Oak, just 'twixt twelve and one,
20   Must my sweet Nan present the Fairy Queen –
The purpose why is here – in which disguise,
While other jests are something rank on foot,
Her father hath commanded her to slip
Away with Slender, and with him at Eton
Immediately to marry. She hath consented.
Now, sir,
Her mother – ever strong against that match
And firm for Doctor Caius – hath appointed
That he shall likewise shuffle her away,
30   While other sports are tasking of their minds,
And at the deanery, where a priest attends,
Straight marry her. To this her mother's plot
She, seemingly obedient, likewise hath
Made promise to the doctor. Now thus it rests:
Her father means she shall be all in white,
And in that habit, when Slender sees his time
To take her by the hand and bid her go,
She shall go with him. Her mother hath intended,
The better to denote her to the doctor –
40   For they must all be masked and vizarded –
That quaint in green she shall be loose enrobed,
With ribands pendent, flaring 'bout her head;
And when the doctor spies his vantage ripe,
To pinch her by the hand, and, on that token,
The maid hath given consent to go with him.

HOST
Which means she to deceive, father or mother?

138

FENTON

    Both, my good host, to go along with me.

    And here it rests – that you'll procure the vicar

    To stay for me at church 'twixt twelve and one,

    And, in the lawful name of marrying,   50

    To give our hearts united ceremony.

HOST

    Well, husband your device. I'll to the vicar.

    Bring you the maid, you shall not lack a priest.

FENTON

    So shall I evermore be bound to thee,

    Besides, I'll make a present recompense.   *Exeunt*

*

    Enter Falstaff and Mistress Quickly   V.1

FALSTAFF Prithee no more prattling. Go. I'll hold. This
is the third time; I hope good luck lies in odd numbers.
Away; go. They say there is divinity in odd numbers,
either in nativity, chance, or death. Away.

MISTRESS QUICKLY I'll provide you a chain, and I'll do
what I can to get you a pair of horns.

FALSTAFF Away, I say; time wears. Hold up your head,
and mince.   *Exit Mistress Quickly*

    Enter Ford disguised as Brook

How now, Master Brook! Master Brook, the matter will
be known tonight or never. Be you in the Park about 10
midnight, at Herne's Oak, and you shall see wonders.

FORD Went you not to her yesterday, sir, as you told me
you had appointed?

FALSTAFF I went to her, Master Brook, as you see, like
a poor old man. But I came from her, Master Brook, like
a poor old woman. That same knave Ford, her husband,

hath the finest mad devil of jealousy in him, Master
Brook, that ever governed frenzy. I will tell you: he
beat me grievously, in the shape of a woman; for in the
20 shape of man, Master Brook, I fear not Goliath with a
weaver's beam, because I know also life is a shuttle. I
am in haste. Go along with me. I'll tell you all, Master
Brook. Since I plucked geese, played truant and whipped
top, I knew not what 'twas to be beaten till lately.
Follow me. I'll tell you strange things of this knave
Ford, on whom tonight I will be revenged. And I will
deliver his wife into your hand. Follow. Strange things
in hand, Master Brook! Follow.   *Exeunt*

V.2   *Enter Page, Shallow, and Slender*

PAGE Come, come. We'll couch i'th'Castle ditch till we
see the light of our fairies. Remember, son Slender, my
daughter.

SLENDER Ay, forsooth. I have spoke with her, and we have
a nay-word how to know one another. I come to her in
white, and cry 'mum'; she cries 'budget'; and by that
we know one another.

SHALLOW That's good too. But what needs either your
'mum' or her 'budget'? The white will decipher her
10 well enough. It hath struck ten o'clock.

PAGE The night is dark. Light and spirits will become it
well. Heaven prosper our sport! No man means evil but
the devil, and we shall know him by his horns. Let's
away. Follow me.   *Exeunt*

V.3   *Enter Mistress Page, Mistress Ford, and Doctor Caius*

MISTRESS PAGE · Master Doctor, my daughter is in green.
When you see your time, take her by the hand, away

with her to the deanery, and dispatch it quickly. Go before into the Park. We two must go together.

CAIUS I know vat I have to do. Adieu.

MISTRESS PAGE Fare you well, sir.   *Exit Caius*
My husband will not rejoice so much at the abuse of Falstaff as he will chafe at the doctor's marrying my daughter. But 'tis no matter. Better a little chiding than a great deal of heartbreak.   10

MISTRESS FORD Where is Nan now, and her troop of fairies, and the Welsh devil Hugh?

MISTRESS PAGE They are all couched in a pit hard by Herne's Oak, with obscured lights, which, at the very instant of Falstaff's and our meeting, they will at once display to the night.

MISTRESS FORD That cannot choose but amaze him.

MISTRESS PAGE If he be not amazed, he will be mocked. If he be amazed, he will every way be mocked.

MISTRESS FORD We'll betray him finely.   20

MISTRESS PAGE
Against such lewdsters and their lechery,
Those that betray them do no treachery.

MISTRESS FORD The hour draws on. To the Oak, to the Oak!   *Exeunt*

Enter Evans disguised as a Satyr, and others as V.4
Fairies

EVANS Trib, trib, fairies. Come. And remember your parts. Be pold, I pray you. Follow me into the pit, and when I give the watch-'ords, do as I pid you. Come, come; trib, trib.   *Exeunt*

141

V.5   *Enter Falstaff disguised as Herne, with a buck's*
       head upon him

FALSTAFF The Windsor bell hath struck twelve; the
minute draws on. Now, the hot-blooded gods assist
me! Remember, Jove, thou wast a bull for thy Europa.
Love set on thy horns. O powerful love, that in some
respects makes a beast a man, in some other a man a
beast. You were also, Jupiter, a swan for the love of
Leda. O omnipotent love, how near the god drew to the
complexion of a goose! A fault done first in the form of a
beast – O Jove, a beastly fault – and then another fault
in the semblance of a fowl – think on't, Jove, a foul fault!
When gods have hot backs, what shall poor men do?
For me, I am here a Windsor stag, and the fattest, I
think, i'th'forest. Send me a cool rut-time, Jove, or who
can blame me to piss my tallow? Who comes here?
My doe?

       Enter Mistress Ford and Mistress Page

MISTRESS FORD Sir John! Art thou there, my deer, my
male deer?

FALSTAFF My doe with the black scut! Let the sky rain
potatoes. Let it thunder to the tune of 'Greensleeves',
hail kissing-comfits, and snow eringoes. Let there come
a tempest of provocation, I will shelter me here.

       He embraces her

MISTRESS FORD Mistress Page is come with me, sweetheart.

FALSTAFF Divide me like a bribed buck, each a haunch.
I will keep my sides to myself, my shoulders for the
fellow of this walk, and my horns I bequeath your
husbands. Am I a woodman, ha? Speak I like Herne
the Hunter? Why, now is Cupid a child of conscience;
he makes restitution. As I am a true spirit, welcome!

       A noise of horns

142

MISTRESS PAGE Alas, what noise?   30
MISTRESS FORD Heaven forgive our sins!
FALSTAFF What should this be?
MISTRESS FORD *and* MISTRESS PAGE Away, away!
> *They run off*

FALSTAFF I think the devil will not have me damned, lest
  the oil that's in me should set hell on fire. He would
  never else cross me thus.
> *Enter Evans as a Satyr, Mistress Quickly as the*
> *Queen of Fairies, Pistol as Hobgoblin, Anne Page and*
> *boys as Fairies. They carry tapers*

MISTRESS QUICKLY *as Queen of Fairies*
  Fairies black, grey, green, and white,
  You moonshine revellers, and shades of night,
  You orphan heirs of fixèd destiny,
  Attend your office and your quality.   40
  Crier Hobgoblin, make the fairy oyes.

PISTOL *as Hobgoblin*
  Elves, list your names; silence, you airy toys.
  Cricket, to Windsor chimneys shalt thou leap.
  Where fires thou findest unraked and hearths unswept,
  There pinch the maids as blue as bilberry.
  Our radiant Queen hates sluts and sluttery.

FALSTAFF
  They are fairies; he that speaks to them shall die.
  I'll wink and couch; no man their works must eye.
> *He lies down upon his face*

EVANS *as a Satyr*
  Where's Bead? Go you, and where you find a maid
  That, ere she sleep, has thrice her prayers said,   50
  Raise up the organs of her fantasy,
  Sleep she as sound as careless infancy.
  But those as sleep and think not on their sins,
  Pinch them, arms, legs, backs, shoulders, sides, and shins.

MISTRESS QUICKLY *as Queen of Fairies*
About, about!
Search Windsor Castle, elves, within and out.
Strew good luck, ouphes, on every sacred room,
That it may stand till the perpetual doom
In state as wholesome as in state 'tis fit,
60   Worthy the owner and the owner it.
The several chairs of order look you scour
With juice of balm and every precious flower.
Each fair instalment, coat, and several crest,
With loyal blazon, evermore be blest!
And nightly, meadow-fairies, look you sing,
Like to the Garter's compass, in a ring.
Th'expressure that it bears, green let it be,
More fertile-fresh than all the field to see;
And *Honi soit qui mal y pense* write
70   In emerald tufts, flowers purple, blue, and white,
Like sapphire, pearl, and rich embroidery,
Buckled below fair knighthood's bending knee.
Fairies use flowers for their charactery.
Away, disperse! But till 'tis one o'clock,
Our dance of custom round about the oak
Of Herne the Hunter let us not forget.

EVANS *as a Satyr*
Pray you, lock hand in hand; yourselves in order set;
And twenty glow-worms shall our lanterns be,
To guide our measure round about the tree.
80   But stay – I smell a man of middle earth.

FALSTAFF Heavens defend me from that Welsh fairy,
lest he transform me to a piece of cheese.

PISTOL *as Hobgoblin*
Vile worm, thou wast o'erlooked even in thy birth.

MISTRESS QUICKLY *as Queen of Fairies*
With trial-fire touch me his finger-end.
If he be chaste, the flame will back descend
And turn him to no pain; but if he start,

It is the flesh of a corrupted heart.

PISTOL *as Hobgoblin*

A trial, come.

EVANS *as a Satyr*

        Come, will this wood take fire?

   They burn him with their tapers

FALSTAFF O, O, O!

MISTRESS QUICKLY *as Queen of Fairies*

Corrupt, corrupt, and tainted in desire!   90

About him, fairies, sing a scornful rhyme,

And, as you trip, still pinch him to your time.

          THE SONG

   Fie on sinful fantasy!

   Fie on lust and luxury!

   Lust is but a bloody fire,

   Kindled with unchaste desire,

   Fed in heart, whose flames aspire,

   As thoughts do blow them, higher and higher.

   Pinch him, fairies, mutually,

   Pinch him for his villainy.   100

Pinch him, and burn him, and turn him about,

Till candles and starlight and moonshine be out.

  During this song they pinch Falstaff; and Doctor
  Caius comes one way, and steals away a boy in green;
  Slender another way, and takes off a boy in white;
  and Fenton comes, and steals away Anne Page. A noise
  of hunting is made within; and all the Fairies run
  away. Falstaff pulls off his buck's head, and rises up.
  Enter Page, Ford, Mistress Page, and Mistress Ford

PAGE

Nay, do not fly; I think we have watched you now.

Will none but Herne the Hunter serve your turn?

MISTRESS PAGE

I pray you, come, hold up the jest no higher.

Now, good Sir John, how like you Windsor wives?

She points to the horns
See you these, husband? Do not these fair yokes
Become the forest better than the town?

FORD Now, sir, who's a cuckold now? Master Brook,
110 Falstaff's a knave, a cuckoldy knave. Here are his
horns, Master Brook. And, Master Brook, he hath
enjoyed nothing of Ford's but his buck-basket, his
cudgel, and twenty pounds of money, which must be
paid to Master Brook. His horses are arrested for it,
Master Brook.

MISTRESS FORD Sir John, we have had ill luck; we could
never meet. I will never take you for my love again, but
I will always count you my deer.

FALSTAFF I do begin to perceive that I am made an ass.
120 FORD Ay, and an ox too. Both the proofs are extant.

FALSTAFF And these are not fairies? I was three or four
times in the thought they were not fairies; and yet the
guiltiness of my mind, the sudden surprise of my
powers, drove the grossness of the foppery into a
received belief, in despite of the teeth of all rhyme and
reason, that they were fairies. See now how wit may be
made a Jack-a-Lent when 'tis upon ill employment.

EVANS Sir John Falstaff, serve Got and leave your desires,
and fairies will not pinse you.
130 FORD Well said, fairy Hugh.

EVANS And leave your jealousies too, I pray you.

FORD I will never mistrust my wife again till thou art able
to woo her in good English.

FALSTAFF Have I laid my brain in the sun and dried it,
that it wants matter to prevent so gross o'erreaching as
this? Am I ridden with a Welsh goat too? Shall I have
a coxcomb of frieze? 'Tis time I were choked with a
piece of toasted cheese.

EVANS Seese is not good to give putter. Your belly is all
   putter.   140
FALSTAFF 'Seese' and 'putter'? Have I lived to stand at
   the taunt of one that makes fritters of English? This is
   enough to be the decay of lust and late-walking through
   the realm.
MISTRESS PAGE Why, Sir John, do you think, though we
   would have thrust virtue out of our hearts by the head
   and shoulders, and have given ourselves without scruple
   to hell, that ever the devil could have made you our
   delight?
FORD What, a hodge-pudding? A bag of flax?   150
MISTRESS PAGE A puffed man?
PAGE Old, cold, withered, and of intolerable entrails?
FORD And one that is as slanderous as Satan?
PAGE And as poor as Job?
FORD And as wicked as his wife?
EVANS And given to fornications, and to taverns, and
   sack, and wine, and metheglins, and to drinkings, and
   swearings and starings, pribbles and prabbles?
FALSTAFF Well, I am your theme. You have the start of
   me. I am dejected. I am not able to answer the Welsh   160
   flannel. Ignorance itself is a plummet o'er me. Use me as
   you will.
FORD Marry, sir, we'll bring you to Windsor, to one
   Master Brook, that you have cozened of money, to whom
   you should have been a pander. Over and above that
   you have suffered, I think to repay that money will be a
   biting affliction.
PAGE Yet be cheerful, knight. Thou shalt eat a posset
   tonight at my house, where I will desire thee to laugh at
   my wife that now laughs at thee. Tell her Master Slender 170
   hath married her daughter.
MISTRESS PAGE (aside) Doctors doubt that. If Anne Page

be my daughter, she is, by this, Doctor Caius's wife.

Enter Slender

SLENDER Whoa, ho, ho, father Page!

PAGE Son, how now? How now, son? Have you dispatched?

SLENDER Dispatched? I'll make the best in Gloucestershire know on't. Would I were hanged, la, else!

PAGE Of what, son?

180 SLENDER I came yonder at Eton to marry Mistress Anne Page, and she's a great lubberly boy. If it had not been i'th'church, I would have swinged him, or he should have swinged me. If I did not think it had been Anne Page, would I might never stir! And 'tis a postmaster's boy.

PAGE Upon my life, then, you took the wrong.

SLENDER What need you tell me that? I think so, when I took a boy for a girl. If I had been married to him, for all he was in woman's apparel, I would not have had him.

190 PAGE Why, this is your own folly. Did not I tell you how you should know my daughter by her garments?

SLENDER I went to her in white, and cried 'mum', and she cried 'budget', as Anne and I had appointed. And yet it was not Anne, but a postmaster's boy.

MISTRESS PAGE Good George, be not angry. I knew of your purpose, turned my daughter into green; and indeed she is now with the Doctor at the deanery, and there married.

Enter Doctor Caius

CAIUS Vere is Mistress Page? By gar, I am cozened. I ha'
200 married *un garçon*, a boy; *un paysan*, by gar, a boy. It is not Anne Page. By gar, I am cozened.

MISTRESS PAGE Why? Did you take her in green?

CAIUS Ay, by gar, and 'tis a boy. By gar, I'll raise all Windsor. *Exit*

FORD This is strange. Who hath got the right Anne?

PAGE

My heart misgives me. Here comes Master Fenton.
Enter Fenton and Anne Page
How now, Master Fenton?

ANNE

Pardon, good father. Good my mother, pardon.

PAGE Now, mistress, how chance you went not with
Master Slender?   210

MISTRESS PAGE

Why went you not with Master Doctor, maid?

FENTON

You do amaze her. Hear the truth of it.
You would have married her most shamefully
Where there was no proportion held in love.
The truth is, she and I, long since contracted,
Are now so sure that nothing can dissolve us.
Th'offence is holy that she hath committed,
And this deceit loses the name of craft,
Of disobedience, or unduteous title,
Since therein she doth evitate and shun   220
A thousand irreligious cursèd hours
Which forcèd marriage would have brought upon her.

FORD

Stand not amazed. Here is no remedy.
In love the heavens themselves do guide the state.
Money buys lands, and wives are sold by fate.

FALSTAFF I am glad, though you have ta'en a special
stand to strike at me, that your arrow hath glanced.

PAGE

Well, what remedy? Fenton, heaven give thee joy!
What cannot be eschewed must be embraced.

FALSTAFF

When night-dogs run, all sorts of deer are chased.   230

MISTRESS PAGE

    Well, I will muse no further. Master Fenton,
    Heaven give you many, many merry days.
    Good husband, let us every one go home,
    And laugh this sport o'er by a country fire;
    Sir John and all.

FORD   Let it be so. Sir John,
    To Master Brook you yet shall hold your word,
    For he tonight shall lie with Mistress Ford.   *Exeunt*

COMMENTARY

THE Act and scene divisions are those of the Folio. Biblical quotations are from the Bishops' Bible (1568 etc.). In the Commentary, the Account of the Text, and the Collations 'Q' refers to the Quarto text of *The Merry Wives of Windsor* (1602) and 'F' to the text in the first Folio of 1623. Quotations from these texts are not modernized, except for the printing of long 's' (ʃ) as 's'.

I.1   This opening scene is, for part of its course, something of a false start. It gives the impression that Shallow's complaint against Falstaff is going to be one of the play's main concerns. In fact, however, once the scene is over, nothing more is made of the matter. It is Falstaff's meeting with Mistress Ford and Mistress Page that launches the principal intrigue, and Evans's plan for a match between Slender and Anne Page that introduces the secondary action of the comedy. Nevertheless, Shakespeare knew what he was doing in beginning as he did. For an audience familiar with *1 Henry IV* the mere mention of Falstaff in the first speech would have been full of promise, catching their attention at once – a matter of prime importance on the open stage of the Elizabethan theatre, where there were no lights to go down. And, skilled man of the theatre that he was, Shakespeare would know that winning the interest of his audience at the outset was far more necessary than fulfilling all the expectations roused in doing it. He could rely on his failure to make anything further of the Falstaff–Shallow relationship going unnoticed in performance, provided that there was other matter to take its place. Moreover, the deer-stealing motif looks forward to the subsequent action, where Falstaff seeks to steal those who are dear to Page and Ford.

1   *Sir Hugh.* Parsons were normally addressed as 'Sir', a title of respect in Shakespeare's England.
    persuade me not don't try to dissuade me

2   *Star-Chamber.* The Court of Star Chamber, so called because the ceiling of the room in which it sat was decorated with stars, tried cases which did not come under the jurisdiction of the ordinary courts of law. Offences such as riot and charges involving noble-men came within its purview.

3   *abuse* wrong, ill-use

4   *Esquire.* In Shakespeare's day this title meant that the owner of it held a definite place in the social hierarchy. He was immediately below a knight in rank.

6   *Coram.* This word is a corrupt form of the Latin *Quorum* ('of whom'). It was used to designate certain justices whose presence was necessary to constitute a bench of magistrates.

7   *cousin* kinsman. According to what Slender says at III.4.38, Shallow is his uncle.
    Custalorum. The *Custos Rotulorum*, of which *Custalorum* is a corruption, was the keeper of the rolls, the chief of the justices in a county, having in his care the records of the sessions.

8   *Ratolorum* (Slender's version of *Rotulorum*)

9   *writes* designates, signs
    Armigero Esquire, one entitled to bear heraldic arms

10 *bill* bill of exchange, money order
    quittance receipt, acknowledgement of discharge from debt
    obligation bond, contract

11–12   *Ay, that I do, and have done any time these three hundred years.* Shallow means that his family has borne arms for three centuries.

13   *hath.* Shakespeare on occasions uses this form of the third-person plural.

15   *give* display

       luces pikes (the fresh-water fish)

       coat coat of arms

17   *louses.* It is not clear whether this is a genuine mistake on the part of Evans, whose pronunciation of English is not his strong point, or whether he is punning.

18   *passant* (heraldic) walking

       familiar beast to man salvation that is on a family footing with man. 'A louse is a man's companion' was a common proverb.

20–21   *The salt fish is an old coat.* Shallow seems to be alluding to Evans's pronunciation of 'coat' as 'cod', but the joke, if there is one, is by no means clear.

22   *quarter* add another family's coat of arms to my own

       coz kinsman

25   *Not a whit* not at all, not in the least

26   *py'r lady* by our lady (as Evans pronounces it). F reads 'per-lady'.

27   *skirts* lower part of a coat or gown taking the form of four panels

31   *atonements* reconciliations

32   *Council* Privy Council (sitting as the Court of Star Chamber)

33   *meet* fitting, proper

35–6   *Take your vizaments in* take account of, consider. By *vizaments* Evans means 'advisements'.

37   *O'my* (colloquial) on my

39   *swort.* F reads 'Sword', but *swort* seems to be needed because Evans is quibbling on 'sword' and 'sort', meaning 'issue' or 'outcome'.

42   *George.* F reads '*Thomas*', but as Page is called 'George' whenever his name occurs elsewhere in the play the change seems necessary. It is quite possible

that Shakespeare began by thinking of him as 'Thomas' and then changed his mind.

45   *small* in a soprano voice

46   *'orld* (Evans's pronunciation of 'world'; he habitually omits the initial 'w')
      just exactly

48   *is* did. Evans has trouble with auxiliary verbs.

51   *pribbles and prabbles* empty chatter and petty quarrels. *Prabbles* is Evans's version of 'brabbles', and *pribbles* a word of his own making.

54-5 *Did her grandsire leave her seven hundred pound?* F allots this speech to Slender, but it is Shallow who is more interested in Anne Page's fortune.

56   *is make her a petter penny* will provide her with much more in addition

57-8 *I know the young gentlewoman. She has good gifts.* Like lines 54-5, these words are given to Slender in F; but it is plain from what he says at line 44 that he has no real knowledge of Anne. The speech is therefore allotted to Shallow in this edition.

58   *gifts* qualities of mind and body

59   *possibilities* prospects of inheriting wealth

66   *your well-willers* those who wish you well

72   *tell you another tale* have something further to say to you

78   *ill killed* not killed in the proper manner. There seems to be a suggestion here that the deer from which the venison came was one of those killed by Falstaff, but nothing is made of it.

79   *la!* indeed! (exclamation used to emphasize a conventional phrase)

83   *fallow* fawn-coloured

84   *Cotsall* (the Cotswold Hills in Gloucestershire, a great centre for coursing matches)

85   *judged* determined, fairly decided

87   *'Tis your fault.* The meaning of this phrase is disputed. Some think *fault* means 'misfortune', as it does at

III.3.206; others are of the opinion that it means 'the check caused by a dog's losing the scent of his quarry'. The latter explanation would seem to be ruled out because greyhounds hunt by sight not scent. To the present editor the most probable meaning appears to be: 'You are mistaken, you are in the wrong'. 'Fault' in the sense of 'mistake' is common in Elizabethan English.

97   *in some sort* to some extent

100   *at a word* in short

103   *of* about

108   *lodge* (house in a park or forest occupied by the keeper)

108   *pin* trifle

        shall be answered must be atoned for

109   *straight* (1) immediately; (2) straightforwardly

112–13 *in counsel* in private, in secret

114   *Pauca verba* (Latin) few words. Evans refers to two Elizabethan proverbs: 'Few words show men wise' and 'Few words are best'.

        worts (1) words (as pronounced by Evans); (2) cabbages (the sense in which Falstaff takes it)

116   *broke your head* drew blood by breaking the skin of your head

        matter subject of complaint

117   *matter* (1) matter of consequence; (2) pus

118   *cony-catching* cheating, swindling (rogues' cant – the dupe of a confidence trick being described as a cony or rabbit)

119–20 *They carried me . . . my pocket.* This sentence is taken from Q . That the copy for F, from which it is omitted, must once have contained it, or something very like it, is made almost certain by Falstaff's question to Pistol at line 141: *did you pick Master Slender's purse?* See the Account of the Text, pages 210–11.

119   *carried* led, conducted

121   *Banbury cheese* (a scornful allusion to Slender's figure – Banbury cheeses being proverbially thin)

123   *Mephostophilus* (the name of the devil in Marlowe's play *Doctor Faustus*; used here as a term of abuse)

125   *Slice* (1) slice of cheese; (2) cut to pieces

        humour temperament, mood. The word 'humour' seems to have been badly overworked in the last decade of the sixteenth century. Through Nym, who uses it *ad nauseam* with no sense of its original meaning, Shakespeare appears to be satirizing the excessive use of it.

130   *fidelicet* videlicet (Latin for 'namely')

134   *prief* brief, summary, abstract

139   *tam* (Evans's version of 'dam')

143   *great chamber* main living room

144   *seven groats in mill-sixpences*. A groat was worth fourpence; and a mill-sixpence was a sixpence made by a mechanical process in a stamping mill, instead of being hammered into shape as coins had been in the past. Slender seems rather confused about it all, because *seven groats* amount to two shillings and fourpence, a sum that is not divisible by six.

144–5   *Edward shovel-boards* old broad shillings, dating from the reign of Edward VI (1547–53), used in the game of shovel-board, in which coins were sent sliding along a polished board into holes at the end of it. Worn smooth with age, shillings issued under Edward VI would have been well adapted for use in this game, and, judging by the price that Slender has paid for his, would seem to have been much prized on this account.

146   *Yed* (shortened form of the name Edward, like 'Ned')

148   *it is false, if it is*. Evans means to say 'he is false, if he is'.

149   *mountain-foreigner* (abusive periphrasis for 'Welshman')

150   *combat challenge of* challenge to trial by combat

        latten bilbo man whose sword (*bilbo*) is made of brass (*latten*)

151   *labras* lips. Pistol's Latin is not very good – the word should be *labra*.

154   *Be advised* take my advice, think carefully
      pass good humours make the best of it, behave properly

155   *Marry trap with you*. The precise meaning of this cant phrase, which occurs only here, is not known. Dr Johnson takes it to be 'an exclamation of insult, when a man is caught in his own trap'; others have suggested that it means 'be off with you'. It is clear from the context that it expresses contempt.

155–6 *run the nuthook's humour on me* threaten me with the constable. 'Nuthook' was a cant term for the catchpole or constable.

156   *very note of it* truth of the matter. The reference is to a musical note; and the literal meaning is 'the right tune of it'.

160   *Scarlet and John*. Scarlet and Little John were two of Robin Hood's 'merry men'. The main allusion here is to Bardolph's scarlet complexion, but Falstaff also seems to be suggesting that Bardolph combines the thieving propensities of both the outlaws.

162   *five sentences* (Bardolph's blundering version of 'five senses')

164   *fap* (West Midland dialect) drunk
      cashiered relieved of his cash, robbed. Normally in Shakespeare's work 'cashier' has its usual meaning of 'discard from service' (compare its use at I.3.6); but here Bardolph appears to be punning on a compound word of his own devising, 'cash-sheared', a rather neat equivalent for 'fleeced'. Bardolph relies, of course, on Slender's not understanding what he says.

165   *conclusions passed the careers* the things that finally happened to him went far beyond what he had planned, matters got out of hand. The word *career* is employed here, it would seem, in the sense of a fixed course laid out for a gallop.

166 *in Latin*. Slender means that Bardolph's use of thieves' cant was 'Greek to him' then, just as it is now.

167 *but* except

171 *'udge* judge (as pronounced by Evans)
     mind sentiment, intention

179 (stage direction) *He kisses her*. This direction is adapted from Q, which reads: '*Syr* Iohn kisses her'; but it is implicit in F's 'By your leaue good Mistris', for kissing, as Erasmus noticed with pleasure on his first visit to England in 1499, was the usual form of greeting between a man and a woman.

181 *to* for

183 *had rather* would rather

183–4 *Book of Songs and Sonnets*. Slender is referring to one of the many anthologies of love poetry that were available in Shakespeare's day. The most famous of them was the *Songes and Sonettes* published by Richard Tottel in 1557 and frequently reprinted. Slender needs it, of course, in order to cull from it some choice expressions of devotion that he can use on Anne Page. Courtly compliments do not come readily to his simple mind.

189 *Allhallowmas* (All Saints' Day, 1 November)

190 *Michaelmas* (St Michael's Day, 29 September). Simple, it is worth noticing, characteristically gets the two feasts the wrong way round and halves the interval between them in the process.

191 *stay* wait

192 *Marry* (a mild oath of interjection, coming originally from the name of the Virgin Mary)

193 *tender* proposal of marriage
     afar off indirectly, in a roundabout manner

195 *reasonable* fair-minded. Slender is under the impression that Evans's *tender* is for some kind of accommodation between him and his enemies.

199 *motions* proposals

203 *country* district, part of the country

simple though as sure as

210   *demands* request

212   *divers* some, several

213   *parcel* part

214   *carry your good will to* feel affection for, love

219   *Got's lords and his ladies!* This strange oath appears to be one of Evans's inventions.

220   *possitable* (Evans's version of 'positively')

220–21   *carry her your desires towards her* direct your affection towards her. The curious expression *carry her* may be yet another instance of Evans's imperfect command of English, or it may be his pronunciation of *career*, meaning 'gallop'.

222   *upon good dowry* on the strength of a good dowry being forthcoming. The bride's dowry, a normal part of the marriage settlement in Shakespeare's England, was the money and estate that she brought with her to her husband. It was, of course, provided by her father.

226   *conceive me* understand me, realize my meaning

230   *decrease.* Slender means 'increase' and is alluding to the proverb 'Marry first and love will come after'.

234   *dissolved* (Slender's mistake for 'resolved')

dissolutely (for 'resolutely', as Evans notices, missing the previous error over 'resolved')

235   *fall* fault, mistake

240   *Would I* I wish I

244   *wait on him* join him

245   *'Od's* God's

250   *attends* awaits

252   *sirrah* sir (used only in addressing social inferiors or boys)

for all although

252–3   *wait upon* serve, attend

254   *beholding* beholden, under obligation

256   *till my mother be dead.* Slender's mother evidently curbs his desire to cut a figure.

256   *what though* what of it, no matter

264-5   *playing at sword and dagger with a master of fence.*
        Fencing with a rapier in one hand and a dagger in the
        other was introduced into England in the last decade
        of the sixteenth century and became very fashionable.
        Italian fencing masters set up schools in London.
        Mercutio, in *Romeo and Juliet* (II.4.19–35), pours
        scorn on the craze and on the technical terms be-
        longing to it.

265   *master of fence* fencing master
        veneys bouts

265-6   *a dish of stewed prunes* (the prize for the winner).
        Slender, without being aware of it, is speaking baw-
        dily, since 'stewed prunes' was a common term for
        prostitutes.

266   *by my troth* by my faith (a mild oath)

268   *i'th'* (colloquial) in the

270   *the sport* (bear-baiting, in which a chained bear was
        attacked by dogs)

270-71 *quarrel at* object to, take exception to. Slender is
        evidently a puritan of sorts, for it was the Puritans
        who, to their credit, disapproved of the barbarous
        sport of bear-baiting.

275   *Sackerson* (name of a famous bear belonging to the
        Paris Garden, a well known bear-baiting ring not far
        from the Globe Theatre)

277   *passed* surpassed all belief, beggared description

278   *ill-favoured* ugly-looking

283   *By cock and pie* (an oath of asseveration). 'Cock' is a
        perversion of 'God', and 'pie' a late medieval word
        meaning 'directory for divine service'.
        shall not choose must

288   *keep on* go ahead

289-90 *do you that wrong* insult you in that way, be so im-
        polite to you

292   *I'll rather be unmannerly than troublesome.* Slender is
        resorting to proverbs again; 'Better be unmannerly

than troublesome' was a common saying of the time.

I.2.1   *Caius* (pronounced to rhyme with 'try us')

3   *dry nurse* housekeeper

4   *laundry* laundress

7   *altogether's acquaintance* is thoroughly acquainted

11   *pippins* apples

cheese. This is the reading of both F and Q at this point. Most editors emend to 'seese' in order to bring the pronunciation into line with that indicated by F's 'Seese' at V.5.139.

I.3.2   *bully rook* brave fellow

4   *turn away* discard, dismiss

6   *wag* go off, go their ways

8   *sit at* live at the rate of, am spending

9   *Thou'rt* (colloquial) thou art

Keisar (old form of 'Kaiser') emperor

Pheazar person of overwhelming presence. This word is either the Host's version of 'vizier' or a word of his own making derived from the verb 'pheeze' meaning 'frighten away'.

10   *entertain* employ

draw draw liquor

tap serve as a tapster

11   *Hector* (the Trojan hero, often cited in Shakespeare's works as the model of valour)

14   *froth* (create a large head of foam on a mug of beer in order to cheat the customer with short measure)

lime (adulterate wine with lime in order to make it sparkle). Compare *1 Henry IV*, II.4.120, where Falstaff says to the drawer Francis: 'You rogue, here's lime in this sack too.' This reading is taken from Q. The F version is 'liue', which makes good sense but

does not carry the overtone of 'cheating' which seems
necessary in this context.

14   *I am at a word* I mean what I say, with me it's a case
of no sooner said than done

16   *An old cloak makes a new jerkin* (an adaptation of the
proverb 'His old cloak will buy you a new kirtle')
jerkin (close-fitting jacket, worn by men in Shakespeare's day)

19   *Hungarian wight* beggarly fellow. 'Hungarian' was an
Elizabethan cant term for 'beggarly' through its
punning association with 'hungry'.
spigot peg (in the faucet of a barrel)

20   *gotten in drink* begotten when his parents were drunk

20–21   *Is not the humour conceited?* isn't that a clever turn of
phrase? isn't that an ingenious witticism?

22   *acquit* rid, freed
tinderbox (alluding to Bardolph's red nose and flaming
complexion)

23   *open* obvious, easily detected

25   *good humour* right trick of the trade
at a minute's rest in the space of a minute. The
emendation of *minute's* to 'minim's' is an attractive
one; but both F and Q read 'minutes'.

26   *Convey* (thieves' cant) steal
it call call it. Pistol is much given to inversion. His
syntax, like his verse, owes much to the ranting plays
of the period 1570–90.

27   *fico* (1) fig; (2) female genitals. This Italian word was
used as an insult and was commonly accompanied by
an obscene gesture.

28   *out at heels* (1) penniless, destitute (the sense in which
Falstaff uses the phrase); (2) in a state where the heels
of the shoes or stockings are worn through (the sense
in which Pistol takes it)

29   *kibes* chilblains

30   *cony-catch* take to cheating

31   *shift* resort to stratagems, live by my wits

32   *Young ravens must have food.* Pistol is alluding to the proverb 'Small birds must have meat'. The *Young ravens* he has in mind are, of course, himself and Nym.

34   *ken* know

    of substance good well off, a man of means

35   *about* (1) engaged in, planning (the sense in which Falstaff means it); (2) about the waist, in circumference (the sense in which Pistol takes it)

40   *entertainment* (1) kindness, readiness to meet advances; (2) a source of provision

    discourses is affable, talks with familiarity

41   *carves minces her words*, speaks affectedly

    leer of invitation inviting glance, come-hither look

41–2   *construe the action of her familiar style* interpret the meaning of her familiarities of speech and behaviour

42   *hardest voice* harshest judgement, most severe interpretation. There is an elaborate grammatical pun in this sentence turning on the use of *construe* and *voice*.

45   *will* (1) intention; (2) sexual desires; (3) legal will

46   *honesty* chastity

    into English. There may well be a pun here on the verb 'ingle', meaning 'to cuddle'. Pistol would then be saying that Falstaff has transformed Mistress Ford from an honest woman into one who is now 'ingle-ish' – ready for and responsive to his advances.

47   *The anchor is deep.* The precise meaning of this remark is not known, though Nym clearly thinks it very clever. The likeliest interpretation is 'This is a deep plot'.

    Will that humour pass? what do you think of that for a neat phrase?

49   *legion.* F reads 'legend'; but most editors prefer *legion*, which is supported by the reading 'legians' in Q.

    angels. This is one of the commonest of Elizabethan puns. An 'angel' was a gold coin, bearing the figure of Michael the archangel and worth about ten shillings.

50   *As many devils entertain* let as many devils do battle
with them. Pistol implies that Falstaff is a legion of
devils in himself.

    To her, boy (cry of encouragement to a dog engaged in
hunting)

53   *writ me* written, I'd have you notice. The *me* (ethic
dative) is really superfluous, but it is added by the
speaker – Nym does it in the previous line – as a means
of calling attention to himself and adding colour and
liveliness to what he is saying.

54   *even now* just now

    good eyes approving glances

55   *parts* appearance

    œillades looks of love. F reads 'illiads', a form that
represents the Elizabethan pronunciation of this word,
newly borrowed from the French.

60   *course o'er* examine, run her eye over

64   *Guiana.* Sir Walter Ralegh had made an expedition to
Guiana in 1595, and had published an account of his
discoveries in the following year, emphasizing the
wealth and fertility of the land.

    cheaters (1) escheators (officers of the Crown, whose
task was to notify the Exchequer when lands fell due to
the King); (2) sharpers

70   *Sir Pandarus.* By Shakespeare's day Pandarus, the
uncle of Cressida in Chaucer's *Troilus and Criseyde*
who brings the lovers together, had become the type
of the pander, a word that derives from his name. It
is in this role that he is portrayed in Shakespeare's own
Troilus and Cressida.

71   *And by my side wear steel* and still keep my reputation
as a soldier

73   *haviour of reputation* appearance of respectability

74   *tightly* safely (like a 'tight' ship)

75   *pinnace* (small fast-sailing ship, often in attendance on
a larger ship)

76   *avaunt* be off with you, be gone

77   *o'th'hoof* (colloquial contraction of 'on the hoof') on foot

pack be off, take yourselves off

78   *humour* fashion. This is the Q reading. F has 'honor', which does not give a satisfactory apposition to 'French thrift'.

79   *French thrift* (perhaps an allusion to the fashion of discarding several servingmen and replacing them by a single French page)

skirted wearing a coat with full skirts

80   *gripe* seize on

gourd and fullam (kinds of false dice used by cheaters)

holds hold good, can still be relied on. Shakespeare often uses the form of the third-person singular when two or more singular nouns precede the verb.

81   *high and low* (false dice weighted in such a way as to throw high or low numbers as required)

82   *Tester* sixpenny piece

83   *Phrygian Turk* (a term of abuse – the Turks being the inveterate enemies of Christendom)

84   *operations* (probably Nym's version of 'inspirations') plans

85   *welkin* sky

86   *With wit or steel* by ingenuity or by force

humours methods

87   *discuss* disclose, make known

87, 88   *Page ... Ford*. These are both Q readings. F reads 'Ford ... Page', which does not correspond to what happens in II.1. Nym's speech at line 92 would, however, be much more appropriate if it were about Ford. It could well be that at this stage Shakespeare meant Nym to address Ford, and Pistol Page, but then changed his mind.

88   *eke* also

90   *prove* test the fidelity of

92   *Page*. F reads '*Ford*'.

93   *deal with* make use of, resort to

93   *possess* fill
      yellowness jealousy
94   *the revolt of mine* my revolt
95   *Mars* (Roman god of war)

I.4.5 *old* plentiful
7   *posset* (a drink made of hot milk curdled with wine or
       ale)
8   *soon at night* as soon as night comes
8–9   *sea-coal fire* (fire made with mined coal brought by
       sea from Newcastle)
11   *withal* with
12   *breed-bate* trouble-maker
13   *something* somewhat
       peevish silly, foolish
16   *for fault of* for lack of, in default of
22   *Cain-coloured* reddish-yellow (the traditional colour of
       Cain's beard in tapestries). 'Caine colourd' is the
       reading of F; Q has 'kane colored', which some
       editors prefer, taking it to mean 'yellowish' (the colour
       of a cane).
23   *softly-sprighted* gentle-spirited
24   *as tall a man of his hands* as brave a man in action (a
       proverbial phrase)
25   *between this and his head* in these parts (another pro-
       verbial phrase)
26   *warrener* keeper of a warren (piece of land used for
       breeding and preserving game, especially rabbits)
36   *shent* scolded , rebuked
37   *closet* private room, study
40   *doubt he be* fear he is
42   *And down, down, adown-a, etc.* (a popular refrain sung
       to many songs of the time – compare Ophelia's use of
       it in *Hamlet*, IV.5.167–8. The implication of *etc.*
       would seem to be that Mistress Quickly goes on
       repeating the refrain until Caius interrupts her.)

166

43	*toys* silly trifling
45	*Do intend* do you hear (French *entendre*)
48	*horn-mad* furious with rage (like a mad bull prepared to horn anyone)
49–50	*Ma foi ... la grande affaire* (French) by my faith, it is very hot. I'm going to the court – important business
52	*Oui, mette-le au mon pocket. Dépêche* yes, put it in my pocket. Hurry
60	*trot* troth (as pronounced by Caius)
	'Od's me God save me
60–61	*Qu'ai-je oublié* what have I forgotten
61	*simples* medicines made from herbs. Though Caius does not yet know it, there is indeed a Simple in his closet.
64	*mad* angry, mad with rage
65	*diable* devil
66	*Larron* thief
68	*content* calm, quiet
73	*phlegmatic* (Mistress Quickly's mistake for 'choleric')
74	*of an* on an
85	*put my finger in the fire, and need not* meddle where there is no need to (a proverbial expression)
86	*baille* fetch
89	*throughly* thoroughly, really
	moved angered
90	*melancholy.* Mistress Quickly means 'choleric' (compare line 73), but she invariably hits on any 'humour' but the right one.
91	*you* for you, since you ask me
94–5	*dress meat* prepare food
96	*charge* burden, load of work
98	*avised* aware
105	*jack'nape* (Caius's version of 'jackanapes', meaning 'tame monkey')
106	*gar* (Caius's pronunciation of 'God')
	troat throat (as pronounced by Caius)
107	*make* interfere
109	*cut all his two stones* castrate him

109   *stones* testicles

114   *Jack* knavish, contemptible

115   *measure our weapon* act as umpire in our duel

118–19 *What the good-year.* The meaning of this expression has not been satisfactorily explained, though here something like 'What the deuce' seems to be intended.

123   *An* (1) Anne; (2) an

128   *trow* wonder

        Come near enter

135   *honest* chaste

        gentle full of good qualities

        your friend favourably disposed towards you

141   *Have not your worship.* Mistress Quickly is mixing two constructions: 'Have not you' and 'Has not your worship'.

145   *it is such another Nan* Nan (diminutive form of 'Anne') is such a merry girl

        detest (Mistress Quickly's version of 'protest')

147   *but* except

148   *allicholy* (a corruption of 'melancholy')

149   *go to* come

151   *voice* good word, support

155   *confidence* (for 'conference')

159–60 *Out upon't* (an exclamation of dismay)

II.1.1 *'scaped* escaped, been free from

2   *holiday time* gay festive time, prime

5   *precisian* austere spiritual adviser, puritan minister. Falstaff is thinking of Love as a king who asks the opinion of Reason but does not make him a member of his privy council.

7   *sympathy* agreement, common ground between us

8   *sack* (the general name for a class of white wines imported from Spain and the Canaries)

19   *Herod of Jewry* audacious villain. In the miracle plays, which were still being acted occasionally in the late

sixteenth century, Herod was portrayed as an out-and-out villain, delighting in his own wickedness.

21 *What an unweighed behaviour* what unguarded action, what ill-judged piece of behaviour

22 *Flemish drunkard.* The Flemings were often cited (in the England of Shakespeare's day) as the most drunken race in Europe.

23 *conversation* behaviour in his company

24 *assay me* assail my virtue with words, address me with proposals of love

25 *should I say* can I have said

26 *amorous propos*

27 *putting down* suppression (possibly with bawdy implications)

29 *puddings* sausages, stuffing

30 *Trust me* believe me

33 *ill* (1) annoyed, savage (the sense in which Mistress Page means it); (2) unattractive (the sense in which Mistress Ford takes it)

34–5 *have to show* have something (the letter) to show

42 *respect* consideration
    come to attain, achieve
    honour rank, position of dignity

44 *Dispense with* disregard, have done with

45 *go to hell* (for committing adultery)

48 *hack.* The precise sense of this word is doubtful, but, when its use here is related to its use at IV.1.61, it seems likely that some meaning such as 'make a hackney (prostitute) of a woman' is intended. There could also be a quibble on 'hack', meaning 'strike with a weapon', employed with sexual connotations.

49 *article of thy gentry* character of your rank

50 *burn daylight* (proverbial) waste time, engage in futilities

52–3 *make difference of* discriminate between

53 *liking* physical appearance, looks

55 *uncomeliness* improper behaviour

56   *disposition* character
       gone to been in keeping with, accorded with
57   *adhere* agree, accord
59   *Greensleeves* (a popular love song, sometimes associated with harlotry in Shakespeare's day, to the tune of which numerous lyrics were set)
       trow wonder
62   *entertain him* engage his thoughts, fill his mind
67   *ill opinions* (Falstaff's belief that the wives are light women)
68   *inherit* take possession (of Falstaff's offer)
69–73 *I warrant ... us two.* On the significance of this passage, see the Introduction, pages 24–5.
72   *out of doubt* indubitably
73   *press* (1) printing-press; (2) pressure of sexual intercourse
74   *Mount Pelion* (mountain in Thessaly). In classical mythology the Titans, when they rebelled against the gods, sought to reach the top of Olympus by piling Mount Ossa on Pelion. In revenge the gods buried them under the mountains they had sought to move.
75   *turtles* turtle-doves (proverbially true to their mates)
80   *wrangle* quarrel
       honesty chastity
       entertain treat
81   *withal* with
82   *strain* tendency, quality
83   *boarded* accosted, made advances to (the figurative use of 'to board' in the nautical sense)
       fury impetuous fashion
88   *comfort* encouragement
89   *a fine-baited delay* delaying tactics full of tempting allurements
91   *villainy* sharp practice
92–3   *chariness of our honesty* scrupulous integrity of our good names
95–6   *good man* husband

103   *curtal dog* dog that has had its tail docked (with the result that it is no longer a 'true' dog but an unreliable one)

104   *affects* loves, feels an inclination for

107   *one with another* indiscriminately, promiscuously

108   *gallimaufry* whole lot

        perpend consider, take note

110   *liver* (supposed to be the seat of love in Shakespeare's time)

        Prevent take counter-measures

111   *Sir Actaeon.* Actaeon, in classical mythology, while out hunting, accidentally came upon Diana, the goddess of chastity, as she was bathing. To revenge this intrusion on her privacy, the goddess turned him into a stag and had him torn to pieces by his own hounds. Actaeon thus became identified with the horned man, the cuckold.

        he. This superfluous pronoun is added for emphasis.

        Ringwood (a traditional name for a hound in England)

112   *the name* (the name 'Actaeon', signifying 'cuckold')

114   *horn* (mark of the cuckold)

115   *foot* walk

116   *cuckoo-birds do sing.* The song of the cuckoo, which lays its eggs in the nests of other birds, was thought of as a warning to the cuckold or potential cuckold.

117   *Away* come away

119   *find out* inquire into

121–2   *should have borne* was expected to bear, was ordered to bear

127–8   *and there's the humour of it.* These words, which are not found in F, have been added from Q. Their inclusion seems necessary so that Page can pick them up and comment on them in his speech after Nym has made his exit.

129   *'a* (colloquial) he

130   *his* its

132   *affecting* affected

135   *Cataian* scoundrel, sharper (literally, a native of Cathay, the old name for China)

144   *crotchets* strange notions, queer ideas

146   *Have with you* I'm coming

151   *fit it* fit the part, be the right person for the job

162   *offer it* try to do such a thing

163   *yoke* pair

167   *lie* lodge

170   *turn her loose to him* leave her free to do as she likes with him (a farmyard reference to the turning loose of a cow and a bull in the same pasture)

171-2   *lie on my head* (1) be my responsibility; (2) appear on my head (in the form of the cuckold's horns)

173   *misdoubt* have doubts about the character of

174   *turn them together* (carries on the farmyard allusion of *turn her loose to him*)
         confident trusting

181   *Cavaliero justice* gallant justice (from Spanish *caballero*, meaning 'gentleman trained in arms')

182-3   *Good even and twenty* good day and twenty such greetings. 'Even' was used in Elizabethan English for any time after noon. Nevertheless, there would seem to be a mistake here, because Mistress Page's remark *You'll come to dinner, George?* (lines 146-7) makes it plain that the time is morning, since dinner, the main meal of the day, was eaten about eleven a.m.

191   *had the measuring of their weapons* been made umpire in their duel

192   *contrary* different

197-9   *None, I protest ... for a jest.* In F this speech is allotted to Shallow; but Q, while printing a garbled version of it, rightly gives it to Ford.

197   *protest* declare, assure you
         pottle two-quart tankard

197-8   *burnt sack* mulled sack, white wine heated over a fire

198   *recourse* access

199   *Brook.* This, though misprinted as '*Rrooke*' on this

occasion, is the reading of Q here and on all subsequent occasions when the name is used. F has
'*Broome*' throughout; but it is evident that *Brook* is
the original name. See the Account of the Text,
pages 208–9.

202   *Ameers* emirs. F reads 'An-heires', which makes no
sense. *Ameers* has been adopted in this edition because
it is in keeping with the Host's fondness for high-
flown titles such as *Caesar, Keisar, and Pheazar*
(I.3.9), but the emendation 'mynheers' (Dutch for
'sirs') is equally plausible.

207   *pass . . . pass* (used indefinitely, not with reference to
persons present)
   stand on make much of, attach great importance to
   distance (regulation space that had to be kept between
two fencers)
   passes lunges
   stoccadoes thrusts

209–10   *long sword.* This heavy weapon had gone out of fashion
by the time the play was written, having been ousted
by the lighter and more deadly rapier.

210   *made you four tall fellows skip* made four lusty fellows
skip, I can tell you. The *you* here, meaning 'for you',
gives extra emphasis to the boast.

212   *wag* go

213   *Have with you* I'll go along with you

215   *secure* over-confident

215–16   *stands so firmly on his wife's frailty* trusts so firmly in
what may really be frailty in his wife

218   *made* did, got up to

219   *sound* measure the depth of, search into

220   *honest* chaste
   lose waste

II.2.4   *I will retort the sum in equipage.* This line, stamped with
Pistol's characteristic idiom, is only to be found in Q,

where it appears as line 2 in response to Falstaff's
'*I*le not lend thee a penny.' It is included in this
edition because it completes the dramatic effect of
Pistol's speech. Pistol begins with a brag, proclaiming
his independence, but then changes his tune, offering
to pay back.

4   *retort* repay (in Pistol's inflated jargon)

      in equipage. The normal meaning of this term is 'in
military array'; but Pistol seems to think it means 'in
equal payments' on the instalment plan.

6   *lay my countenance to pawn* borrow money on the
strength of my patronage of you

      grated upon pestered, importuned

8   *coach-fellow* companion, yokefellow

9   *grate* prison-bars

      geminy of pair of twin

11   *tall* brave

12   *the handle of her fan*. Fans at the time when the play
was written often had very long handles made of gold,
silver, or ivory.

      took't swore, took an oath

15   *Reason* with good reason

17   *short knife* (the cutpurse's tool)

18   *throng*. Cutpurses prefer to operate where there is a
crowd.

      Pickt-hatch (a disreputable district of London)

19   *stand upon* become punctilious over, quibble about

20   *unconfinable* imitless, infinite

21–2   *terms of my honour precise* my honour unstained

22   *I, I, I*. This is the reading of F. Most editors emend to
'Ay, ay, I', because 'I' is the normal spelling of 'Ay',
as well as of 'I', in F. In this case, however, the change
seems unnecessary, since Falstaff is making the most of
the contrast between himself and Pistol.

22–3   *leaving . . . on the left hand* disregarding

24   *fain* obliged, compelled

      shuffle resort to shifts

hedge prevaricate, become evasive
lurch steal

25 *yet you, you rogue.* F reads 'yet, you Rogue', which editors render as 'yet you, rogue', assuming that the comma is misplaced. To the present editor it seems far more likely that the compositor, confronted by two consecutive 'you's, overlooked the first one. Falstaff has already called Pistol *you rogue* twice in this speech.
ensconce hide, find protective covering for

25-6 *cat-a-mountain* wildcat, ferocious

26 *red-lattice* ale-house. Lattices painted red were the sign of an ale-house.

27 *beating* battering (like blows)

29 *relent* comply, give way

34 *an't* if it

39 *vouchsafe.* This word, as Falstaff points out in his answer, is used improperly by Mistress Quickly, since it implies the granting of something to an inferior in rank by a superior.

46 *on* say on, continue

59 *canaries.* Precisely what Mistress Quickly means by this word is not known, though something like 'state of excitement' must be intended. She appears to be confusing 'quandary' with 'canary', the name of a lively Spanish dance and of a light sweet wine from the Canary Islands.

65 *rushling* rustling

66 *alligant.* Mistress Quickly seems to be muddling 'eloquent' and possibly 'elegant' with 'alicant', a Spanish wine made at Alicante.

70 *angels* (gold coins bearing the figure of the archangel Michael)
defy despise, reject

71 *sort* manner

74 *pensioners* gentlemen of the royal bodyguard

77 *she-Mercury* messenger (Mercury being the messenger of the gods in classical mythology)

80	*gives you to notify* bids you take notice
81	*absence* (Mistress Quickly's version of 'absent')
84	*wot* know
87	*frampold* disagreeable
92	*messenger* (for 'message')
94	*fartuous* (for 'virtuous')
100	*charms* spells, magic powers
103	*parts* personal qualities of mind and body
104	*for't* (colloquial) for it
111	*of all loves* for love's sake (a phrase of strong entreaty)
112	*infection* (for 'affection')
115	*list* pleases
118	*no remedy* beyond all question
122	*nay-word* password, watchword
	that so that, in order that
128	*yet* still
131	*punk* harlot, strumpet
	Cupid's carriers Cupid's messengers (Cupid being the god of love in classical mythology)
132	*fights* (screens used to conceal and protect the crew of a vessel during a naval engagement)
133	*ocean whelm* let the ocean overwhelm, let the ocean drown
136	*look after* look lovingly on
138	*grossly* (1) clumsily, obviously; (2) by a fat man
	so so long as, provided that
	fairly successfully
141	*would fain* much desires to
149	*encompassed* got round, outwitted
	via (a word of encouragement to a horse or soldiers) go on
152	*make bold* presume, venture
	so little preparation so unexpectedly and with so little ceremony
154	*What's your will?* what do you want?
155	*Give us leave* leave us alone

160–61	*charge you* cause you expense
163	*unseasoned* ill-timed, unseasonable
164	*if money go before, all ways do lie open* (a common proverb)
165	*on* go forward, march ahead
168	*carriage* burden
177	*discover* reveal, disclose
181	*register* record, list, catalogue
182	*sith* since
189–90	*observance* reverence, deference, dutiful attention
190	*engrossed opportunities* seized every opportunity
	fee'd purchased
193–4	*would have given* would like to be given, would like as a present
197	*meed* reward
201–2	*Love like a shadow . . . what pursues* (an adaptation of the proverb 'Love, like a shadow, flies one following and pursues one fleeing')
201	*substance* (1) true affection; (2) money, wealth
208	*quality* nature, kind
209–11	*Like a fair house . . . I erected it.* A building erected on another man's land belonged legally to him.
214	*honest* chaste
215	*enlargeth her mirth so far* gives such free scope to her sense of fun
215–16	*there is shrewd construction made of her* her behaviour is open to malicious interpretation, she has a bad reputation
218–19	*of great admittance* admitted freely into the best of company
219	*authentic* entitled to respect
220	*allowed* approved of, praised
221	*preparations* accomplishments
225	*of it* for it
226	*amiable* amorous
	honesty chastity
229	*apply well to* fit in with, be consistent with

232   *dwells so securely* stands so confidently

233   *folly* wantonness

235   *against* directly at (like the sun)

       detection evidence of infidelity

236   *had* (subjunctive) would have

       instance evidence, precedent

238   *ward* guard, defence

239   *other her defences* other defences she has

247   *Want* lack, go short of

254   *speed* succeed, fare

259   *wittolly* cuckoldy

259–60 *for the which* on account of which

260   *well-favoured* good-looking, attractive

262   *harvest-home* profit gathered

265   *mechanical* base, vulgar (originally 'one engaged in manual labour')

       salt-butter cheap-living, cheese-paring (salt-butter, imported from Flanders, being cheaper than English butter)

267   *meteor* (regarded as an ominous portent in Shakespeare's day)

268   *predominate* (an astrological term, developing the idea already present in *meteor*) be in the ascendancy

270   *soon at night* this very night

270–71 *aggravate his style* add to his title (by turning him from a knave into a cuckold)

273   *Epicurean* lecherous, sensual

275   *improvident* rash and baseless

280–81 *stand under the adoption of abominable terms* suffer being called detestable names

282–3 *Amaimon ... Lucifer ... Barbason* (names of devils). Amaimon and Lucifer are coupled together by Falstaff in *1 Henry IV* (II.4.329–30).

283   *additions* titles

284   *Wittol* contented cuckold

285   *secure* over-confident

287–8 *a Fleming ... Parson Hugh ... an Irishman.* Flemings were proverbially fond of butter, Welshmen of cheese, and the Irish of strong liquor.

289   *aqua-vitae* (spirits such as brandy and whisky)
       walk lead or ride (a horse) at walking pace
295   *detect* expose
296   *about* set about, go about
297   *Fie* (an exclamation of disapproval)

II.3.11   *herring.* 'Dead as a herring' was already a stock phrase in Shakespeare's day.
17   *Save* God save
21   *foin* thrust (in fencing)
22   *traverse* move back and forth
23   *pass* employ
       punto thrust with the point of the sword
       stock thrust with the point of the dagger
       reverse backhand blow with the sword
       distance interval of space to be kept between two fencers
24   *montant* upright thrust or blow
25   *Francisco* Frenchman
       Aesculapius (god of medicine in classical mythology)
26   *Galen* (ancient Greek physician still regarded as an authority on medicine in Shakespeare's day)
       heart of elder coward. The Host is taking advantage of Caius's ignorance of English idiom in order to insult him with a seeming compliment. Unlike 'heart of oak' which is hard, *heart of elder* is very soft.
27   *stale* (1) dupe, laughing-stock; (2) urine of horses (referring to the use of urine for diagnostic purposes)
28   *Jack* base, common
30   *Castalion-King-Urinal.* This is another string of insults thinly veiled as a compliment. The Castilian king was Philip II of Spain, who died in 1598 and was not regarded with favour in England. The spelling of F ('Castalion') is retained in this edition, because it

indicates a further pun on *stale* and, possibly, on 'stallion'.

30–31   *Hector of Greece*. The Host betrays his own ignorance here. Hector was, of course, the Trojan hero who fought the Greeks, and who was, for the Elizabethans, the very type of the true soldier.

36   *against the hair* contrary to the natural tendency, against the grain

40   *Bodykins* God's little body (a mild oath)

42   *make one* join in, take part

43   *salt* vigour

52–3   *Mockwater*. This invented name seems to combine mockery of the physician's pretensions to be able to diagnose diseases from an examination of the urine with a reference to 'making water' as a manifestation of fear or cowardice. It would be tempting to read 'Make-water', were it not for the fact that F ('Mockewater') and Q ('mockwater') are in complete agreement.

57   *jack-dog* mongrel

59   *clapper-claw* maul, thrash
    tightly soundly, thoroughly

64   *wag* go on his way

68   *Frogmore* (a place to the south-east of Windsor)

81   *Cried game?* isn't the game afoot? (The image is that of hounds giving cry upon sight of their quarry.)

85   *adversary* (the Host's mistake for 'emissary')

III.1.5   *the pittie-ward* (towards Windsor Little Park)
      the park-ward (towards Windsor Great Park)

6   *Old Windsor* (a village south of Frogmore)

11   *chollors* (Evans's version of 'cholers' – angry passions)

13   *urinals* (glass vessels in which urine was kept for medical inspection)

14   *costard* head (originally a large kind of apple)

16–25   *To shallow rivers . . . To shallow, etc.* These lines are a garbled version of part of the most famous of all Elizabethan lyrics, Christopher Marlowe's 'The Passionate Shepherd to His Love'. The first three stanzas run thus:

> Come live with me, and be my love,
> And we will all the pleasures prove
> That valleys, groves, hills and fields,
> Woods, or steepy mountain yields.

> And we will sit upon the rocks,
> Seeing the shepherds feed their flocks
> By shallow rivers, to whose falls
> Melodious birds sing madrigals.

> And I will make thee beds of roses,
> And a thousand fragrant posies,
> A cap of flowers, and a kirtle,
> Embroidered all with leaves of myrtle.

An instrumental version of the tune to which Marlowe's poem was sung appeared in William Corkine's *The Second Book of Ayres* (1612). It is reproduced, along with another version, in *The British Broadside Ballad and Its Music*, by Claude M. Simpson (New Brunswick, N.J., 1966). The tune is also given by John H. Long in his *Shakespeare's Use of Music. The Final Comedies* (Gainesville, Florida, 1961). But, while the tune has survived, it is impossible to say whether Shakespeare meant Evans to use it, because the metrical version of Psalm 137 (see the note to line 23) is also running through the Parson's mind. The best comic effect can probably be achieved by having the love song sung to the psalm tune.

19   *posies* bunches of flowers

23   *Whenas I sat in Pabylon*. These words are an intrusion. They come from the first line of Psalm 137 in the Sternhold and Hopkins hymnal (1562), where the opening verse takes the following form:

> Whenas we sat in Babylon, the rivers round about,
> And in remembrance of Sion the tears for grief
>   burst out,
> We hanged our harps and instruments the willow
>   trees upon,
> For in that place men for their use had planted
>   many a one.

The psalm tune is printed by Claude M. Simpson and by John H. Long in the works cited in the note to lines 16–25 above.

24   *vagram* (confusion of 'fragrant' and 'vagrant')

25   *etc.* This word suggests that Evans continues with the song until Simple enters and speaks.

41   *the word* (the Bible)

43   *in your doublet and hose* (without a cloak)
       doublet (close-fitting upper garment)
       hose (close-fitting breeches like tights)

49   *belike* it would seem

50   *at most odds* at the greatest variance

54   *wide of his own respect* indifferent to his own reputation

58–9   *had as lief* would as gladly

61   *Hibocrates* (Hippocrates, ancient Greek physician)

62   *Galen.* See the note on II.3.26.

67   (stage direction) *offer* attempt, prepare

70   *question* debate, discuss

75   *In good time* indeed! what a question!

81   *cogscombs* (Evans's pronunciation of 'coxcomb' meaning 'head')

81–2   *for missing your meetings and appointments.* This is the reading of Q; the words, which seem essential for the completion of the sentence, are omitted from F.

89   *Gallia and Gaul* Wales and France

93   *politic* cunning, diplomatic
       Machiavel follower of Machiavelli. Niccolò Machiavelli, the great Italian political theorist of the early sixteenth century, was commonly seen in Elizabethan

England as the exponent of an immoral statecraft, largely on the evidence of his best known work, *Il Principe* (1532).

95   *motions* evacuations of the bowels

96   *no-verbs* non-existent words (a coinage of the Host's to describe Evans's misuse of English)

97-8   *Give me thy hand, terrestrial; so. Give me thy hand, celestial; so.* This reading is adopted from Q. F merely has 'Giue me thy hand (Celestiall) so', which destroys the carefully balanced symmetry of the Host's speech. See the Account of the Text, pages 209-10.

99   *art* learning

100   *burnt sack* mulled wine
       issue outcome, conclusion

101   *to pawn* as a pledge, as a security

103   *Trust* believe

106   *sot* fool

108   *vlouting-stog* (Evans means 'flouting-stock, laughing-stock')

110   *scald* scabby, mean

111   *cogging companion* cheating rogue

III.2.1   *keep your way* go on, don't stop

2   *follower* (1) servant; (2) one who goes behind another

3   *Whether had you rather* which of the two would you prefer

12   *as idle as she may hang together* as bored as she can be without falling completely to pieces
       want lack

16   *had you* did you get
       weathercock (indicates that Robin is wearing a feather in his hat)

17   *what the dickens*. This is the earliest recorded use of this phrase, in which *dickens* is probably a form of 'devil'.

18   *had him of* got him from

22   *on's* (colloquial) on his
23   *league* friendship, alliance
30   *point-blank* straight, horizontally
       twelve score at a distance of twelve score (240) yards
30–31 *pieces out* encourages
31   *folly* wantonness
       motion prompting, encouragement
32   *advantage* favourable opportunity
33–4 *hear this shower sing in the wind* divine that trouble is
       brewing
35   *revolted* faithless, disloyal
36   *take him* take him by surprise, catch him out
38   *divulge* proclaim, reveal
39   *secure* over-confident
       Actaeon cuckold. See the note on II.1.111.
40   *cry aim* shout applause, give approval. Spectators
       encouraged archers by crying 'Aim!' when they were
       about to shoot.
46   *knot* company, band
       cheer fare
50   *break with* break my word to
56   *stand wholly for* entirely support
62   *speaks holiday* uses choice language, talks gaily
63   *carry't* win the day, succeed
       'Tis in his buttons. The meaning is uncertain, but 'it is
       predestined' seems likely. The phrase is unknown
       outside this passage, and the F reading, 'buttons', is
       probably a compositor's error for some other word –
       'browes' perhaps. Q is of no assistance here, since it
       has 'betmes', which is not a word at all.
66   *is of no having* has no property, is of no substance
66–7 *the wild Prince and Poins* (Prince Hal and his companion
       Poins in *1* and *2 Henry IV*. See the Introduction, pages
       37–8.)
67   *region* rank, social standing
68   *knit a knot in* strengthen, augment
70   *simply* as she is, without a dowry

waits on is subject to

80   *canary* (1) sweet wine from the Canaries (which is what the Host means); (2) a lively Spanish dance (referred to by Ford when he says *I'll make him dance*)

81   *pipe-wine* (1) wine from the pipe (a cask holding four barrels); (2) whine of the pipe (in the sense of a musical instrument used for the dance). Ford is using elaborate puns to convey his intention of beating Falstaff, the pipe of wine, until he howls and dances.

82   *gentles* gentlemen

I.3.2   *buck-basket* dirty-linen basket

3   *Robert.* F reads '*Robin*', but as the little page does not enter until line 18 the emendation seems obvious.

6   *charge* (1) order; (2) load

13   *whitsters* bleachers of linen

   Datchet Mead (a meadow between Windsor and the Thames)

16   *ha'* (colloquial) have

20   *eyas-musket* young male sparrow-hawk

24   *Jack-a-Lent* puppet (literally the figure of a man dressed in bright clothes that was set up in the season of Lent for boys to throw stones at)

28–9   *turn me away* discard me, dismiss me

38   *pumpion* pumpkin

39   *turtles* turtle-doves (proverbially faithful to their mates)

   jays light women (because the jay has a gaudy plumage and is given to chatter)

40   *Have I caught thee, my heavenly jewel?* Falstaff is quoting, not quite accurately, for the word *thee* is not in the original, the opening line of the Second Song in Sir Philip Sidney's *Astrophil and Stella* (1591).

42   *period* goal, conclusion

44   *cog* tell smooth lies, flatter

52   *becomes* suits, goes well with

53   *ship-tire* elaborate woman's head-dress shaped like a ship

        tire-valiant fanciful head-dress

53–4 *tire of Venetian admittance* head-dress fashionable in Venice

55   *kerchief* (cloth used to cover the head, female head-dress of an unpretentious kind)

56   *become* fit

58   *absolute* perfect, accomplished

        fixture placing

60   *semi-circled farthingale* (skirt with hoops of whalebone which made it extend behind but not in front of the body)

60–61 *I see what thou wert if Fortune, thy foe, were – not Nature – thy friend.* I can imagine how celebrated you would be if Fortune, now your enemy since it has placed you in the middle class, had been your friend, and not merely Nature, which has given you beauty but not the rank that should go with it. 'Fortune my foe' was a popular tune.

67   *hawthorn-buds* fops, young dandies

68   *Bucklersbury* (London street where herbalists had their shops)

68–9 *simple-time* midsummer (the time when apothecaries were supplied with herbs or 'simples', as they were called)

74   *Counter-gate.* The Counter was the debtors' prison, and prisons were notorious for the bad smells that emanated from them.

        reek smoke, vapour

83   *presently* immediately

84   *ensconce me* hide myself

85   *arras* (hanging screen of tapestry placed round the walls of rooms)

90   *overthrown* ruined

93   *well-a-day* alas

97–8 *Out upon you* (an exclamation of reproach)

109 *clear* innocent, clear of guilt
friend lover
110 *convey him out* get him away secretly
amazed confused, bewildered
112 *good life* respectable position in society
117 *stand* waste time over
123 *bucking* washing
whiting-time bleaching-time
131–2 *and none but thee.* These words, which are not found in
F, are taken from Q. They are included in the present
text because they add force to Falstaff's efforts to
reassure Mistress Page of his love for her.
139 *cowl-staff* (stout pole used for carrying a basket slung
between two men)
drumble dawdle
141 *come near* come in, enter
146 *what have you to do* what is it to do with you, what
concern of yours is it
147 *buck-washing* (process of washing dirty linen by
soaking it in an alkaline lye and then beating and rinsing
it in clear water)
148–9 *Buck? ... I warrant you, buck.* Three senses of the
word 'buck' are involved here: (1) clothes for washing;
(2) male deer (symbolizing cuckoldry); (3) to copulate.
150 *of the season* in the rutting season
151 *tonight* last night
153–4 *unkennel the fox* dislodge the fox from its hole
155 *escape.* F reads 'vncape'; but there is no known
example of this word elsewhere. Assuming that it is
addressed to Page and the rest, some editors gloss it as
'uncouple the hounds', while others emend to 'uncope' or 'uncase'. The present editor takes the view
that the word is addressed to Falstaff, who, Ford thinks,
is now imprisoned in the house. He therefore emends
'uncape' to *escape*, meaning 'escape if you can'.
156 *be contented* restrain yourself
156–7 *wrong yourself* put yourself in the wrong

163   *issue* outcome, result

168   *taking* fright, state of alarm

170–71   *I am half afraid he will have need of washing.* Mistress Ford is implying that Falstaff's terror may have made him befoul himself.

174   *strain* nature, disposition

178   *try* test

180   *obey* yield to, respond to

181   *carrion* (used as a term of contempt)

187   *that* that which

188   *compass* bring about, accomplish

195   *wrong* discredit, disgrace

199   *presses* cupboards, clothes presses

203   *suggests* prompts you to, tempts you to
        imagination mad idea, baseless suspicion

204   *distemper* disturbance of mind, deranged condition
        in this kind of this sort, of this species

206   *fault* misfortune, weakness

218   *a-birding* (hawking with a sparrow-hawk at small birds, which were driven into a bush and then shot)

219   *for the bush* for driving birds into the bush

III.4.2   *turn* direct, refer

5   *state* estate
    galled chafed away, injured, much reduced
    expense extravagant spending, squandering

6   *only* as my sole purpose (in asking for your hand)

7   *bars* objections to my claim

8   *wild societies* association with wild companions

10   *property* means to an end

12   *heaven so speed* as heaven may prosper

16   *stamps in gold* golden coins

17   *very* true

22   *Break* break off, interrupt

24   *make a shaft or a bolt on't* try it one way or the other. (Shafts and bolts were two kinds of arrows.)

	'Slid by God's eyelid
32	*ill-favoured* ugly
36	*To* go to
	coz kinsman
42	*cousin* kinsman
46	*come cut and long-tail* no matter who comes, let them all come (a common proverbial expression, used originally of dogs and horses, to express a whole category)
46–7	*under the degree of* in the rank of
49	*jointure* (the part of a husband's estate which he settled on his wife in the marriage contract, in order to provide for her widowhood in case he died before her)
56	*'Od's heartlings* God's little heart (a very mild oath)
62	*motions* proposals
62–3	*happy man be his dole* good luck to the man who wins you (a proverbial expression meaning literally 'may his lot be that of a happy man')
76	*for that* because
78	*checks* reproofs
79	*advance the colours* raise the standard (as a preliminary to battle)
82	*mean* intend
84	*quick* alive
89	*affected* inclined
96	*once* at some time
105	*speciously* (Mistress Quickly's version of 'specially')
106	*must of* must go on. Verbs of motion are often omitted after 'must'.
108	*slack it* put it off, be so remiss about it

III.5.3	*toast* piece of hot toast (to warm the drink)
4	*barrow* barrow-load
7–8	*new-year's gift*. In Elizabethan England New Year was the traditional time for the giving of presents.

8   *slighted me* slid me slightingly. Q reads 'slided me'. It looks very much as though Shakespeare has created a portmanteau word here combining the senses of 'to slide' and 'to slight'.

9   *remorse* pity, compunction

13   *shore* bank

       shelvy made of sandbanks, shelving

16   *mummy* dead flesh, mass of pulp

21   *reins* loins, kidneys

23   *cry you mercy* beg your pardon

25   *chalices* drinking cups, small goblets

25–6   *a pottle* two quarts

28   *Simple of itself* unmixed with anything else

       I'll I'll have

29   *brewage* concocted drink

36   *take on with* scold

37   *erection* (Mistress Quickly's mistake for 'direction')

40   *that* so that

41   *yearn* grieve

51   *miss* fail

62   *sped you* were you successful

63   *ill-favouredly* badly

64   *determination* mind, decision

65   *peaking cornuto* sneaking cuckold (*cornuto* meaning literally 'the horned one')

66   *dwelling* existing

67   *'larum* perturbation, fear

       me (ethic dative)

68   *encounter* amatory meeting

70   *rabble* pack

71   *distemper* bad temper

82   *smocks* slips, linen undergarments

83   *that* so that

90   *knaves* menials

       hinds servants

100   *with* by

       bell-wether ram with a bell on his neck who leads the

flock. Ford made a lot of noise, led the pack, and was, in Falstaff's eyes, a horned man, a cuckold.

101 *compassed* bent in the form of a circle

bilbo sword from Bilbao (noted for the temper and elasticity of its blade)

102 *peck* round vessel used as a peck measure

103 *stopped in* fastened in, stoppered in

104 *fretted* rotted, fermented

105 *kidney* constitution

106 *dissolution* melting, liquefaction

107 *in the height* at the highest pitch

109 *Dutch dish* Dutch cooking was thought of as greasy.

113 *good sadness* all seriousness

114 *desperate* hopeless

115 *undertake* have to do with

119 *embassy* message

122 *address me* betake myself

130 *There's a hole made in your best coat* (a proverbial phrase meaning 'your reputation is badly flawed')

135 *halfpenny purse* (diminutive purse for holding small silver halfpence)

140 *horn-mad* furious with rage at being a cuckold

IV.1 There is nothing whatever in Q to correspond to this scene. The obvious reason for its complete omission from that text is that it is a self-contained episode, totally unrelated to the rest of the action. What it offers is an amusing picture of the Elizabethan school-boy and of the kind of education he was subjected to, together with a lot of bawdy innuendo. It has been suggested that Shakespeare wrote it as a sophisticated titbit for a courtly audience, the only audience, it is argued, that would have the knowledge of Latin necessary for a proper appreciation of the blunders and of the improprieties they give rise to. The answer to this view is in the scene itself. Little William, the son

191

of a citizen, already has enough Latin for the purpose. All that is required is an elementary acquaintance with Lily's *Latin Grammar*, the standard authority in schools at the time. It is not William's defective Latin that lets him down, leaving him in a state of innocent ignorance, but the fact that he has hitherto, it would seem, been shielded from contact with some of the grosser and more indecent terms in the English language. Clearly this is a deficiency that will soon be remedied. A citizen audience of grown-up Williams would have no difficulties with the scene.

4   *courageous* (probably associated in Mistress Quickly's mind with 'raging')

6   *suddenly* at once

7–8   *but bring* merely accompany

12   *let the boys leave to play* asked that the boys be given a holiday

15   *profits nothing in the world at his book* makes no progress at all in his studies

16   *accidence* (rudiments of Latin grammar)

23   *'Od's nouns* God's wounds (an oath)

24   *Peace your tattlings* silence your idle prattle

26   *Polecats* (a slang term for 'prostitutes')

43   *hung, hang, hog* (Evans's pronunciation of *hunc, hanc, hoc*)

44   *'Hang-hog' is Latin for bacon* (an allusion to an old saying: 'Hog is not bacon until it be hanged')

49   *caret* (Latin) is lacking. Mistress Quickly confuses this word with the English word 'carrot'.

57   *Vengeance of Jenny's case* fie on Jenny's situation. Some complicated misunderstandings, with very bawdy implications, are going on here. Mistress Quickly takes *Genitive case* as a reference to the occupation of Jenny, the local prostitute, and to the female genital organs; thinks *horum* means 'whore'; and finds yet another sexual allusion in *harum*, 'hare' being a slang term for 'harlot'.

61 *to hick and to hack*. The precise meaning of these words is not known, but 'to drink (causing hiccups) and to wench' seems likely. For *hack*, compare *These knights will hack* (II.1.47–8).

73 *preeches* (Evans's version of 'breeched', meaning 'flogged on the bare buttocks')

77 *sprag* (for 'sprack', meaning 'lively, alert')

IV.2.2 *sufferance* suffering, pain
   obsequious devoted, zealous

1 *in a doit's breadth* exactly, precisely

4–5 *accoutrement* suitable formalities (literally 'equipment')

5 *complement* accompaniment, external shows

12 *people* servants, household

20 *lines* role, part (a theatrical allusion). Many editors, not recognizing the reference to an actor's part, emend to 'lunes', meaning 'fits of lunacy', but the Q reading, 'in his old vaine againe', shows that *lines* is correct.

22 *complexion* appearance, colour of the skin

23 *Peer out* (a reference to the budding horns of the cuckold)

32 *experiment* trial, test

42 *should* can

43 *bestow* dispose of

47 *that* so that

49 *make you* are you doing

52–3 *use to discharge their birding pieces* are in the habit of firing off the guns they use for shooting birds. This method of chimney-sweeping is put to good dramatic use in Thomas Middleton's play *The Changeling* (1622).

54 *Creep into the kiln-hole*. F gives these words to Mistress Ford, but in view of what she says at lines 56–60 Mistress Page seems the likelier speaker.
   kiln-hole oven

57   *press* clothes cupboard

58   *abstract* list, register

62–3 *If you go ... go out disguised.* F allots this speech to
      Mistress Ford, thus giving two consecutive speeches
      to the same character, which is plainly wrong.

67   *muffler* (kind of scarf or wrapper worn by women in
      Shakespeare's day to cover part of the face and the
      neck)

68   *extremity* extravagance

69   *mischief* calamity

70–71 *the fat woman of Brainford.* Q reads 'Gillian of
      Brainford', thus giving the fat woman's identity.
      Gillian of Brainford (the modern Brentford, twelve
      miles east of Windsor) is the central figure in *Jyl of
      Breyntfords Testament*, by Robert Copland, a ribald
      piece of work published about 1560 but probably
      written twenty years earlier.

73   *thrummed hat* (hat made of, or perhaps fringed
      with, 'thrums', the soft waste ends of the weaver's
      warp)

76   *look* look for, search for

78   *straight* immediately

86   *good sadness* all seriousness

88   *try* test, make an experiment on

96   *dishonest* lewd, unchaste

99   *honest* chaste

100   *act* commit adultery, fornicate

101   *Still swine eats all the draff* the quiet pig eats all the
      swill (a proverbial expression to describe the demure
      hypocrite)

103   *hard at* close to

109   *unfool me* take the reproach of folly away from me

110   *Youth in a basket* (proverbial) fortunate lover

111   *panderly* pimping, procuring
      knot band
      ging (old form of 'gang')
      pack plotting confederacy

112   *Now shall the devil be shamed* (an allusion to the proverb 'Speak the truth and shame the devil')

115   *passes* goes beyond all bounds, beats everything

126   *Hold it out* keep it up

132–3   *take up your wife's clothes.* Evans blunders again. He means 'pick up your wife's dirty clothes', but what he says is 'lift up your wife's dress', the preliminary to sexual intercourse.

139   *intelligence* information

140   *Pluck me out* pluck out for me

144   *By my fidelity* on my word of honour

145   *strange diseases*

146   *pray* (in order to drive out the devil by whom Ford is, Evans thinks, possessed)

151   *show no colour for my extremity* admit no excuse for my extravagant behaviour

152   *table sport* laughing-stock of the company

154   *leman* lover, paramour (with a pun on 'lemon')

161   *quean* jade, woman of questionable reputation
        cozening cheating, deceiving

162   *of errands.* Ford suspects the fat woman is a bawd.

165   *by th'figure* (either by using astrological diagrams or by making effigies in wax for the purpose of enchantment)
        daubery specious methods, false shows, trickery

166   *beyond our element* out of our sphere, beyond our comprehension

169   *not strike.* F omits 'not'; but it is clearly demanded by the sense, and was inserted in the second Folio (1632).

172   *prat her* beat her buttocks ('prats' being a slang word for 'buttocks')

173   *rag* worthless creature. 'Ragge' is the reading of F. Many editors prefer 'hag', the reading of the third Quarto (1630), which is based on F, and of the third Folio (1664).

174   *polecat* whore
        ronyon (an abusive term for a woman, probably meaning 'scabby old wretch')

174   *conjure* charm, bewitch
178–9 *'Tis a goodly credit for you* it does you great credit (ironical)
185   *issue* final outcome
       cry out bark (like a hound in full cry)
186   *trail* track, scent
       open give tongue (hunting language)
187   *obey his humour* give way to his whim
197   *wantonness* lust
198–9 *in fee simple, with fine and recovery* (legal terminology) in complete possession, under the fullest legal sanction
199–200 *in the way of waste* as mere objects to be exploited. Mistress Page is carrying on the legal terminology in suggesting that Falstaff has been treating them both as though they were a piece of common land. There is probably a quibble on 'waist'.
204   *figures* idle fancies, phantasms
206   *ministers* agents
208   *period* limit, fitting conclusion

IV.3   This scene introduces the horse-stealing episode, which is never properly worked out or fully integrated into the structure of the play. See Introduction, pages 27–8.
9   *sauce them* make them pay dearly, make it hot for them
9–10   *at command* reserved
11   *come off* pay up

       'Tis she is
       best discretions of a 'oman most discreet women
3   *at an instant* at the same time
6   *with* of
10   *submission* (four syllables)
24   *use* treat, deal with
27   *Sometime* once, formerly

29   *ragg'd* rugged, jagged

30   *blasts* blights, withers

       takes bewitches

31   *milch-kine* dairy cattle

34   *eld* people of olden times

35   *Received* accepted (from the past)

37   *want not* are not lacking

39   *device* plan, contrivance

41   *Disguised like Herne, with huge horns on his head.*
       Omitted from F, this line preserved in Q is essential,
       for without it Page's words *And in this shape* (line 43)
       make no sense.

47   *growth* size, stature

48   *urchins* goblins

       ouphes elves

49   *rounds* circlets

52   *sawpit* (pit used for sawing timber)

53   *diffusèd* confused, disorderly

56   *pinch.* Pinching was the traditional way in which
       fairies punished those who incurred their displeasure.

59   MISTRESS FORD. F gives this speech to Ford.

60   *sound* soundly

66   *jackanapes* (properly 'tame monkey', but Evans must
       mean 'satyr', since this is the form he actually
       takes)

67   *taber* (Evans's version of 'taper')

68   *vizards* masks

73   *Eton* (across the river from Windsor)

76   *properties* (in the theatrical sense)

77   *tricking* costumes, ornaments

85   *affects* likes

IV.5.2   *discuss* declare, make known

6   *truckle-bed* (small bed on castors, which could be
       pushed under the larger *standing-bed* when not in
       use)

7   *Prodigal* (the Prodigal Son in the Bible)

8   *Anthropophaginian* man-eater, cannibal

11   *be so bold as stay* venture so far as to wait

16   *Ephesian* boon companion

18   *Bohemian-Tartar* barbarian, wild man
          tarries waits for

23   *wise woman* witch and fortune-teller

25   *mussel-shell* empty-headed useless fool

28   *thorough* through

29   *beguiled him of* cheated him out of, robbed him of

34   *cozened* cheated

35   SIMPLE. F, mistakenly, allots this speech to Falstaff.

40   *conceal* (Simple's mistake for 'reveal')

50   *like who more bold* as bold as the boldest

53   *clerkly* scholarly, a man of learning

57   *was paid* suffered, was beaten

59   *mere* absolute, nothing but

60   *varletto* rascal (the Host's attempt to turn 'varlet' into
          Italian)

64   *Doctor Faustuses* (an allusion to the hero of Marlowe's
          play *Doctor Faustus,* who practised black magic)

69   *Have a care of your entertainments* (Evans means
          'beware of your guests, keep a sharp eye on the people
          you entertain')

71   *cozen-germans* (1) first cousins; (2) cozening Germans,
          German cheats. The reading of Q is 'cosen gar-
          mombles', which has led to much learned speculation.
          It has been seen as a reference to Frederick, Count of
          Mömpelgart, who visited England in 1592 and became
          very desirous of being made a member of the Order of
          the Garter. He was finally elected to the Order in
          1597, by which time he had become the Duke of
          Würtemberg, but the investiture took place in his
          absence, and Queen Elizabeth did not bother to send
          on the insignia of the Order to him. There may be
          something in this; but Q is so inaccurate that 'gar-
          mombles' could well be nothing more than the re-

porter's version of 'German nobles' or something of that kind.

Readins (Evans's version of 'Reading')

72   *Colebrook* (modern Colnbrook, a village not far from Windsor)

73   *for good will* out of friendship (ironical)

74   *vlouting-stocks* (Evans means 'flouting-stocks, laughing-stocks')

      convenient right, proper, fitting (ironical)

77   *doubtful* apprehensive

81   *that the court is know to come* (Caius's attempt at 'whom coming the court knows of')

83   *Hue and cry* (shout calling for general pursuit of a felon or felons)

      villain (addressed to Bardolph)

90   *liquor* grease, oil

92   *forswore myself* lied (about my cards)

93   *primero* (a card game)

93–4 *to say my prayers.* Omitted from F, these words, which are essential to the sense, have been preserved in Q.

102   *speciously* (for 'specially')

103   *that* so that

109   *action* movements and behaviour

117   *crossed* thwarted

IV.6.10   *answered* responded to, requited

11   *far forth* far

12   *to* according to

13   *contents* (stress on the second syllable)

14   *larded with my matter* intermixed with the matter that concerns me

17   *image* main idea

18   *at large* as a whole

20   *present* represent, play the part of

22   *something rank on foot* going forward in some profusion

29   *shuffle* spirit, use trickery to get

30   *tasking of* occupying, making demands on

31   *attends* awaits

34   *it rests* matters stand

36   *habit* dress

38   *intended* planned, arranged

40   *vizarded* disguised

41   *quaint* elaborately, elegantly

42   *flaring* streaming loose

43   *vantage* opportunity

44   *token* sign, signal

48   *here it rests* this remains to be done

51   *united ceremony* the union of the marriage rite

52   *husband your device* manage your plan prudently

54   *bound* indebted, under obligation

55   *present recompense* immediate reward

V.1.1   *hold* keep my word, keep the appointment

2   *third time* (alluding to the proverb 'The third time pays for all')

3   *divinity* oracular power, divination

7   *wears* wears on, passes

8   *mince* walk off in an affected manner

12   *yesterday.* Shakespeare has nodded here; the beating of Falstaff took place on the morning of this same day.

20–21   *Goliath with a weaver's beam* (an allusion to 1 Samuel 17.7: 'The shaft of his [Goliath's] spear was like a weaver's beam')

21   *life is a shuttle.* Falstaff, whose knowledge of the Bible is impressive, is here quoting from the Book of Job 7.6: 'My days pass over more speedily than a weaver's shuttle.'

V.2.1   *couch* lie hidden

5   *nay-word* password, watchword

6   *mum ... budget*. The two words together form 'mumbudget', meaning 'silence'.

9   *decipher* indicate, distinguish

11   *become* suit, fit

V.3.7   *abuse* ill-usage

12   *the Welsh devil Hugh*. The F reading is 'the Welch-deuill Herne', but Herne is not a Welsh devil, and the emendation is accepted by most editors.

13   *couched* hidden

17   *cannot choose but amaze* is bound to frighten

20   *betray* deceive

21   *lewdsters* lascivious persons, lechers

V.5   (stage direction) *Enter Falstaff ... upon him*. This direction is adapted from that in Q, which reads '*Enter sir Iohn with a Bucks head vpon him*'.

2   *hot-blooded* amorous, lecherous

3   *Jove, thou wast a bull for thy Europa*. In classical myth Jove, the king of the gods, abducted Europa by appearing to her in the form of a milk-white bull. He seemed so gentle that after garlanding his horns with flowers she climbed on to his back. Thereupon he dashed into the sea and swam away with her.

6–7   *Jupiter, a swan for the love of Leda* (referring to another of Jove's amorous exploits: his seduction of Leda by appearing to her in the guise of a swan)

8   *complexion* appearance

11   *hot backs* carnal desires, strong sexual urges

13   *rut-time* (season of the year in which the male deer become sexually excited)

14   *to piss my tallow* if I urinate my fat away (alluding to the fact that stags grow thin in the rutting season)

18   *scut* (short tail of a deer or rabbit)

19   *potatoes* yams, sweet potatoes (regarded as an aphrodisiac in Elizabethan times)

19   *Greensleeves.* See the note on II.1.59.

20   *kissing-comfits* perfumed sugar-plums (used to sweeten
        the breath)

        eringoes sweetmeats made from the candied root of sea
        holly (thought to be an aphrodisiac)

21   *provocation* erotic stimulation

24   *bribed* stolen

25-6   *the fellow of this walk* the keeper in charge of this part
        of the forest. Falstaff is quibbling; he means (1) that
        his shoulders are the perquisite of the keeper; (2) that
        he will use them to shoulder off the keeper, should he
        turn up.

27   *woodman* (1) hunter, one skilled in woodcraft; (2)
        woman-hunter; (3) woodwose (wild man of the woods),
        like Herne

28   *Cupid* (god of love in classical mythology)

        of conscience who is conscientious, who keeps his word

36   *cross* thwart

38   *shades* phantoms, spirits

39   *orphan* (probably an allusion to the belief that fairies
        had no fathers)

40   *Attend your office and your quality* apply yourselves to
        your proper function and business

41   *oyes* hear ye (call of the public crier, from the French
        oyez)

42   *list* listen for

        toys trifles, things of no substance

44   *unraked* (where the embers have not been covered with
        ashes so as to keep the fire going all night)

46   *sluttery* sluttishness

48   *wink* close my eyes

        couch lie hidden

51   *Raise up the organs of her fantasy* stimulate her
        imagination (so that she has pleasant dreams)

52   *Sleep she* may she sleep, let her sleep

        careless free from cares, untroubled by anxieties

53   *as who*

55   *About* get to work, bestir yourselves
57   *ouphes* elves
58   *perpetual doom* Day of Judgement
59   *wholesome* sound
60   *Worthy* worthy of, befitting
       the owner (Queen Elizabeth)
61   *The several chairs of order* each of the chairs of the order
       order order of knighthood (in this case the Order of the
       Garter)
       look make sure, take care that
63   *instalment* place or seat wherein a person is installed,
       stall
       coat coat of arms
       several crest separate heraldic device
64   *blazon* armorial bearings
66   *compass* circle
67   *expressure* impression, picture
69   *Honi soit qui mal y pense* (French – the motto of the
       Order of the Garter) shamed be he who thinks evil of it
70   *tufts* bunches
73   *charactery* (pronounced to rhyme with 'refractory')
       writing
75   *dance of custom* customary dance
79   *measure* dance
80   *man of middle earth* mortal (*middle earth* being the
       earth seen as midway between heaven and hell)
82   *a piece of cheese.* The Welshman's fondness for cheese
       was the subject of a number of 'merry tales' in the
       sixteenth century, a stock joke. Compare II.2.287–8.
83   *o'erlooked* looked upon with the evil eye, bewitched
84   *trial-fire* testing fire (as in the trial by ordeal)
86   *turn* put
92   *still* continually
       THE SONG. The original music for this song has not
       survived.
94   *luxury* lechery, lasciviousness
95   *bloody fire* fire in the blood

99   *mutually* jointly, all together

102   (stage direction) *During this song ... Mistress Ford.*
      There is, as usual, no stage direction in F at this point.
      Q, from which the direction in this edition is adapted,
      reads as follows: '*Here they pinch him, and sing about
      him, & the Doctor comes one way & steales away a boy
      in red. And Slender another way he takes a boy in
      greene: And Fenton steales misteris Anne, being in white.
      And a noyse of hunting is made within: and all the
      Fairies runne away. Falstaffe pulles of his bucks head,
      and rises vp. And enters M. Page, M. Ford, and their
      wiues, M. Shallow, Sir Hugh.*' The reference to
      Shallow is particularly interesting, because in F he
      has no lines to speak in this scene, and there is therefore
      no warrant for bringing him on, though in keeping with
      Shakespeare's general practice in comedy one would
      expect him to be present at the denouement, especially
      as his 'wise cousin' is so intimately involved in it.
      Q, on the other hand, gives him a speech as well as an
      entrance. He is the first of the company to address
      Falstaff, saying to him '*God saue you sir Iohn Falstaffe.*'
      It seems highly probable that these words, or something
      like them, were part of the text, but were omitted from
      F.

103   *watched you* caught you in the act

105   *hold up* prolong, continue
      higher further, longer

107   *yokes.* Mistress Page means Falstaff's horns, of course,
      but also the idea of the cuckold's horns which has so
      obsessed Ford.

114   *arrested* seized on a legal warrant

120   *ox* fool. 'To make an ox of one' was to make a fool of
      him.
      proofs (horns)
      extant (1) in existence; (2) conspicuous, standing out
      to view, protuberant

124   *powers* intellectual faculties

foppery deceit, dupery

125   *received belief* article of faith, absolute conviction

     in despite of the teeth of contrary to, in spite of

126   *wit* inventiveness of mind

127   *Jack-a-Lent* (puppet dressed up for boys to throw stones at in Lent; compare III.3.24)

135   *wants matter* lacks the capacity, has no means

136   *ridden with* harassed by, tyrannized over by

     Welsh goat. For the Elizabethan English the important place which the goat had in the rural economy of Wales was an indication of the poverty of that country. Compare Glendower's remark: 'The goats ran from the mountains' (*1 Henry IV*, III.1.36).

137   *coxcomb of frieze* fool's cap of coarse woollen cloth (of the kind made in Wales)

142   *makes fritters* makes a hash

143   *decay* ruin, cause of destruction

     late-walking staying out late (to keep assignations with women)

146–7   *by the head and shoulders* violently, headlong

150   *hodge-pudding* large sausage made of numerous ingredients

151   *puffed* inflated, blown up

152   *intolerable* excessive

154–5   *Job* (the biblical figure). See Job 1.9–11, where Satan slanders him, and Job 2.9, where his wife tempts him to curse God.

157   *metheglins* Welsh mead

158   *starings* swaggerings, efforts to stare one out of countenance

     pribbles and prabbles. See the note on I.1.51.

159   *start* advantage

160   *dejected* cast down, humbled

161   *is a plummet o'er me* has sounded me, has got to the bottom of me

     plummet (1) woollen fabric (quibbling on *flannel*); (2) plummet-line (used for sounding depths at sea)

165   *should* were to
       that that which

168   *posset* (drink made of hot milk curdled with ale, wine, or the like)

172   *Doctors doubt that* (a traditional phrase expressing disbelief)

175-6 *dispatched* settled the business

178   *on't* (colloquial) of it

181   *lubberly* clumsy, loutish

182   *swinged* (pronounced to rhyme with 'fringed') beaten, thrashed

184-5 *postmaster's boy* boy of the man who has charge of the post horses

200   *un paysan* (French) a yokel, a peasant

212   *amaze* perplex, bewilder

215   *contracted* betrothed

216   *sure* firmly united (in marriage)

219   *unduteous title* name of undutifulness

220   *evitate* avoid

227   *stand* (station taken up by a hunter)
       glanced missed its mark

231   *muse* grumble

AN ACCOUNT OF THE TEXT

The Merry Wives of Windsor first saw print in 1602, when it was published as a quarto. The title-page, which is not without its interest, runs, when modernized, thus: *A most pleasant and excellent conceited comedy of Sir John Falstaff and the Merry Wives of Windsor, intermixed with sundry variable and pleasing humours of Sir Hugh the Welsh knight, Justice Shallow, and his wise cousin Master Slender, with the swaggering vein of Ancient Pistol, and Corporal Nym. By William Shakespeare. As it hath been divers times acted by the Right Honourable my Lord Chamberlain's Servants, both before her majesty and elsewhere.* This is evidently a publisher's blurb, singling out the characters that could be expected to have an immediate appeal to anyone who knew the two parts of *Henry IV* and *Henry V*. It is also curiously erratic. The description of Slender, a new character, could hardly be bettered, yet that of Evans, the other new character named, suggests that whoever was responsible for it had neither seen nor read the play. The text itself has something of the same hit-and-miss quality. Nevertheless, it was reprinted, with a few minor alterations, in 1619. Then, in 1623, came the Folio edition of the plays, in which *The Merry Wives of Windsor* appears as the third of the Comedies, between *The Two Gentlemen of Verona* and *Measure for Measure*. The text of the Folio is very different from that of the Quarto. It is almost twice the length, running to over 2,700 lines as compared with a mere 1,600. It contains five scenes – IV.1 and V.1–4 – which are not to be found at all in the Quarto. It introduces one character, Page's son little William, who does not appear in the Quarto, and allots a speaking part to another, Falstaff's page Robin, who is mute in the text of 1602. Moreover, it is carefully divided into Acts and scenes, whereas the Quarto has no such divisions. Most important of all, however, the Folio presents a much fuller, better written, and far more coherent play than does the Quarto.

The superiority of the Folio text was soon recognized at a very practical level. The Quarto of 1602 had been printed for a bookseller called Arthur Johnson. In January 1630 Johnson made over his rights in *The Merry Wives of Windsor* to another bookseller, R. Meighen. But, when Meighen had the play reprinted as a quarto, later in the same year, it was not the 1602 text, or the 1619, which he used, but that of the Folio. The judgement about the relative values of the two texts, implicit in this choice, is one that all editors of the comedy have concurred with; they are unanimous in basing their texts on that of the Folio.

This does not mean, however, that the editor can afford to ignore the Quarto completely. Rowe did so in his edition of 1709, the first edited Shakespeare that we have, but only for the simple reason that he did not know of its existence. Pope, Shakespeare's second editor, though unaware of the 1602 version, knew that of 1619, and recognized that at one point it offered a demonstrably better reading than the Folio. When Ford asks the Host for his connivance in Ford's plan to present himself to Falstaff under an assumed name, he says in the Folio: 'tell him my name is *Broome*: onely for a iest' (II.1.198–9). Thereafter in the Folio the name under which he talks to Falstaff is consistently 'Broome'. In the Quarto Ford's request is: 'tell him my name|Is *Rrooke*, onlie for a Iest'. The Host's reply, 'thy|Name shall be *Brooke*', makes it clear that the improbable 'Rrooke' is merely a misprint; and from this point onwards the name is always 'Brooke' in the Quarto. At this stage in the action there is nothing to indicate which of the two names is the one that Shakespeare originally wrote, though 'Brooke' has obvious associations with 'Ford' while 'Broome' has none. The issue is settled in the next scene. At II.2.140–48, the following exchanges between Bardolph and Falstaff occur in the Folio:

Bar. Sir *Iohn*, there's one Master *Broome* below would faine
  speake with you, and be acquainted with you; and hath sent
  your worship a mornings draught of Sacke.
Fal. Broome is his name?
Bar. I Sir.
Fal. Call him in: such *Broomes* are welcome to mee, that
  ore'flowes such liquor. . . .

Falstaff's final speech here makes no sense. It is evident that
something has gone wrong. The corresponding passage in the
Quarto runs thus:

Bar. Sir heer's a Gentleman,
  One M. *Brooke*, would speak with you,
  He hath sent you a cup of sacke.
Fal. M. *Brooke*, hees welcome: Bid him come vp,
  Such *Brookes* are alwaics welcome to me. . . .

The Quarto clearly has the name right; the substitution of
'Brooke' for 'Broome' turns the Folio nonsense into a characteristically Falstaffian jest. In every other respect, however, the
Quarto text is plainly inferior to that of the Folio here. Quite
apart from the fact that it prints prose as though it were verse,
it almost ruins the joke by missing out Falstaff's explanation of
why 'Such *Brookes*' are welcome to him. Moreover, its
repetition of the word 'welcome' is feeble. The lively, natural
quality of the Folio's dialogue, with its use of question and
answer, has been flattened out and made pedestrian. The
Quarto version here – and it is representative of the general
level of the Quarto as a whole – has all the appearance of
something inadequately remembered.

Pope, while realizing that 'Brooke' is the correct reading,
missed the other instance in which the Quarto text preserves
what Shakespeare wrote. It was spotted by the dramatist's
third editor, Lewis Theobald (1733). At III.1.92, the Host,
seeking to reconcile Caius and Evans, whom he has already
addressed as '*Gallia* and *Gaule*, *French* & *Welch*, Soule-Curer,

and Body-Curer' (III.1.89–90), puts his plea to them in the following form in the Folio:

> Peace, I say: heare mine Host of the Garter,
> Am I politicke? Am I subtle? Am I a Machiuell?
> Shall I loose my Doctor? No, hee giues me the Potions and the Motions. Shall I loose my Parson? my Priest? my Sir *Hugh*? No, he giues me the Prouerbes, and the No-verbes. Giue me thy hand (Celestiall) so: Boyes of Art, I haue deceiu'd you both. . . .

The Quarto version of this same speech is:

> Peace *I* say, heare mine host of the garter,
> Am *I* wise? am I polliticke? am *I* Matchauil?
> Shall *I* lose my doctor? No, he giues me the motions
> And the potions. Shall *I* lose my parson, my sir *Hu*?
> No, he giues me the prouerbes, and the nouerbes:
> Giue me thy hand terestiall,
> So giue me thy hand celestiall:
> So boyes of art I haue deceiued you both. . . .

The words 'Give me thy hand, terrestrial' – the form 'terestiall' is merely a mis-spelling – are demanded by the action, since the Host wishes to end the quarrel, and by the whole structure of the speech, which is built on carefully contrived antitheses. Moreover, it is easy to see how the compositor, or the scribe who prepared the text of the play for the printer, came to miss these five words. He set the first four of them, and then his eye jumped from the Host's appeal to Caius to his appeal to Evans, which starts with the same four words.

There are other instances in which the Quarto offers a reading that is tempting, but none of them has the patent rightness of the two just cited. For example, in the opening scene Slender answers Falstaff's brazen query 'What matter have you against me?' (I.1.116) by saying in the Folio text: 'Marry sir, I haue matter in my head against you, and against your cony-catching Rascalls, *Bardolf*, *Nym*, and *Pistoll*.' The Quarto at this point is far more explicit. It reads: 'I haue matter in my head against you and your cogging companions, *Pistoll* and *Nym*. They carried mee to the Tauerne and made mee drunke, and afterward picked my pocket.' To the present editor it appears that the second sentence, not to be found in the Folio, is required to lead on to Falstaff's question 'Pistol, did you pick Master Slender's purse?' (I.1.141). It has, however, been argued that a much subtler effect is achieved here if Slender, as in the Folio, has not yet made any specific complaint, since Falstaff's question then reveals that he knows perfectly well that Slender's purse was picked. This is undoubtedly true; so how does one decide whether to include the sentence from the Quarto or not? The answer will depend on whether one sees *The Merry Wives of Windsor* as a play of broad humour, written for an audience that needed to have things spelled out, or whether one regards it as a sophisticated comedy, designed for a learned queen and her court.

The whole problem would have been easier had the Folio text been set up from Shakespeare's own manuscript of the play, or even from the playhouse prompt-copy. It was not. Two features of it are bound to strike anyone who looks at it with a little care. In the first place, there is only one stage direction within the scene in the entire play. This occurs at V.5.36, in the form '*Enter Fairies*.' Secondly, the only other entrances marked come at the beginning of each scene, and they name all the characters who take part in that scene, irrespective of whether they are on stage from the outset or do not appear until later. The Folio text, as it stands, cannot be used as a prompt-book. It is not the work of a man of the theatre. The 'massed entries', as they are called, together with certain other peculiarities, such as the prodigal use of parentheses, have led modern scholars to the conclusion that the copy which the printers of the Folio had at their disposal was a transcript made by a professional scribe, Ralph Crane. Crane has done the work of tidying-up so thoroughly that it is impossible to say what sort of manuscript he was working from. What is practically certain is that he must have introduced some errors of his own in the process of copying.

The Folio text also represents a version of the play that has been submitted to some form of censorship. One mark of this is the substitution in it of 'Broome' for the 'Brooke' of the Quarto. The most likely reasons for it are either that the use of 'Brooke' somehow gave offence to the powerful family of that name, or that it was thought unwise to remind James I, who had *The Merry Wives of Windsor* performed before him at court on 4 November 1604, of this same family, which had been implicated in the Bye Plot and the Main Plot. The change of the name could well be the work of Shakespeare himself. The other evidence of censorship is the weakness of the oaths in the Folio as compared with those in the Quarto. For example, when Falstaff is describing his adventure in the buck-basket to the disguised Ford, he says in the Folio, replying to Ford's incredulous question 'A Buck-basket?', 'Yes: a Buck-basket' (III.5.80–81). In the Quarto, however, his answer to the same question is 'By the Lord a buck-basket', which sounds much more convincing. The purging of oaths of this kind from the text, which again may well be the work of Shakespeare himself, probably took place after the passing of an act, in 1606, to prohibit the profane use of God's name on the stage.

Pope thought of the Quarto as an early draft of the comedy, which Shakespeare later revised and expanded. This remained, with some modifications, the general view of scholars until 1910, when W. W. Greg, in a brilliant piece of textual analysis, showed that the peculiarities of the 1602 text could be explained far more satisfactorily by the hypothesis that it represents a version of the Folio put together from memory by an actor, or actors, who had taken part in performances of it. The prime culprit he identified as an actor who had played the Host, because his speeches, as the one quoted at page 210 amply demonstrates, are remarkably close to their counterparts in the Folio. The part of Falstaff, though not quite so well preserved as that of the Host, is also fairly full and accurate, as are the entire scenes in which one or the other of these two characters is involved. When neither of them is on stage, things fall apart. Passages from one scene find their way into another; the point of jokes is lost; and there is much feeble repetition. There are some differences between the two texts, however, which cannot be explained by this theory alone. The complete omission of the examination in Latin grammar (IV.1) and of the first four scenes of Act V shows that there was also deliberate abridgement. Greg's view, with which the present editor fully agrees, is that the Quarto was vamped up by two actors, who had played the parts of the Host and Falstaff, in order to put together a shortened version of the play suitable for production in the provinces. Greg thinks further that the report was compiled by someone other than the two actors, who drew on the recollections of each of them. Some such assumption is made necessary by the extraordinary reading the Quarto provides of the Host's speech at IV.5.83. In the Folio it runs:

Huy and cry, (villaine) goe: assist me Knight, I am vndone: fly, run: huy, and cry (villaine) I am vndone.

In the Quarto it takes the following form:

I am cosened H*ugh*, and coy *Bardolfe*, Sweet knight assist me, *I* am cosened.

The nonsensical 'H*ugh*, and coy *Bardolfe*' seems to be the work of an amanuensis mishearing and misunderstanding the Host's 'Hue and cry, Bardolph'.

The Quarto is, in fact, a 'Bad Quarto', and, as such, wholly unreliable and of no authority. Yet it is not without its uses and its delights.

COLLATIONS

The following lists are *selective*. They do not include corrections of obvious misprints or changes of punctuation.

I

The readings listed below derive from the Quarto of 1602, not from the Folio. Stage directions are not included in this list; they are given separately in list 3. The reading to the left of the bracket is that of the present edition; the reading to the right of it that of F.

I.1.	119–20	They carried me to the tavern, and made me drunk, and afterward picked my pocket] *not in* F
	150	latten] Latine
I.3.	14	lime] liue
	49	a legion] (Q: legians); a legend
	78	humour] honor
	87	Page] *Ford*
	88	Ford] *Page*
II.1.	127–8	and there's the humour of it] *not in* F
	197	FORD] *Shal.*
	199	(*and for the rest of the play*) Brook] *Broome*
II.2.	4	I will retort the sum in equipage] (*line 2 in* Q); *not in* F
	23	God] heauen
	29	wouldst] would
	51, 55	God] heauen
	293	God] Heauen
II.3.	52	word] *not in* F
III.1.	80	urinals] Vrinal
	81	cogscombs] (Q: cockcomes); Cogs-combe
	81–2	for missing your meetings and appointments] *not in* F
	97	Give me thy hand, terrestrial; so] *not in* F
	101	lads] Lad
III.3.	131–2	and none but thee] *not in* F
III.5.	81	By the Lord] Yes
IV.3.	7	them] him
	9	house] houses

IV.4. 41 Disguised like Herne, with huge horns on his head] *not in* F

IV.5. 93–4 to say my prayers] *not in* F

2

The following list contains the substantial departures from the text of F, other than those given above, that are to be found in the present edition. The F reading is to the right of the bracket. Stage directions are not included. Readings thought to be peculiar to the present edition are marked '*this edition*'.

THE CHARACTERS IN THE PLAY] (*this list is not in* F *of* Q)

I.1. 31 per-lady] per-lady
     31 compromises] compremises
     39 swort] sword
     42 George] *Thomas*
  54, 57 SHALLOW] *Slen.*
     70 Got's] go't's
 111, 113 Council . . . counsel] Councell . . . councell
    165 careers] Car-eires

I.3. 55 œillades] illiads
     77 o'th'] ith'
     92 Page] *Ford*

I.4. 44 *un boîtier vert*] vnboyteene verd
  49–50 *Ma foi, il fait fort chaud. Je m'en vais à la cour – la grande affaire*] mai foy, il fait for ehando, Ie man voi a le Court la grand affaires
     52 *Dépêche*] de-peech
     86 *baille*] ballow
    119 good-year] good-ier

II.1. 1 have I 'scaped] haue scap'd
     54 praised] praise
     58 Hundredth Psalm] hundred Psalms
  195–6 guest cavaliero] guest-Caualiere
    202 Ameers] An-heires

II.2. 25 you, you rogue] (*this edition*); you Rogue
    225 exchange] enchange

II.3.	26	Galen] *Galien*
	73	PAGE, SHALLOW, *and* SLENDER] *All.*
III.1.	110	scald] scall
III.2.	45	ALL] *Shal. Page, &c.*
III.3.	3	Robert] *Robin*
	145	JOHN *and* ROBERT] *Ser.*
	155	escape] (*this edition*); vncape
	181	foolish] foolishion
III.4.	12	FENTON] *not in* F
	66	Fenton] *Fenter*
III.5.	28	pullet-sperm] Pullet-Spersme
IV.1.	32	pebble] Peeble
	43	*hung*] *hing*
	57	Jenny's] Ginyes
	64	lunatics] Lunaties
	72–3	*quae . . . quaes*] *que . . . Ques*
IV.2.	54	MISTRESS PAGE] *not in* F
	62	MISTRESS PAGE] *Mist. Ford.*
	93	direct] direct direct
	97	misuse him enough] misuse enough
	110	villains] villaine
	111	ging] gin
	118	this] thi
	169	him not strike] him strike
IV.3.	1	Germans desire] Germane desires
IV.4.	6	cold] gold
	31	makes] make
	59	MISTRESS FORD] *Ford.*
	64	ne'er] neu'r
	81	Quickly] quickly
IV.5.	40	SIMPLE] *Fal.*
IV.6.	27	ever] euen
	39	denote] deuote
V.2.	2–3	my daughter] my
V.3.	12	Welsh devil Hugh] Welch-deuill Herne
V.5.	68	More] Mote
	70	emerald tufts] Emrold-tuffes

192 white] greene
196 into green] into white
200 *un garçon*] oon Garsoon
     un paysan] oon pesant
202 green] white

3

The stage directions of the Folio are of such a kind (see page 211) as to make them almost useless to the editor or producer. The stage directions in the present edition are therefore mainly editorial. A considerable number of them, however, derive from the Quarto, which is far more helpful in this respect. Indeed, some of the Quarto directions are of great interest, since they indicate what the reporters could remember of the actual stage business that had occurred in productions they had taken part in. The following list contains the stage directions of the present text which have some basis in the Quarto and/or Folio. The reading of this text is to the left of the bracket; that of the Quarto and/or Folio to the right of it. When no Folio direction is given, none exists.

I.i.   0 *Enter Justice Shallow, Slender, and Sir Hugh Evans*] *Enter Iustice* Shallow, *Syr* Hugh, *Maister* Page, *and* Slender. Q; *Enter Iustice* Shallow, Slender, *Sir* Hugh Euans, *Master* Page, Falstoffe, Bardolph, Nym, Pistoll, Anne Page, *Mistresse* Ford, *Mistresse* Page, Simple. F

     102 *Enter Sir John Falstaff, Bardolph, Nym, and Pistol*] *Enter Syr* Iohn Falstaffe, Pistoll, Bardolfe, *and* Nim. Q

     173 *Enter Anne Page, with wine, Mistress Ford, and Mistress Page*] *Enter Mistresse* Foord, *Mistresse* Page, *and her daughter* Anne. Q

     179 *He kisses her*] *Syr* Iohn kisses her. Q

     182 *Exeunt all except Slender*] *Exit ail, but* Slender *and mistresse* Anne. Q

I.1. 279 *Enter Page*] *Enter Maister* Page. Q
      293 *Exeunt*] *Exit omnes.* Q ; *Exeunt.* F
I.2.   0 *Enter Evans and Simple*] *Enter sir* Hugh *and*
           Simple, *from dinner.* Q ; Enter *Euans, and*
           Simple. F
       11 *Exeunt*] *Exit omnes.* Q ; *Exeunt.* F
I.3.   0 *Enter Falstaff, Host, Bardolph, Nym, Pistol, and*
           Robin] *Enter sir* Iohn Falstaffes *Host of the Garter*,
           Nym, Bardolfe, Pistoll, *and the boy.* Q ; *Enter*
           Falstaffe, Host, Bardolfe, Nym, Pistoll, Page. F
       14 *Exit*] *Exit Host.* Q
       19 *Exit Bardolph*] *Exit Bardolfe.* Q (*after line* 18)
       79 *Exeunt Falstaff and Robin*] *Exit Falstaffe, and the*
           Boy. Q
       95 *Exeunt*] *Exit omnes.* Q ; *Exeunt.* F
I.4.   0 *Enter Mistress Quickly and Simple*] *Enter*
           Mistresse Quickly, *and* Simple. Q ; *Enter Mistris*
           Quickly, Simple, Iohn Rugby, Doctor, Caius,
           Fenton. F
       38 *She shuts Simple in the closet*] *He steps into the*
           Counting-house. Q
       42 *Enter Doctor Caius*] *And she opens the doore.* Q
       54 *Enter Rugby*] *Enter Iohn.* Q
       87 *He writes*] *The Doctor writes.* Q
      122 *Exeunt Caius and Rugby*] *Exit Doctor.* Q
      160 *Exit*] *Exit omnes.* Q ; *Exit.* F
II.1.   0 *Enter Mistress Page, with a letter*] *Enter Mistresse*
           Page, *reading of a Letter.* Q ; *Enter Mistris*
           Page, *Mistris* Ford, *Master* Page, *Master* Ford,
           Pistoll, Nim, Quickly, Host, Shallow. F
       29 *Enter Mistress Ford*] *Enter Mistresse* Foord. Q
      101 *Enter Ford with Pistol, and Page with Nym*]
           Enter Ford, Page, Pistoll and Nym. Q
      118 *Exit*] *Exit Pistoll:* Q
      128 *Exit*] *Exit Nym.* Q
      147 *Enter Mistress Quickly*] *Enter Mistresse Quickly.* Q
           (*after line* 139)

156 *Exeunt Mistress Page, Mistress Ford, and Mistress Quickly*] *Exit Mistresse* Ford, *Mis.* Page, *and* Quickly. Q

176 *Enter Host*] *Enter Host and Shallow.* Q

189 *They go aside*] Ford *and the* Host *talkes.* Q

214 *Exeunt Host, Shallow, and Page*] *Exit Host and Shallow.* Q

221 *Exit*] *Exit omnes.* Q; *Exeunt.* F

II.2.   0 *Enter Falstaff and Pistol*] *Enter Syr Iohn, and Pistoll.* Q; *Enter* Falstaffe, Pistoll, Robin, Quickly, Bardolffe, Ford. F

31 *Enter Mistress Quickly*] *Enter Mistresse* Quickly. Q

129 *Exeunt Mistress Quickly and Robin*] *Exit Mistresse* Quickly. Q

139 *Enter Bardolph*] *Enter Bardolſe.* Q

149 *Enter Bardolph, with Ford disguised as Brook*] *Enter* Foord *disguised like* Brooke. Q

272 *Exit*] *Exit Falstaffe.* Q

297 *Exit*] *Exit* Ford. Q; *Exti.* F

II.3.   0 *Enter Doctor Caius and Rugby*] *Enter the Doctor and his man.* Q; *Enter* Caius, Rugby, Page, Shallow, Slender, Host. F

15 *Enter Host, Shallow, Slender, and Page*] *Enter* Shallow, Page, *my* Host, *and* Slender. Q

74 *Exeunt*] *Exit all but the* Host *and* Doctor. Q

89 *Exeunt*] *Exit omnes.* Q; *Exeunt.* F

III.1.   0 *Enter Evans and Simple*] *Enter Syr Hugh and Simple.* Q; *Enter* Euans, Simple, Page, Shallow, Slender, Host, Caius, Rugby. F

34 *Enter Page, Shallow, and Slender*] *Enter Page, shallow, and Slender.* Q

66, 67 *Enter Host, Caius, and Rugby . . . Evans and Caius offer to fight*] *Enter* Doctor *and the* Host, *they offer to fight.* Q (*after line* 64)

102 *Exit*] *Exit Host.* Q

114 *Exeunt*] *Exit omnes* Q

III.2.   0 *Enter Mistress Page and Robin*] Mist. Page,
              Robin, Ford, Page, Shallow, Slender, Host,
              Euans, Caius. F

           8 *Enter Ford*] Enter M. Foord. Q

          44 *Enter Page, Shallow, Slender, Host, Evans, Caius,
              and Rugby*] Enter Shallow, Page, host, Slender,
              Doctor, and sir Hugh. Q

          77 *Exeunt Shallow and Slender*] Exit Shallow and
              Slender, Q

          80 *Exit*] Exit host. Q

          83 *Exeunt*] Exit omnes. Q ; Exeunt F

III.3.   0 *Enter Mistress Ford and Mistress Page*] Enter
              Mistresse Ford, with two of her men, and a great
              buck busket. Q ; Enter M. Ford, M. Page,
              Seruants, Robin, Falstaffe, Ford, Page, Caius,
              Euans. F

          18 *Exeunt John and Robert*] Exit seruant. Q

          39 *Enter Falstaff*] Enter Sir Iohn. Q

          87 *Falstaff hides himself*] Falstaffe stands behind the
              aras. Q
              Enter Mistress Page] Enter Mistresse Page. Q
              (*after line* 75)

         129 *Aside to him*] A side. Q

         133 *He gets into the basket ; they cover him with foul
              linen*] Sir Iohn goes into the basket, they put
              cloathes ouer him, the two men carries it away:
              Foord meetes it, and all the rest, Page, Doctor,
              Priest, Slender, Shallow. Q

         164 *Exeunt Page, Caius, and Evans*] Exit omnes. Q

         186 *Enter Ford, Page, Caius, and Evans*] Enter all. Q

         227 *Exeunt*] Exit omnes : Q ; Exeunt. F

III.4.   0 *Enter Fenton and Anne Page*] Enter M. Fenton,
              Page, and mistresse Quickly. Q ; Enter Fenton,
              Anne, Page, Shallow, Slender, Quickly, Page,
              Mist. Page. F

          64 *Enter Page and Mistress Page*] Enter M. Page his
              wife, M. Shallow, and Slender. Q

99 *Exit Fenton*] *Exit Fen.* Q

108 *Exit*] *Exit.* Q; *Exeunt* F

III.5.   0 *Enter Falstaff and Bardolph*] *Enter Sir Iohn Falstaffe.* Q; *Enter Falstaffe, Bardolfe, Quickly, Ford.* F

22 *Enter Mistress Quickly*] *Enter Mistresse Quickly.* Q

52 *Exit*] *Exit mistresse Quickly.* Q

55 *Enter Ford disguised as Brook*] *Enter Brooke.* Q

127 *Exit*] *Exit Falstaffe.* Q

140 *Exit*] *Exit omnes.* Q; *Exeunt.* F

IV.1.   0 *Enter Mistress Page, Mistress Quickly, and William*] *Enter Mistris Page, Quickly, William, Euans.* F

80 *Exeunt*] *Exeunt.* F

IV.2.   0 *Enter Falstaff and Mistress Ford*] *Enter misteris Ford and her two men.* Q; *Enter Falstoffe, Mist. Ford, Mist. Page, Seruants, Ford, Page, Caius, Euans, Shallow.* F

9 *Exit Falstaff*] *He steps behind the arras.* Q
   Enter Mistress Page] *Enter mistresse Page.* Q *(after line 7)*

78 *Exit Falstaff*] *Exit Mis. Page, & Sir Iohn.* Q

107 *Enter Ford, Page, Shallow, Caius, and Evans*] *Enter M. Ford, Page, Priest, Shallow, the two men carries the basket, and Ford meets it.* Q

169, 172, 175 *Enter Falstaff in woman's clothes, and Mistress Page ... He beats Falstaff ... Exit Falstaff*] *Enter Falstaffe disguised like an old woman, and misteris Page with him, Ford beates him, and hee runnes away.* Q *(after line 167)*

188 *Exeunt Ford, Page, Shallow, Caius, and Evans*] *Exit omnes.* Q

211 *Exeunt*] *Exit both.* Q; *Exeunt* F

IV.3.   0 *Enter Host and Bardolph*] *Enter Host and Bardolfe.* Q; *Enter Host and Bardolfe.* F

11 *Exeunt*] *Exit omnes.* Q; *Exeunt* F

IV.4.   0 *Enter Page, Ford, Mistress Page, Mistress Ford,*

		and Evans] Enter Ford, Page, their wiues, Shallow, and Slender. Syr Hu. Q; *Enter Page, Ford, Mistris Page, Mistris Ford, and Euans.* F
IV.4.	88	*Exit] Exit omnes.* Q
IV.5.	0	*Enter Host and Simple] Enter Host and Simple.* Q; *Enter Host, Simple, Falstaffe, Bardolfe, Euans, Caius, Quickly.* F
	20	*Enter Falstaff] Enter Sir Iohn.* Q
	58	*Enter Bardolph] Enter Bardolfe.* Q
	66	*Enter Evans] Enter Sir Hugh.* Q (*after Caius's exit*)
	75	*Exit] Exit.* Q (*before line* 83) *Enter Caius] Enter Doctor.* Q (*after line* 64)
	82	*Exit] Exit.* Q (*before Evans's entry*)
	84	*Exeunt Host and Bardolph] Exit.* Q
	94	*Enter Mistress Quickly] Enter Mistresse Quickly.* Q
	118	*Exeunt] Exit omnes.* Q; *Exeunt.* F
IV.6.	0	*Enter Fenton and Host] Enter Host and Fenton.* Q; *Enter Fenton, Host.* F
	55	*Exeunt] Exit omnes.* Q; *Exeunt* F
V.1.	0	*Enter Falstaff and Mistress Quickly] Enter Falstaffe, Quickly, and Ford.* F
	28	*Exeunt] Exeunt.* F
V.2.	0	*Enter Page, Shallow, and Slender] Enter Page, Shallow, Slender.* F
	14	*Exeunt] Exeunt.* F
V.3.	0	*Enter Mistress Page, Mistress Ford, and Doctor Caius] Enter Mist. Page, Mist. Ford, Caius.* F
	24	*Exeunt] Exeunt.* F
V.4.	0	*Enter Evans disguised as a Satyr, and others as Fairies] Enter Euans and Fairies.* F
	4	*Exeunt] Exeunt.* F
V.5.	0	*Enter Falstaff disguised as Herne, with a buck's head upon him] Enter sir Iohn with a Bucks head vpon him.* Q; *Enter Falstaffe, Mistris Page, Mistris Ford, Euans, Anne Page, Fairies, Page, Ford, Quickly, Slender, Fenton, Caius, Pistoll.* F

15 *Enter Mistress Ford and Mistress Page*] Enter
mistris Page, and mistris Ford. Q

29 *A noise of horns*] There is a noise of hornes, the
two women run away. Q

36 *Enter Evans as a Satyr, Mistress Quickly as the
Queen of Fairies, Pistol as Hobgoblin, Anne Page
and boys as Fairies. They carry tapers*] Enter sir
Hugh like a Satyre, and boyes drest like Fayries,
mistresse Quickly, like the Queene of Fayries: they
sing a song about him, and afterward speake. Q;
Enter Fairies. F

88 *They burn him with their tapers*] They put the
Tapers to his fingers, and he starts. Q

102 *During this song they pinch Falstaff; and Doctor
Caius comes one way, and steals away a boy in
green; Slender another way, and takes off a boy
in white; and Fenton comes, and steals away Anne
Page. A noise of hunting is made within; and all the
Fairies run away. Falstaff pulls off his buck's head,
and rises up. Enter Page, Ford, Mistress Page, and
Mistress Ford*] Here they pinch him, and sing
about him, & the Doctor comes one way & steales
away a boy in red. And Slender another way he
takes a boy in greene: And Fenton steales misteris
Anne, being in white. And a noyse of hunting is
made within: and all the Fairies runne away.
Falstaffe pulles of his bucks head, and rises vp.
And enters M. Page, M. Ford, and their wiues,
M. Shallow, Sir Hugh. Q

173 *Enter Slender*] Enter Slender. Q (but after the
entry of Caius)

198 *Enter Doctor Caius*] Enter the Doctor. Q (but
preceding the entry of Slender)

206 *Enter Fenton and Anne Page*] Enter Fenton and
Anne. Q

237 *Exeunt*] Exit omnes. Q; Exeunt. F

AN ACCOUNT OF THE TEXT

4

The following list contains some of the more interesting and
plausible emendations, not adopted in the present edition, which
have been made by editors from the time of Nicholas Rowe
(1709) onwards. Those which originate in modern scholarly
editions are acknowledged. The reading to the left of the
bracket is that of the present edition; the reading to the right of
the bracket is the rejected emendation.

I.1.   21   coat] cod (*Sir A. T. Quiller-Couch and J. Dover
               Wilson, 1921*)
         232   content] contempt
         235   fall] fault
I.2.   11   cheese] seese
I.3.   25   minute's] minim's; minim- (*Sir A. T. Quiller-
               Couch and J. Dover Wilson, 1921*)
I.4.   21   wee] whey-
          22   Cain-coloured] cane-colour'd
II.1.   5   *precisian*] physician
         129   'The humour of it'] The 'humour' of it (*H. J.
               Oliver, 1971*)
         202   Ameers] (An-heires F); myn-heers
II.2.   22   I, I, I] I, ay, I; Ay, ay, I (*Sir A. T. Quiller-
               Couch and J. Dover Wilson, 1921*)
          27   bold beating] bull-baiting
II.3.   52-3   Mockwater] Make-water (*C. J. Sisson, 1954*)
III.2.   63   buttons] fortunes (*C. J. Sisson, 1954*)
III.3.   155   escape] (vncape F); uncouple; uncope (*Sir A. T.
               Quiller-Couch and J. Dover Wilson, 1921*);
               uncase (*C. J. Sisson, 1954*)
IV.2.   20   lines] lunes
V.5.   117   meet] mate (*Sir A. T. Quiller-Couch and J.
               Dover Wilson, 1921*)